"Go away—"
She grabbed at the bundle.

He saw the shame then, and cursed himself roundly. "What are you doing here?" he demanded.

"Please," she said in a strained whisper. "Just go."

Zane laughed, though with no amusement. "You've got to be kidding. I just can't walk away and leave you to—" His arm sketched out utter astonishment. "This."

"It's my home." Her voice was nearly too soft to be heard.

"Lady, I don't know what the deal is here, but you're coming with me. Surely someone in town has a room for the night." Seeing her shoulders stiffen, he remembered the old man's scornful treatment of her. *Roan O'Hara was always too high on herself.*

What was going on? And why did he care? All he wanted was a nice quiet road trip. Some time to think, to get his head on straight after—

Movement arrested his jumbled thoughts.

The woman was already halfway to the cabin that looked as if it would fall down if she opened the door.

Sighing loudly, Zane followed. He closed the distance, but she leaped up the steps like a gazelle while he stumbled on a broken one before recovering barely quickly enough to avoid a gaping hole in the porch.

She slammed the door in his face.

The only good news was that the house didn't fall with the impact.

Dear Reader,

Some of you have met Zane MacAllister before in *The Healer*—a happy-go-lucky younger brother living a charmed life as Hollywood's favorite heartthrob. When some of you asked for a story for him, I decided that Zane needed a challenge.

In Roan O'Hara he has one. She's a woman with a troubled past, struggling to come to terms with a serious problem, all too aware that this could be her last chance to save herself. The last thing she needs in her life is a pampered playboy.

Enter Zane, larger than life, twice as handsome. He can't remember the last time a woman wanted nothing to do with him, but Zane has a good heart and a solid upbringing; he's not a man who can walk away from someone in trouble. He's all too aware that his brothers are the real heroes; he only plays them on the screen.

What makes a real hero—the splashy coupe, the big rescue? The quiet valor to endure? Is it putting your own needs aside for the sake of another? Finding the courage to dream again when you've lost faith in dreams?

I salute the courage of those tackling Roan's challenge and their loved ones fighting a different but equally difficult battle. I hope that they will feel that this story, within the limitations of its format, pays honor to their struggle.

This is the fourth installment of my DEEP IN THE HEART series. I've received numerous requests for Jesse's story, and I'm pleased to say it's coming up next.

I love to hear from readers. Please contact me via my Web site, www.jeanbrashear.com, or www.eHarlequin.com, or at P.O. Box 3000 #79, Georgetown, TX 78627-3000.

All my best,

Jean

A Real Hero
Jean Brashear

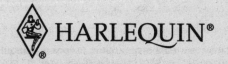

HARLEQUIN®

TORONTO • NEW YORK • LONDON
AMSTERDAM • PARIS • SYDNEY • HAMBURG
STOCKHOLM • ATHENS • TOKYO • MILAN • MADRID
PRAGUE • WARSAW • BUDAPEST • AUCKLAND

ISBN 0-373-71190-5

A REAL HERO

To Paula Eykelhof, for her commitment to quality and her courage in taking risks. Her vision has resulted in an extraordinary team of editors and authors who operate in an environment of respect, professionalism and encouragement that is a writer's dream.

And, as always, for Ercel…my own real hero.

PROLOGUE

Manhattan

"ZANE, IS IT TRUE that you and Gisella had a secret wedding last weekend in Cancún?" the blond reporter from the *Star* shouted. The noise level rocketed as camera crews and microphones crowded the hotel ballroom at the press conference for Zane MacAllister's latest film.

Zane resisted a groan. He'd known that the snapshot of him with the supermodel would be fresh meat for the tabloids. "Thanks for the vote of confidence, Heather, but I just met the woman a week ago when we attended the same preview party." He winked. "I'm sure a famous beauty like her can do better than some ole small-town Texas boy."

The assembled reporters hooted. The blonde named Heather batted her eyelashes at him. Fresh off an Oscar nomination and just named "Sexiest Man Alive" by *People* magazine, Zane MacAllister was the hottest star in Hollywood at the moment. Life was sweet. He was enjoying the heck out of it, but the man who'd been a skinny, brainy runt of the litter was only too aware of what life could be like on the flip side of good looks and fame. And if he forgot, his older brothers, Diego, Jesse and Cade, would gladly bring him back to earth.

He missed them, missed his mother and father, his pesky younger sister, Jenna. Two more stops on this publicity tour for his new release, then he had six weeks off before his next film. He couldn't wait to head home to Texas and hibernate for a while.

As the director fielded questions, Zane listened with half an ear, scanning the crowd without really seeing. He was so tired. His ex-girlfriend Kelly's middle-of-the-night call had kept him tossing in his bed. They hadn't been an item in months, not since he'd finally realized that she didn't want to kick her cocaine habit, that no matter what help he offered, she wasn't ready to accept. It frustrated the hell out of him. The waste of it sickened him. He'd seen too many people in his business dragged down by the fast life. Kelly was well on her way to being another casualty, no matter how hard Zane had fought to save her.

"Zane has no comment on that."

The tension in his publicist Annie Schaefer's voice alerted Zane that he'd missed a question.

That the room had fallen unnaturally silent.

"So she's just another disposable girlfriend?" jeered a voice from the back.

"What?" Zane turned to Annie. "What's he talking about?"

"Get up and leave—now," she whispered, hand over Zane's microphone. "I'll handle this."

Zane almost obeyed—he'd had plenty of experience with the landmines the press could plant—but something in the gathering buzz of the audience, something about the shock in Annie's eyes, kept him in place. "Tell me what's going on," he demanded.

A reporter spoke up first. "Her brother says it's your fault, Zane. That Kelly Mason killed herself because you abandoned her when she told you she was pregnant. Not exactly what we've come to expect from All-American Zane MacAllister, is it?"

Dead? Zane couldn't speak. Kelly…*pregnant?* His mind went white. How could—Last night she'd cried on the phone but refused to tell him why. She'd begged him to come back, but she'd been high and hysterical and—

He jerked the mike toward him. "When she called, she never mentioned—"

The buzz leaped to a roar.

"You mean she called you before she did it?"

"What did you say to make her kill herself?"

"You didn't want the baby?"

How could it be his? They hadn't made love in—

Annie grabbed the mike back. "This news comes as a terrible shock to all of us. Mr. MacAllister will have a statement later." She flipped off the microphone, nudging him none too gently to his feet. "You know better than to hand them something like that. Let's get out of here."

"But—" Zane looked out at the crowd as though somewhere in it lay the answers.

"Forget them—" she snapped. "They're piranhas, ready to feed." Her tone gentled. "You're rattled. I don't blame you. I'll phone some sources from the suite, see what I can find out."

He turned blind eyes to her. "She never said—" He glanced away. "I didn't let her finish. I thought it was just the same old—"

The crowd still clamored, shouting questions as he walked through the door in a daze.

He'd hung up on Kelly in disgust only hours ago. Given up on her, at last.

In so doing, had he driven her to give up on herself?

CHAPTER ONE

Great Smoky Mountains
North Carolina

TWO WEEKS LATER, a man who looked very little like
Zane MacAllister drove down the deserted road he'd
taken off the Blue Ridge Parkway on his way south
to Asheville. Brushing an unfamiliar, newly dark
mustache with one finger, hair shaggy and no longer
blond, he contemplated the dense thickets of rhodo-
dendron, the towering beeches and maples bearing
hints of coming scarlet and gold. The Appalachians
were ancient compared with the mountains he knew
out West, and time had been a pumice stone, wearing
steep peaks down to round, blue-shadowed waves ex-
tending as far as he could see. Near at hand, endless
green slopes on either side of the road would break
for a bald knob of charcoal rock.

Stunning it was, but almost too rich for the eye.
With a sudden ache, he longed for the starkness of
the Davis Mountains of Texas, which were home.

His parents and siblings had called him every day
since Kelly's death. Mama Lalita, the wise old healer
who was as much his grandmother as if they shared

genes, had even made one of her rare forays on the telephone, performing a long-distance diagnosis.

"*Cielito,*" she'd said. *Little sky,* the pet name she'd given him as a child. She'd always said his sunny nature made her think of a cloudless sky, *cielito sin nuves.* "Come home. You should be with those who love you." Ordering him, in no uncertain terms, to present himself with all haste for a *limpia,* or spiritual cleansing.

His sky was no longer cloudless; he had blood on his hands that would never wash out. Thank God Kelly's brother had been lying about her being pregnant, but that relief didn't lessen Zane's responsibility for her death. He carried the weight of it on his chest until he couldn't sleep at night for the smothering press of it.

He should have realized the last episode was different. He should have stopped her. Should have—

All the reassurances others offered dissolved to nothing in the face of knowing that he was the last person who had spoken to Kelly, the one to whom she'd reached out while her demons dug their claws into her throat and choked the life out of her. He could hardly remember the sunny, energetic starlet whose joy had attracted him so on the set of his first big hit.

Damn drugs. Try as he might, he could not understand how a person could know the damage they wreaked and still keep using them. He'd been there for Kelly, paid for rehab twice, would gladly have spent whatever necessary to fix her.

But he couldn't understand what it was that needed fixing, not really. Life threw things at you. You dealt with them. Sure, a beer now and then was nice, but—

Too damn wholesome, Zane. A friend had leveled that charge once. *You've never been tested in your entire charmed life.*

It was true. His half brother Diego had almost died in a Special Forces ambush and still bore scars and a limp. His other half brother, Jesse, was a hostage negotiator, had seen the darker side of life in his years in law enforcement. Even his photographer brother, Cade, had faced dangerous animals and treacherous mountain peaks.

And here Zane was, with more money and women than any man should have, simply because of his looks. Dodging only reporters, not bullets. Disguising himself with dark-brown dye on hair long past its usual razor cut, he was reduced to driving down back roads, seeking some time to think without the constant questions, the screaming headlines.

His brothers were the heroes. He just played them.

Ladyville, the sign up ahead said. Gratefully, Zane turned from pondering the demise of the All-American Boy to wondering if this burg would have a café where he could take a leak and grab a bite to eat. His jeans were loose on his waist, the casualty of too many sleepless nights and no appetite.

He hadn't even been able to attend the funeral to

say goodbye to Kelly for fear of turning it into a circus. Her grieving family had deserved better.

Suddenly, Zane longed for his own family, wanted a taste of his mother's biscuits badly enough to whip the car around and catch the nearest plane to Texas. Wanted to forget the time alone he'd thought he needed and instead sit in her sunny kitchen and let her fuss over him, listen to his kid sister Jenna's early-morning grumbles. Walk out to the barn and hook a boot heel over a fence while comparing notes on the livestock with his dad.

But home was a good eighteen hundred miles away yet, and he had to buy gas and make a pit stop. This one-horse town was no bigger than tiny La Paloma, where Mama Lalita and Diego lived, and there'd be nowhere to spend the night. Best to gas up and go, then get serious about heading straight to Texas in the morning.

That decided, he swerved into the parking lot of the only store in Ladyville and pulled up to the lone pump.

ROAN O'HARA placed her purchases on the scarred wooden counter and waited for the ancient, beak-nosed proprietor, Noah Crabill, to turn around. She opened her cheap billfold with shaking fingers and counted the meager funds inside. She debated if she should spend the money on the gas required to drive to a bigger town with discount stores.

But she couldn't leave, not yet. Couldn't go back

into the world, not this soon. Deep in her bones, she
knew that making a stand here was her last chance.
Gran's ramshackle cabin was in no condition for
winter, but with enough hard work, Roan could render it so, and thereby prove that she was worthy of
surviving.

She stood on the edge of a crumbling cliff, and
she would hang on—

Or she would fall. For the last time.

Roan fingered the sturdy leather gloves she'd chosen over the meat her body needed for strength.
Gran's old shotgun and her .22 rifle stood in a corner
of the cabin. Until Roan could force herself to use
them, the remaining home-canned goods in the root
cellar would have to suffice, rationed with the corn,
beans and other staples on the counter.

"Excuse me?" she said.

Noah didn't respond. Maybe he'd grown hard of
hearing in the long years since she'd been back.

"Excuse me?" A little louder. "Noah?"

No sign he'd heard her. She started to move down
to the end where he stood, when the screen door
opened with a squeak.

Noah swiveled toward the sound and, despite being barely six feet away from her, never looked at
her once. Instead, he fixed his gaze on the newcomer.
"Can I help you with something?"

The stranger, a tall, too-handsome man with un-
kempt dark hair and a mustache, hesitated, nodding
at her. "She was here first."

"She can wait," Noah said.

The stranger frowned. "Ladies first is how I was raised."

"She ain't no lady."

The stranger cast her a questioning glance.

Roan ducked her head, shame a burn in her throat. "It's all right. I don't mind."

"I do," the stranger replied.

Noah shook his head. "Left a good woman to die alone. Too fancy for the likes of us," he said, in that graveled voice he'd had since she could remember. "Do her good to be taken down a notch."

Roan's whole body quivered with the need to hide, to seek sweet oblivion for a little while, just for—

No. This was where it all stopped. She touched the interrupted scar on her left wrist as if it were a magic totem. Held on tight.

Life. She'd chosen life.

One tanned arm reached past her, lifting her burdens. "Then I'll pay for my gas and these," the stranger said.

"No—" she managed.

"That's not your—" Noah began.

The stranger's jaw tightened. "I already pumped my gas. You take the money for it, you take the money for *my* groceries." His stance dared Noah to argue.

Roan couldn't move. "I can't let you—"

A wink from him rendered her mute from shock.

In the midst of tension so thick she could sink her fingers into it, a dimple appeared in his cheek.

Winked.

Roan whirled away, shame riding hard alongside fury. This was a game to him? She was almost to the door, blindly searching for—

"Ma'am? Wait a minute, ma'am—"

At that moment, Roan thought she might burst into laughter. Not because any of this was funny, but because it was the ultimate indignity that he would speak to her in tones of respect like some dowager. *Ma'am.* She knew she looked a thousand years old. Now she felt it.

Stop. Just…stop.

She needed those items on the counter. Gran's cabin was falling down around her ears. She'd walked down the mountain because her ancient pickup was nearly out of gas. She had no job, no friends, no home. She'd spent too much of the morning trying to remember which plants Gran had once taught her were edible and which would kill. In her former life as Ben Chambers's trophy wife, she'd had no use for hunting and foraging skills.

For a moment, the urge to lie down and give up was almost more than she could resist.

"Ma'am?" came a voice, gentle now. "Are you all right?"

The tears rose then; with clenched jaw, she willed them back. Straightened her spine and tried to remember the elegant lady she was once thought to be.

"Fine," she managed, but couldn't yet turn around.

His hand gripped her upper arm.

Roan flinched as though he'd struck her.

He dropped his hand immediately. "Where's your car? I'll carry these for you."

At the edge of her vision, she saw two paper sacks held in one muscled arm. Her reach was tentative; a quick move might make him snatch them away. "How much?" she murmured, stilling her trembling fingers.

He didn't answer, and finally she had to look up. Kind, worried green eyes met hers. "How 'bout if you have supper with me, and we'll call it even." He grinned so easily, as if nothing serious had happened here. As though she wouldn't have a worse encounter with Noah the next time, thanks to his meddling.

Her fingers tightened on a worn brown bag. "How much?"

His smile faded. "Forget it. It was nothing."

Nothing? The amount was a huge chunk of her sparse funds. She gazed out at the luxury SUV he was driving, and knew he hadn't lied. To him, the money was probably no big deal at all. Once it would have been the same for her.

But now that money represented what little self-respect she had left.

Since he wouldn't tell her, she fumbled in her bill-fold and extracted what she'd calculated, rounded up to the next even dollar for her pride and shoved the bills at him.

"I don't want your money," he said, all humor fled.

"And I don't want your help." She grabbed her bags.

Then she ran.

ZANE STOOD out on the weathered porch and watched her go, her gait jerky and stiff. What the hell was that about?

Behind him, the proprietor spoke. "Forget about her. Roan O'Hara was always too high on herself."

The woman Zane had seen was anything but conceited. Tall but rail-thin, short black hair looking as though she'd whacked it herself without benefit of a mirror, she'd seemed nothing as much as defeated, barely clinging to raveling threads of pride.

He opened his mouth to ask about her, then shut it abruptly. Given how much he hated having his own life laid bare to the world, why would he invade her privacy? And hadn't he just seen the results of his interference in Kelly's life? What made him think he could help this woman?

Besides, she'd made it clear his assistance wasn't wanted.

He glanced back over his shoulder. "You got any-place to eat in this town? A café of some sort?"

The old man shook his head. "Folks around here fix their own food. We're not some tourist trap. We leave that to places like Asheville or Boone. We're workin' people.'' He nodded toward his shelves. ''Got some jerky there. Made it myself.''

Zane had grown up hunting and fishing. He'd survived many a trip with his dad or brothers on deer jerky and spring water. ''Don't mind if I do.''

But first he asked for and used the facilities, rusty, cracked and water-stained though they were. Returning, he followed the grizzled proprietor's nod to wooden shelves with peeling paint that must date back to Eisenhower, grabbed several sticks of jerky, then foraged for peanuts and some of those cheese crackers he hadn't had in ages. Two—make that three—Hershey bars and a soft drink for good measure.

His personal trainer, Chuck, who wanted Zane to live on water and zero carbs, would have a coronary if he could see this. It would be worse, in Chuck's eyes, than the Mexican food habit Zane refused to give up.

With multiple close-up love scenes to film in six weeks, he shouldn't be eating like this.

On the other hand, face it, his muscles were as ripped as humanly possible without steroids, something he refused to consider. One junk-food binge wouldn't kill him, and right now, he didn't give a damn. He'd pay later, if needed. One thing about him that could compare with any of his brothers was his work ethic. He played hard, but he worked harder.

Arms full of his booty, Zane scanned the tiny store reeking of mildew and tobacco and time.

"That it?" the old man asked, bushy eyebrows aloft at the size of Zane's bundle.

He'd probably made the guy's take for the whole day. Zane grinned, the tension of the previous encounter fading. "I think so."

"Where you from?"

Zane considered his cliff-top mansion in Malibu, his expensive apartment in Manhattan he'd left just two days ago. Neither was home. "Texas."

The old man nodded. "Thought so. Accent's hard to miss."

Zane, who'd put in a lot of hours to ditch his Texas drawl at the beginning of his career, was unaccountably proud now. "You can take the boy out of Texas, but you can't take Texas out of the boy."

"Hmmph." The old man finished ringing up his purchases on the oldest cash register Zane had ever seen, tarnished but ornate, probably worth a mint to a Beverly Hills designer.

Zane fished out the necessary bills and waited for his change.

"Don't need a bag this time, do you?"

Skinflint. Zane recalled the decrepit paper bags used for the woman's groceries. Then he remembered the frugality of people back home who'd been raised in severe poverty. This was Appalachia, he reminded himself. Beautiful, but filled with pockets of some of the deepest poverty in the country.

He'd lived off the fat of the land too long. "Sure," he said. "No problem." He turned to go, then reversed himself. "You have a good day, now."

"Hmmph." The old man's severe features might have softened, but it was hard to tell.

Zane nudged the screen door open with his shoulder and grinned to himself, filing away the man's speech patterns and mannerisms, the way he held his body with one shoulder a little higher, the hitch to his gait. The world was full of interesting characters, and someday, when he'd grown enough as an actor so that no one cared about his looks, he might get to play a codger just like this one.

ANOTHER HALF MILE down this road, then she would begin the long climb to Gran's cabin. She still couldn't think of it as hers. For the past two days, she'd tiptoed around as though Gran would walk through the door at any minute, fresh from taking one of her potions or salves to a neighbor.

But the mountain's wisewoman would never share those healing treasures again. Herbs still hung from the ceiling in bundles, and the chest carved with Gran's own designs held seeds and leaves and powders Roan wished were more familiar.

Gran had tried to teach her, and as a child, Roan had listened, hung on every word.

But time had changed all that, and too many memories were only feather-light dust in the corners of Roan's mind. She thought she could spot ginseng, goldenseal and sassafras. Sarsaparilla, used to purify the blood, also helpful with infections and burns. Many of them, however, stirred no recognition in her.

Her arms ached from the weight of the bags, but she didn't dare loosen her grip. Noah reused his grocery sacks until they were in shreds, requiring the local people to return one for every bag he grudgingly gave out.

He'd remembered her. She'd known the odds of that were good, hadn't she? Mountain people possessed long memories. A century ago was as real as today. Who your people were was something you never escaped.

Or in her case, she was the one who'd probably been a millstone around Gran's neck. And Mama...

It didn't bear thinking. Mama would just drink until she didn't remember, anyway.

As her head spun from lack of food, Roan focused harder on the ground before her. Mama wasn't her problem anymore; the new husband Roan had never met had itchy feet, and they were currently in Nashville—or was it Knoxville? She couldn't recall.

Didn't care. Mama had seldom emerged from her haze to notice Roan, and Roan had long ago learned not to let it matter. Being ignored was easier to prepare for; the whiplash of love and neglect wore her out. When her mother was on, she could seduce Roan into believing that the days of oblivion, the nights of weeping and clinging, would never return.

But they always did. To expect anything of an alcoholic was a slow death; in rehab, Roan had heard, again and again, that her mother's behavior wasn't her fault, that trust was the first casualty for children of alcoholics. That the cycle of trying to fix the parent and taking the blame for failing to accomplish it was an old story, repeated millions of times every day all over the world.

But Roan had failed at much more than fixing her mother the drunk. She'd miscarried two babies. She'd failed to be the perfect wife she'd promised to the man who'd been her ticket out of these mountains. Then, just as she'd almost found the courage to leave a loveless marriage, she'd finally been granted a miracle. Her chance to make her life count by delivering a child, a little girl who wasn't the boy her husband had wanted but was perfect in Roan's eyes. Beautiful and good and—

Roan stumbled on a stone.

Dead.

Roan's head spun, little black dots dancing before her eyes.

She blinked several times, forcing herself to remember the dainty fingers, the tiny toes. The perfect shell of the ear into which Roan had whispered her love and the secrets Gran had passed down.

Her angel, Elise. Dead because of her—

Swift and sharp as a steel blade, agony struck. It would never be over. Seven years and the wound would never stop bleeding until Roan herself was dead.

Black dots shifted. Grew.

Roan tried to catch herself. Find safe ground.

She couldn't. The bags slid from arms gone weak.

Roan fell into the darkness that was always there. Waiting to claim her.

DRIVING BACK DOWN the road toward the Blue Ridge Parkway, Zane tried his first bite of the old man's jerky. Not bad. Not as good as what Dad made, but—

His gaze narrowed. What was that on the side of the road? It looked like…

Then he blinked. A body. A person—

Her. The faded blue shirt was unmistakable. And the bags of groceries spilled on the ground around her.

Zane jammed on the brakes and was out of the door in a flash, racing to cover the distance between them. *Oh, man.* She'd seemed ill; he'd seen her walking instead of driving. He should have ignored what she said and given her a ride. He should have—

Please. Let her be okay. Don't let another woman die because I didn't—

He fell to his knees beside her, scrambling to find a pulse.

And dropped his head in gratitude.

Alive. Pulse steady.

Zane stripped off the flannel shirt over his T-shirt and placed it on the ground beside her, then eased her over to her back on top of the fabric. She had smudges on her face and more on her arms that he hadn't noticed at the store, and her clothes showed evidence of hard work, so it made no sense to worry about her lying in the dirt.

Though tall, she was so delicately formed. Not an ounce of fat on her, all sinew and bruised shadows and lines of strain. Life hadn't been good to this woman in a long time, if ever.

Roan O'Hara was always too high on herself.

The old man was dead wrong. This woman showed no trace of anything but hard luck.

He felt her arms and legs for fractures, her head for lumps, but she didn't seem injured. He gripped her shoulder and shook her gently. "Hey, there," he said. "Ms. O'Hara. Roan. Can you wake up?"

He saw movement behind her lids, then a slight flutter of her thick black lashes. A hard knot inside his chest eased further. "That's right, Sleeping Beauty. Wake up. Tell me how you feel."

She moaned softly, and Zane cupped one hand against her cheek. Her milk-pale skin and black hair would have told him of her Celtic forebears even if the old man hadn't given her last name. "Open your eyes, Roan. Come back and talk to me," he cajoled.

Slowly, her lashes lifted. In that first moment when she hadn't fully awakened, her eyes held no marks of life's battering. They were a stunning blue that made him think of the morning sky in west Texas, day-bright with promise and possibilities.

"Hey," he said. "How do you feel?"

In a flash, she tensed and made to rise.

Zane held her shoulder. "Not yet. Get your bearings and tell me if anything hurts." He relaxed his grip to banish any worry she might have about his intent.

She seized the opportunity and rolled to her side, then leaped to her feet in a swift, if wobbly, movement.

But once on her feet, she swayed.

Zane was there immediately, steadying her.

"No—" She stepped back. Faltered. "Don't touch me. I don't need—"

"You don't know what you need." Zane grasped her shoulders, afraid she would fall again. "Just give yourself a minute to settle. I'm not going to hurt you."

"I—" She scanned around her at the groceries spilled over hard ground, some landing in the foliage creeping into the roadbed. She whirled and started to lean down. Pain escaped from her in a hiss.

"I'll get them. You sit and figure out if I should take you to a hospital." He nudged her shoulders down.

She shook him off. "I'm fine. And the closest hospital is over an hour from here."

Zane cursed beneath his breath. "Hey—I'm just a regular guy with no agenda. I don't want your food or your money or your body. I'm only trying to help."

She didn't act mollified. "I'm not hurt. I can pick up my own groceries. Don't delay your trip on my account."

Zane ground his teeth and stayed silent. He began gathering the supplies scattered hither and yon. A pitiful sample: dried beans, rice, corn...

She brushed past him, snatching the items from his hands.

He felt almost childish, holding on to one sack of beans. "When's the last time you ate?"

"None of your business," she snapped, bending to retrieve onions and potatoes. She opened one of the bags, shoved the vegetables inside, then lifted the bag.

Everything cascaded to the ground through the hole in the bottom. She stopped, shoulders bowed in defeat.

But in only seconds, she straightened, then began picking the groceries up all over again.

"Listen to me—" Zane barked, turning her toward him. He drew a chocolate bar from the pocket of the shirt on the ground. "You're running on empty. I won't lay a finger on your damn groceries if you'll just sit down and eat this. Rest a minute."

She eyed the fifty-cent chocolate bar as if he'd presented her with Godiva. Swallowing hard, she shook her head. "I can't," she whispered, a plea in her gaze.

"Why the hell not?" Zane shouted, then exhaled loudly, running his fingers through his hair. "Look,

I've got some plastic bags in the car, I think. Just let me get them while you eat this bar. You're pale and shaky, and you're not going to make it much farther. There's no price attached to this chocolate. Hell, I've got two more bars, and you can have everything else I just bought if you'll only let me be certain I'm not driving off and leaving you to faint again.''

"I don't faint," she said.

"Well, you sure did a good imitation of it." He shoved the bar into her pocket and stalked off to his car. "That thing better be at least half-gone by the time I get back over here," he said over his shoulder. "I want to make it to Asheville tonight, and I'm not going until I'm sure you're okay." He resisted the urge to turn and watch to see what she did.

Instead, he leaned into his car and gathered every scrap of food he could find. He stashed her money and two crisp hundred-dollar bills inside one candy bar wrapper, hoping she wouldn't find them until after he'd left.

And emerged from the car, only to see her disappearing into the trees.

With her groceries bundled into his shirt.

Zane just stood there for a minute, wondering why he should bother. He didn't need the grief and could replace the shirt.

Then he swore like a sailor, locked his car and took off after her.

CHAPTER TWO

KEEPING UP WITH HER wasn't that hard. Zane had the sense that only pure will kept her going up the steep incline. Twice she stumbled and barely stayed upright. It was all Zane could do not to close the distance between them, swing her into his arms and carry her the rest of the way to wherever the devil she was heading.

Only two things stopped him: the sure knowledge that she was using all her strength and might hurt herself trying to escape him, and the fact that all his workouts aside, he was feeling the combined effects of the altitude and the sharp angle of her path. His physique might be in superb condition for the camera's unforgiving eye, but when he got back, he was increasing his cardio workouts drastically. His daily two-mile run wasn't enough for what the dense undergrowth and steep ascent required.

He could pick her up and carry her, sure. No problem—on flat ground or the gentle L.A. hills. But in these ancient mountains, he just might embarrass himself.

He had no idea how she kept putting one foot in front of the other, or how much longer he could stand to watch her struggle, despite the potential for humiliating himself.

Just then, she stumbled again. This time, she fell to her knees and remained there, head bent and shoulders hunched.

Zane was beside her in seconds.

She whirled. "No!"

Zane held out his palms. "I only want to help you."

"Stay away from me..." Scrambling backward to escape him, she slipped on the wet leaves.

Zane grabbed her arm and stopped her slide.

She fought him then, a virago using nails and feet and teeth.

"Hey, I'm not going to hurt you..." He renewed his efforts to prevent her from injuring herself or him—or sending them both careering down the treacherous slope. "Ow! Stop it." Finally, he wrestled her to the ground beneath him, using his weight to anchor her torso and legs while trapping her clawing hands at shoulder height.

She went still, gasping for air, her eyes wild. "Please..." She squeezed her lids shut as though waiting for the worst.

Adrenaline surged through him, echoed by blind fury that she could think—

Zane dropped his head and grimaced. Who would believe this? His brothers would be laughing themselves silly that the lover of the silver screen had a woman so terrified and desperate to avoid him.

His mother, all five foot two of her, would blister his ears, and his dad, who had always taught him that women were the finest example of God's grace on earth, would be ashamed of him.

He raised his head to try again to make her understand—

Oh, man. Tears he instinctively knew she'd die before willingly shed leaked from her tightly closed lids.

He leaped away like a scalded cat.

"I'm sorry. I swear I wasn't trying to harm you. I only—"

She rolled, albeit much slower than before, and began, once again, gathering up the makeshift knapsack.

He bit back a curse. It was on the tip of his tongue to tell her who he was, to point out that he could have his pick of women and certainly wasn't reduced to attacking some skinny wraith he'd never take a second glance at.

But she seemed so miserable and stretched to her limits that he held his silence. His ego—bruised as it might be by her reaction to him—didn't need the boost, whereas she looked as if she had lost all right to ego long ago. He wished he knew the reason.

"Please," was at last all he could think to say. "Let me carry those for you. Then I promise I'll leave you alone and you'll never see me again."

Her pale hands stilled, her shoulders sagging.

"Why?" she whispered, facing him fully. "Why would you want to help?"

What blew his mind was that she assumed no one would. Zane's powers of observation had been honed from years of acting, and a close study of her eyes before she glanced away again showed him a woman pushed to the extremes of both loneliness and despair. A woman with a deeply bruised soul, holding on to herself with scratched and bleeding fingers.

Exactly the kind of woman he didn't need to get involved with when he was still struggling to handle his failure to save another woman at the end of her rope.

"Never mind." She turned away again and tried to lift a burden that he could handle with ease.

He grabbed for the bundle, and her strength was no match for his. "My mother," he blurted. "I'd never hear the end of it if I didn't help a lady in distress. And my dad and brothers would horsewhip me—that is, if my little sister let them get to me first." The thought of his family brought a grin to his face.

She frowned. "You can smile about that?"

What kind of life had this woman had that she couldn't understand a family so steeped in love that they'd never have to lay a hand on him because he'd turn himself inside out to avoid disappointing them? "They wouldn't seriously—" He stopped, seeing her wavering on her feet. "How much farther is it?"

Zane barely caught her before she crumpled. He dropped the bundle beside them.

He sank to the ground and pulled the now-unconscious woman onto his lap. Once he assured himself that her heartbeat and breathing were normal, he settled in to give her a few minutes to waken before he started figuring out where she was headed.

The wind rose, and he shivered in his T-shirt. He nestled her closer to him, reaching over to untie the bundle with one hand, dumping the contents, once again, on the ground, so he could wrap his shirt around her. The chocolate bar, he noted, remained uneaten.

He scooted back to settle against a tree trunk, aware that the shadows had lengthened. He'd been raised in other mountains and knew darkness would come quickly as the sun sank behind them. The temperature would drop rapidly.

He would give them both a very few minutes to rest, then he'd awaken her, much as she needed to recuperate, and force her to eat and drink something. Then they'd set off for wherever her destination had been. Once he'd delivered her there, he'd gladly be on his way.

"Ms. O'Hara," the voice insisted. "Roan—"

Roan tried to rise from the deep, dark well into which she'd fallen, but she was so tired. So very tired.

"You have to wake up," she heard. "It's going to be nightfall soon."

She ducked her head, rolling to the side, snuggling deeper into the warmth. Her nose brushed against cloth covering a firm surface that was warm and smelled good. She burrowed her face against it, her lips grazing the cloth.

She heard a gasp. The safe, warm nest—

Clenched.

Her eyes flew open. White cotton stretched over muscles. Lots of them.

Roan scrambled to get away.

Arms tightened around her. "Easy now," the low baritone soothed.

She tensed to fight her way out. Remembered a big body trapping her on the ground, strong hands pinning her wrists—

He sighed loudly. "Save us both some trouble, all right?" Carefully, he set her away from him. "I don't want anything from you but to see you safely home. In case you haven't noticed, the sun is going down. How much farther is your place?"

Roan battled through the exhaustion, forcing muscles already sore from her efforts to make Gran's cabin habitable, now molasses-slow in their responses to this man who said he didn't want to harm her, but...

Green eyes held concern peppered with irritation, but he kept his voice even. "Are you awake enough to move?"

She wasn't sure, but she nodded. "Who are you?"

His gaze darted away. "Only a guy passing through." He locked eyes with her again, resolute. "I'm going to pick up your groceries, then follow you home just long enough to make sure you're okay. Then I'm outta here, got it?" Grabbing her bundle, he rose in one lithe movement and reached out to assist her.

She kept her hands to herself and made her way to her feet, seeing irritation flit across his too-handsome features. It couldn't matter. She had only one goal and could not weaken.

She didn't want his help—couldn't afford to accept it. But she didn't have the strength to argue anymore. He was right; night would come too soon, and her childhood memories of these mountains might not be enough to get her...

Home, she'd been about to say, but it wasn't. Not yet.

It would be, though. It was all she had.

"It's not much farther," she said, hearing the churlish tone and regretting it a little. After all, he'd bought her groceries and raced to her aid when she'd collapsed. He was the only person she'd encountered in weeks who seemed to give a damn.

Which was what made him dangerous. That seductive sense of comfort to which she'd awakened was something she wanted so badly she was afraid of what she'd give up again to have it.

She'd sold herself too often, seeking safe harbor. It had turned out badly every time. No more.

The words of apology were on her lips, but she couldn't afford to bridge the distance between him and herself. He was right—she could feel it; she wouldn't make it the rest of the way carrying that load. Much as being in anyone's debt rubbed, she would accept his help because it was sensible.

But she had nothing to offer in return. If he knew what a bad bargain she was, he'd be running in the other direction already. As matters stood, the condition of Gran's cabin would no doubt do the trick. No one who drove a car like his could do anything but recoil.

So she swallowed the inadequate words and simply put one foot in front of the other, heading uphill toward the place that represented all she'd ever known of home and being loved.

ZANE WAS TOO BUSY keeping an eye on both her and the unfamiliar terrain to notice what lay ahead until she stopped and held out her hand.

"I can handle this now." She wouldn't meet his gaze. "I'm sorry I could see no choice but to take your shirt. If you can wait a minute, I'll give it back. I'm—" She seemed about to say more, but shook her head. "Thank you."

But Zane was too lost in studying the most ramshackle cabin he'd ever seen. He wasn't unaccustomed to the sight of poverty; his own rearing had been solidly middle class, though many of the people of his part of Texas lived barely over the poverty line. But this...

"You can't stay here," he said.

Instantly, she bristled. "It's not your decision."

He took in the ancient weathered logs, the mud used to chink them missing in spots, the rampant vines doing their best to bury the structure itself. "How long has this been uninhabited?"

"Go away!" She grabbed at the bundle.

He saw the shame then, and berated himself. Had he gotten so spoiled that he couldn't imagine living in less than the obscene amount of square footage he inhabited?

That wasn't it. He looked at her and couldn't understand the contrasts she represented. He grabbed one of her hands. She hissed in pain, and he turned the hand over, muttering at the blisters, broken open and bleeding, remembering the gloves in the bundle.

She wasn't used to this. "What are you doing here?" he demanded. "Why isn't anyone helping you?"

She snatched her hand away. "Please," she said in a strained whisper. "Just go."

Zane laughed then, though there was little of amusement in it. "You've got to be kidding. I can't walk away and leave you to—" His arm sketched out utter astonishment. "This."

"It's my home." Her voice was nearly too faint to be heard.

Zane threw his head back, exhaling in frustration. "Lady, I don't know what the deal is here, but you're coming with me. Surely someone in town has a room you can have for the night." Seeing her shoulders stiffen, he remembered for the second time the old man's scornful treatment of her.

Roan O'Hara was always too high on herself.

What was going on?

And why did he care?

He was on his way to his family, and he'd left an expensive car down the hill. He had no business trying to solve the problems of a woman who wouldn't thank him for the attempt.

All he'd wanted was a nice, quiet road trip. A span to think, to get his head back on straight after Kelly—

Movement arrested his jumbled thoughts.

The woman was already halfway to the cabin that looked as if it would fall down around her shoulders if she opened the door.

"Wait—" he shouted.

She didn't slow.

Sighing loudly, Zane once again followed. With long strides, he closed the distance, but she leaped up the steps like a gazelle while he stumbled on a broken one before recovering barely in time to avoid a gaping hole in the porch.

She slammed the door in his face.

The only good news was that the house didn't fall with it.

ROAN HEARD HIM muttering on the other side of the door. Gran had never cared to lock a door in her life; all he had to do was turn the knob. She stared at it as though a serpent bobbed and weaved before her.

She rubbed her temple. Why was he doing this? Why wouldn't he simply wash his hands of her and go away? He'd be glad if he did; he just didn't understand that yet.

I'd never hear the end of it if I didn't help a lady in distress.

Were there really families like that? Too wholesome by far to be believed, no matter how she'd longed to be part of one as a child. How she'd hoped to create one herself until she'd faced the truth of her marriage.

"Lady, if you think I'm just going to walk away…"

Roan couldn't think. She was so tired.

The latch rattled. "Tell me you're all right. I don't want to break down this door, but—"

Before she could respond, the door swung open and there he was, filling the room, frowning as he glanced at the wobbly, chipped porcelain knob.

"Get ou—" She let the words die away and sank to the wooden chair behind her. Suddenly, the effort to battle him was too much.

In a second, he was before her, crouching to look up into her face. Those brilliant green eyes scanned her features, and he frowned, then pulled a chocolate bar from the bundle. "You didn't eat this." He shoved it at her. "Do it now."

She was too hungry to argue. With shaking fingers, she tried to slit the wrapper. With a soft oath, he took it from her and unwrapped it, then broke off a piece.

"When's the last time you ate a decent meal?"

She couldn't speak. The first bite was heaven. The second, bliss. She abandoned all thought of ladylike behavior and wolfed it down.

He drew out another bar and started to open it.

Then swore as he unveiled what looked like the crisp green of money.

"What is that?" she asked.

Color stained his cheeks. "Nothing."

She grabbed for the candy. "How could this get inside—" Her gaze flew to his as understanding dawned. "You." She swallowed hard against humiliation. "I don't need your money, or your pity."

"It wasn't like that—" He broke off, and she knew that it was exactly like that. The rub was that she was desperately short of funds.

But she'd die before accepting. She carefully rewrapped the bar, then handed it back, money, too. "I don't need it. Or your food." She curled her arms around her middle. "You can go now."

Her stomach growled, making a lie of her words.

"I'm not leaving. I'll stay the night."

Startled, she glanced at him. "You can't." Her gaze slid away, landing on the bed pushed against one wall of the two-room cabin.

For the first time, he looked around, and she saw the place through his eyes: ancient logs stained dark with time and the smoke of too many kerosene lamps and fires on the timeworn hearth. The one room served as living area, bedroom and dining space; the second area was the kitchen, which had no running water. The bathroom was an outhouse, and there was no electricity.

Roan shivered. She'd intended to be back hours ago to start the fire that would be her only defense against the night's chill.

He merely shrugged. "I've stayed in worse, hunting with my dad and brothers." His incisive glance caught her shiver, and he gestured toward the fireplace. "Where's the woodpile?"

"You can't—" Seeing the determination on his face, she didn't finish. She was too drained, anyway. "Out there." She indicated the direction with a nod.

"I'll be back," he said. "Don't bother locking the door." He broke off, glaring. "No locks? You're up here alone, and you have no lock on the door?"

"Gran never needed them," she said, staring at the floor, trying to summon the strength to move.

He surprised her again by smiling. "That's how it is at home," he said softly. "I've lived in cities too long."

Where's home?, she wanted to ask.

But didn't. Darkness encroached, and she would do the decent thing and offer shelter for the night, though she herself wouldn't sleep a wink in case the kindness he'd shown was a ruse.

But she wanted to know nothing about this man, even his name. Not where he'd been, where he was headed, nothing.

Except how soon he would go.

Leaving her, as she'd always been, alone.

She just hadn't understood that until far too late.

CHAPTER THREE

ZANE STALKED OUTSIDE after ordering her again to eat the chocolate. She'd refused until he'd stuffed the money back in his wallet.

On the porch, he skirted the hole and stopped on the top step to look around for a moment.

So different from the mountains where he'd grown up. The Davis Mountains rose in the midst of sere desert landscapes that extended for hundreds of square miles of far west Texas. These lush mountains, ripe with towering oaks and pines, thick with rhododendrons and rich emerald grasses, shimmered with starbursts of flagrant scarlet and gold where the foliage was beginning to turn.

To the right, perhaps fifty or sixty yards away, stood an ancient barn with vines creeping over the fence of the enclosed corral. To his left, he spotted what seemed to be the remains of a garden. Weeds flourished, though here and there he could see something resembling the vegetable plants his mother grew each summer.

At the thought of Grace MacAllister, yearning seized him. Spending the night in this place would delay him. Though he'd given his family no timetable, he'd hoped to arrive there in two days, three at the most.

He glanced around, noting the absence of electric lines or telephone wires, thinking wistfully of the cell phone in the middle compartment of his rental car.

Which he'd abandoned on the side of a deserted mountain road.

Zane shrugged. Nothing he could do about it now. The light had faded to the violet gray of what his dad called the gloaming, and if he didn't get his butt in gear, he'd break his neck before he found the woodpile, much less made his way down to the road. With a shake of his head, he set off, carefully avoiding the broken stairs.

Scant minutes later, he knelt before the fireplace, stacking the assortment of logs he'd wrenched from more vine cover. "Please tell me you have matches here," he said. "It's been a long time since I was a Scout."

"You were a Boy Scout—" She clamped off the question, shoving a box of matches at him. Their fingers brushed. She dropped the box into his hands and skittered away.

"Look, I'm getting sick of being treated as if I were some kind of criminal bent on raping you. I'm not that desperate."

At the hurt on her face, he swore beneath his breath. "I didn't—"

"Forget it," she said. "Of course you wouldn't be—I know what I am."

Zane frowned. "What do you mean?"

"Nothing." She shrugged and turned away. "I—excuse me, but I have to go outside." She colored, and her voice dropped. Then she stiffened. "I'm going out to use the facilities." The set of her shoulders dared him to mock her.

"Wait." Zane's hand shot out to grab her arm. He stopped himself, remembering her reaction before. "I wasn't saying—"

But she was already through the door.

Zane sighed. Damn, but she was prickly.

He glanced around once more.

She didn't belong here; those slim, blistered hands made that clear. But everything about her demonstrated that her life hadn't been a cakewalk. What was her story?

He rubbed his face with both hands and vowed not to ask any more questions of her. It wasn't his business; he was only passing through. A stranger stranded for the night but with a clear path toward the future. In six weeks, he'd be filming an action adventure story that could be his highest-grossing picture to date.

Yet as he stood in this dilapidated log cabin whose walls barely slowed the wind, his real life seemed far away indeed. For a minute he experienced an odd vulnerability he hadn't felt since he was a kid on his first camping trip away from home.

He was out here where nature didn't care about the necessities of mere humans, where the night held unseen dangers, where civilization seemed barely to have established a foothold.

Winter was coming, and when it arrived, he would be far away from this place that hovered so close to being swallowed by Mother Earth. He'd be in the desert, or on a soundstage somewhere, minutes from the nearest coffeehouse or a caterer's van, surrounded by people who were paid to accommodate his every wish.

But where would this woman be, this Roan O'Hara of the haunted eyes and gaunt frame?

Mamma mia. Zane shook his head. He couldn't take her on as a cause; she wouldn't like it if he did.

But how would he simply walk away, knowing that she was holding on by the slimmest thread?

She's not your concern. She already said she doesn't want your help.

If he hadn't stopped at that store...

The door creaked open, and there she was, every last bit of uncertainty erased from her frame. "I'll let you stay here tonight, but you'll leave as soon as it's light." Her voice betrayed not the merest quaver.

So be it. "Fine," he said curtly. "I'll sleep on the floor. Have whatever you want of the food I brought. I can get more at that store." He made for the front door, needing fresh air to forestall a temper he seldom displayed.

Once outside, he nearly fell into the stupid hole again.

Sure—just fine and dandy. He'd head out tomorrow—but when he was good and ready. He'd chop her more firewood and fix the porch and steps before she broke her leg, the mule-headed woman.

Zane was halfway to the woodpile, muttering, when he realized that he hadn't thought about Kelly or the press hounds hot on his trail for hours now— the first respite since her death.

Maybe instead of heaping cuss words on Roan's head, he should be thanking the mule-headed woman for aggravating him so much that she'd taken his mind off the reason he'd chosen this detour in the first place.

HE RETURNED to a surprise after chopping wood until he'd gained his own set of blisters and risked cutting off a leg in the growing darkness. Somehow, she'd conjured up an actual meal on the ancient woodstove in the kitchen.

"Where did you find this food?" he asked.

"Gran always canned extra for winter. When she died, it was late summer, I think."

"You don't know when your grandmother died?"

Over her face swept such grief that he was ashamed of blurting the question. "Forget it."

"It's been nearly two years. I've been...out of pocket. I was—" Misery crowded the grief. "The constable's letter, informing me that she'd left this place to me, had to be forwarded."

Zane resisted another survey of the cabin, which

would probably look even worse by full daylight. "So you're here on vacation?"

Her shoulders hunched, then she forced her spine ramrod-stiff. "No. I'm going to live here." Her tone dared him to argue.

Only barely did he bite back the astonishment. *Not my affair,* he reminded himself. *I'm only passing through.*

Instead, he perused the stove. "She teach you to cook on this?"

Her face softened a little. "She said it was the happiest day of her life when she could quit cooking in the fireplace." Fondness colored her tone.

"Amazing. Mama Lalita used to cook on a wood-stove, I remember her saying. But that was before I was born."

"She's a relative?"

"Sort of a grandmother," he answered. "Not by blood, but she might as well be." He smiled, thinking of the tiny woman, so wise and caring. He had grandmothers of his own, but neither had lived nearby when he was growing up. His mother had preserved the ties to her late husband's family even after she'd married his dad, so though Mama Lalita was actually only related by blood to Diego and Jesse, she'd treated all of them as her own.

"You love her," Roan observed.

"Yeah," he answered. "I do. She's a special lady. A *curandera.* Ever heard of that?"

Roan shook her head.

"That's what they call a healer in the Latino culture. It's a tradition going all the way back to the Aztecs. She uses herbs and other methods to care for people."

"Where is she?"

"The Davis Mountains. Far west Texas."

Roan smiled then, and Zane could only stare. Her smile altered everything about her.

"Gran was a wisewoman—some call them *granny women*. She used herbs to help people, too. Gathered some of them wild and raised others in her garden." She stroked an ancient wooden box, one long finger tapping over several tiny drawers. "This was her medicine box, inherited from her own mother. I should oil it." Her head drooped. "She taught me some of what she knew, but I didn't listen well enough. I can't remember much of what she said anymore, and now…" She busied herself with the stove. "It doesn't matter."

But it did; that was obvious from the vanished smile and the way her body telegraphed her misery. That she'd loved her grandmother deeply came through in every word. So why hadn't she known when her grandmother died? And what was she doing here now?

I'm just passing through, he repeated to himself. "Anything I can do to help?"

A faint shake of her head was the only sign she'd heard.

"Then I'll—" He looked around. Too dark to

chop wood or fill the chinks in the walls or anything else he could see to do. "I'll check on the fire," he said.

She shrugged as if it didn't matter.

THEY MADE IT THROUGH the simple meal in near-complete silence. He might as well have been alone but for the sound of her cutlery clinking against ancient, crazed pottery. Zane was shocked to realize just how seldom he got to experience solitude and quiet anymore.

He wasn't much of a cook, though he had an enormous gourmet kitchen in his Malibu house and one easily twice as big as this one even in a less-spacious New York apartment. Most of the time, however, he ate out or ordered in. Food wasn't a big deal to him, only fuel for the body that was his career in a way that made him increasingly uncomfortable. He'd never set out to be a sex symbol; the boy who'd been too thin and worn Coke-bottle glasses would never have dreamed such a thing could happen. He'd tagged along with his brothers and learned to fish and hunt, sure, but he'd been just as happy with his nose stuck inside a book where his fertile imagination could roam, drawing inspiration for the endless *let's pretend* games he'd enlist his brothers or Jenna to play.

No one had been more surprised than him at what had happened when he'd gotten contacts so he could play basketball and his frame had begun to stretch, then fill out—and girls had begun to notice.

Not that he'd complained. He'd been skinny, not stupid.

Still, all his life his brothers had been the ones girls had panted over, so to find himself in college with females who hadn't known the runt had taken some adjusting. He'd gotten so sidetracked by them for a while his dad had had to deliver a stern warning that Zane's family wasn't made of money and he wasn't in college to chase girls.

But man, did he love women…always had. Loved the way they smelled, how they walked; loved the curve of a hip, the sweet rounding of a breast—but even more than that, he found the mind of a woman a subject of endless fascination. He'd never understood them, really, but he sure liked to try.

Despite what his dad said was the brightest mind in the family, Zane had been close to flunking out the semester everything changed. Some scout spotted him on the University of Texas campus and asked him to pose for a calendar. Zane had refused at first, aghast at displaying his body that way—or at what his brothers would say.

But then he'd thought about how much money was being offered and how hard his dad worked—with Zane's sister, Jenna, yet to be put through college. So he said yes, expecting only to defray the costs of the last two years of school. And took his brothers' ribbing.

Except that one thing led to another, some modeling jobs, then a soap opera and a tiny film role. He discovered that all those hours of pretending as a kid served him well; he was a good actor, not just a face and body. He liked acting, relished the challenge of stepping inside a stranger's skin.

Even if he didn't always like the life.

Get real, son, he thought. *Admit it—you love the attention.*

He did, that was true. He'd always had ambition, never been afraid of hard work. Still wasn't. But Kelly's death had bared the dark side of the fairy tale he'd grown accustomed to living.

And he was tired.

"I'll get you some blankets, and you can have the pillow."

Zane jerked out of his thoughts. "What?"

"Since you offered to take the floor, you can have the only pillow." Roan rose and reached for his plate.

Zane grabbed and held on. "You cooked. I'll do the dishes."

A wry smile quirked the tiniest edge of her lips. "Gran did her dishes outside on the porch. No running water, remember?"

"So?"

"I don't see someone like you washing dishes, period—much less having to heat water and use a tin pan on the porch."

He snatched her plate from her hands. "What do

you mean, someone like me?'' She couldn't know who he was. His own mother might not recognize him easily.

One dismissive tilt of a shoulder. ''A rich guy.''

Zane relaxed a little. ''Anyone can rent a car.''

''A sixty-thousand-dollar SUV?'' she asked. ''I don't think so.''

''Doesn't matter,'' he snapped. ''I'm doing the dishes. You sit down.''

Her brows drew close together. ''It's my cabin.''

Zane sought patience. ''Do you hate all men or is it only me?''

She appeared honestly shocked. ''I don't hate men. I just don't need—'' She exhaled. ''Nothing.''

''What's the old man at the store got against you?''

She busied herself poking the fire. ''Doesn't matter.''

''He says you're too high on yourself. Me, I suspect he's dead wrong.''

''I don't care about the opinion of others.''

Zane set the plates on the table and approached her. ''I don't believe that's true. My question is, what are you running from? You wouldn't be in a place like this if you had any option. Are you in trouble?''

She headed for the door. ''It's none of your business.''

''It is when you faint on me twice.'' Zane lambasted himself for pressing her, but he was not a man who could just walk away from someone in trouble, no matter how pointless it was to care. "Talk to me, Roan."

Instead, she jerked the door open and left.

He was getting damn tired of chasing this woman up and down these mountains.

"Let her go, idiot," Zane muttered.

Then he picked up the kerosene lantern and charged into the darkness after her.

ROAN HUDDLED against the side of the house, wishing she'd grabbed one of Gran's quilts before escaping. For two cents, she'd sleep in the barn.

Except she hadn't tackled the barn yet, and God knows what sort of creatures had made it home. Maybe she should tell this guy—what was his name, anyway? She'd been rattled since the moment they'd met. She didn't need his name because she never intended to see him again after sunrise, but still...

His heavy steps pounded on the porch. Light spilled onto her shoulder.

Roan shrank against the logs.

Something moved in the vines trying to devour the porch rail, then skittered over her foot. She leaped away, not quite stifling a scream.

In a second, he was there beside her, his face in the flickering torchlight more worried than angry. "Are you all right?"

Roan froze in place, glancing down quickly, then up again. Afraid to step, wishing she could take both feet off the ground at the same time.

He seemed to understand, closing the gap between them and lifting her with only one arm and carrying her to the porch.

She was so surprised at his strength that she didn't resist him.

"There," he said. "Any idea what it was?"

She studied him, shadows hiding those too-seeing green eyes. "What's your name?"

He hesitated, gaze darting to the side. "Why?"

She frowned. "It's a simple question. You know mine. I don't know what to call you."

He grinned, and the sight took her breath. "So you can personalize it when you tell me to go to hell next time?"

She couldn't help a tiny chuckle. "Maybe so. Look—" She forced herself to meet his gaze squarely. "You've been kind to me, and it isn't that I'm not grateful, but—"

"Harold," he supplied.

She shook her head, distracted. "What?"

"My name is Harold. Since I've been waiting hours for a thank-you, I want to hear my name attached to it." He grinned again, but discomfort flared in his eyes. "It's my dad's name. He's a great guy."

She didn't want to empathize. "There's nothing wrong with Harold."

He shrugged. "I love my dad. Never cared for the name, but he doesn't, either. It doesn't suit him. Everyone calls him Hal."

"What do they call you?" she asked, though there was no reason to care. He'd be gone by morning.

He frowned for a second, then chuckled. "You mean besides 'knothead' or 'pest'?" His eyes turned wistful. "I'm the youngest brother. Mostly they called me a pain in the ass."

"That's unfair. They shouldn't—"

He laughed out loud then. "You obviously don't have brothers. It's how they tell me they love me."

"I'm an only child," she said, and wondered why she had. She pulled away from him and took a step toward the door.

"Hal," he supplied.

"What?"

"You can call me Hal."

"Does your family call you Hal Junior?"

"No." His gaze darted away. "I don't see them as often as I should."

Roan didn't press him on the sadness ghosting over his face. She understood all too well the pain of knowing you'd neglected someone you loved.

But she couldn't afford to get involved. "It's late," she said, opening the door. "I'll help you with the dishes so you can get some sleep. You'll want an early start."

She returned inside.

ZANE ROLLED AGAIN, seeking a comfortable position on the rock-hard floor. He stared into the fire, unsure if she was really asleep or just playing possum. She'd been so tired that she'd barely made it through drying the dishes before she'd sacked out, so he hoped she was having an easier time sleeping than he was. A guilty conscience over the quilts she'd given up when her thin frame needed them much more had combined with his status as unwanted guest to make sleep impossible for him.

He didn't like lying to her about his name, but given that she already wanted him anywhere but here, how much worse would she react if she was aware that he wasn't just the "rich guy" she'd disdained but also someone famous? And what was her beef about money, anyway?

Look around you, Zane. She's got reason enough just in this place.

Part of him itched to solve the mystery of Roan O'Hara, but the saner part of him knew that even if he had the right, he didn't have the energy. All he wanted was to go home to his family and hide out for the next six weeks. Get his head back on straight.

But he wasn't leaving at first light as she assumed, except long enough to retrieve his rental car from the side of the road, pick up some supplies in Ladyville and see who around there would be willing to help her out. Then he'd return with a proper flashlight and a whole bunch of batteries, for one thing, and chop her more wood to tide her over.

After that, conscience clear, he'd leave just as she'd made no bones of wanting him to do.

That settled, Zane punched the paper-thin pillow

again and bunched it beneath his cheek, closing his eyes.

And slowly, listening to the steady sound of her breathing, he, too, relaxed into slumber.

CHAPTER FOUR

"You're back." The old man's tone was flat, but in his eyes, Zane saw a spark of interest. "Thought you was just passin' through."

Zane took a stab at the codger role. "Changed my mind."

"Hmmph."

Nothing more. The old man didn't twitch a muscle, one gnarled hand resting on the counter.

Zane was tempted to smile, but he was sure the humor would be lost on his subject. Instead, he perused the grocery shelves, seeking staple items instead of the junk food he'd gathered last time. He recalled what Roan had had in her bags—beans, corn, flour. She needed more protein. Could use fattening up, too.

He spied burlap sacks stacked against a wall and moved closer. Fifty-pound sacks of pinto beans and corn. Beside them were sacks of flour and rice. He hefted beans and rice over his shoulder, then carried them to the counter. He repeated with two more bags, this time corn and flour. "Got any sugar?"

The old man's eyebrows rose, but he said nothing, simply nodded past Zane's left shoulder.

Zane suppressed a grin and turned that way. He grabbed the largest bag of sugar—twenty-five pounds—and scanned the shelves above it, then filled his arms with canned fruit and vegetables, though he doubted they'd taste as good as her grandmother's. He returned to the counter and dumped this load next to the others.

The old man's eyebrows nearly reached his hairline. Still, he didn't ask.

"What do folks around here do about meat if there's no freezer? Besides jerky, I mean. Yours was good, by the way."

"Hmmph."

"My dad's is better, though—no offense."

Thick, salt-and-pepper eyebrows snapped together. "Not my best batch."

"Hmmph." Zane dealt the old man some of his own medicine.

Silence hummed in the air. In his normal life, Zane was generally in motion, quick to respond, seldom quiet or still, but he found himself enjoying this challenge of meeting the old man on his home ground immensely.

"Most folks salt the meat or smoke it. 'Course, city boy like you could buy some of that canned meat over yonder." He nodded toward the back. "Or he could go down to Asheville to one of them discount stores." No attempt was made to hide his derision.

"When's deer season in these parts?" Zane asked.

"Back home, it won't be for six weeks or so, the beginning of November."

The old man's lip curled. "Damn guv'mint got no right to tell folks when to hunt. Anyone with sense knows not to clean out the stock."

Zane kept his expression sober with effort. In his part of Texas, there had been modern-day efforts to set up a separate republic to flout federal and state control. He understood the "defend the shores, deliver the mail and stay the hell out of our lives" mentality of those accustomed to self-sustaining existences. It was that way where he'd grown up, and this place was smack in the middle of moonshiner country, another reason for them not to like government. Stills hidden back in steep mountain valleys were an ancient tradition, as was the cat-and-mouse game played with "revenooers," the federal agents ready to rob moonshiners of both profit and fun. "Won't get any argument from me."

"Hmmph." But ancient brown eyes sparked.

Zane strolled back to the shelves indicated and loaded up again on canned meats. This time, when he returned, the remaining room on the counter vanished. He could see the questions in the old man's eyes cheek-by-jowl with the determination not to ask.

He had to cough to cover a threatening laugh.

"I didn't expect to need my rifle," he said. L.A. wasn't exactly replete with hunting opportunities, so his dad kept Zane's deer rifle and shotgun at home. "If I take a mind to do some hunting—" he slipped

back into old ways of speaking with ease, surprised
at how welcome it felt after all he'd done to lose his
accent "—where would a body find a weapon and
ammunition?"

He spotted the *why* forming on the old man's lips,
but before he could speak, the screen door creaked
and another voice intervened.

"I got guns I could sell you." A man near his
own age, not quite his height but stocky, his black
beard bristling almost as much as his attitude, let the
screen door slam behind him. "Mornin', Noah." He
nodded to Zane. "That your car outside?" Greed and
contempt shimmered around him thick enough to
see.

Not for the first time, Zane regretted renting a vehicle so noticeable, never imagining he'd be in it
more than two or three days, a stranger passing
through without making contact. He chose not to answer the swarthy man, instead turning back to Noah.
"What about you?"

The old man's gaze darted over to the new arrival,
something like fear in his eyes. "Frank here, he's
got a better supply, don't you, Frank?"

"Depends on who's askin'. You got a name,
boy?"

Boy. Zane's humor fled. He knew jerks like this.
He'd grown up being picked on by them, bullies who
waited until his elder brothers weren't around before
pounding him and Cade—at least, until Cade got big,
too, years before Zane.

Zane had refused to hide behind his brothers. He'd taken his licks and studied his opponents, then used his brains to get the better of them in the end. Not before he'd been bruised and bloodied, of course...but he'd learned.

And Hollywood was full of insecure types who used power as a mask for their shortcomings. Zane smiled and mentally licked his chops. "Depends on who's askin'."

The stockier man stiffened. Bulk that already showed signs of running to fat nonetheless was a threat Zane could not afford to ignore. "Don't sell guns to greenhorns."

Oh, yeah. There was a fight coming, and Zane realized he was spoiling for it. Maybe pounding the bejesus out of this creep was just the release he needed, since he couldn't deck reporters and would never take his hand to a woman.

He smiled sweetly. "I suppose you think you can take me." He shrugged. "Me being a greenhorn and all."

Dark eyes grew wary, but pride overrode. "Know I could."

"Now, Frank, me and this fella, we was just talkin' about huntin'. Reckon he'll be around for a spell," Noah interjected.

Zane glanced at him and could see the old man calculating the bill that would evaporate once Frank bested him, as the old man's fear showed he believed Frank would.

"Where you stayin'?" Frank seized the change of topic with a haste that only confirmed Zane's opinion. This man would fight, no doubt about it, but he preferred it not be with someone his own size.

Zane spoke to Noah, instead. "You got a hammer? Nails?"

"What for?" Frank demanded.

Noah simply pointed.

Zane strolled that way. "I'm helping Roan O'Hara for a few days," he answered.

Both men went rigid, Noah with the disdain he'd shown her before, but something more was going on with Frank.

"She's here?" Frank spat the words, whirling on Noah. "What the hell's she doin' back?"

Noah only shrugged.

Zane grasped the opportunity. "You know her?"

Frank's head whipped around. "Question is, how do you know her?"

There was something nasty and possessive in Frank's tone.

Zane thought about challenging him but decided it was more important to get information—and help for her. "She's up there in her grandmother's cabin without enough wood or food to last the winter, and the cabin's falling down around her ears. Seems to me," he said, looking at Noah now, "that she could use the help of her neighbors."

Frank snorted. "Miss Hoity-toity Bitch won't stay in that cabin, no way. She couldn't wait to leave before. Broke up a marriage to grab a man who could give her the luxuries she thought she deserved. Too good for the likes of us.'' In his voice, Zane heard a man who had quite likely been jilted.

But *hoity-toity?* Broke up a marriage? A woman who required luxuries? Aside from the broken skin of her hands, Zane had seen nothing in Roan O'Hara that vaguely resembled the woman Frank described.

Frank turned to him. "This stuff for her?''

Zane nodded.

Frank chuckled, but it was an ugly sound. "That's rich. You tellin' me she's broke?'' He laughed again, and Noah joined him.

Zane thought about Roan's despair, her struggle with defeat. She'd anticipated that they would feel like this, he saw now. She expected no help from her neighbors, was grimly determined to survive anyhow.

What had driven her to this juncture? Where was that man who'd given her luxuries?

Zane wanted to find out, but he refused to expose Roan to any more ridicule. He was sorry he'd invited this much. If he'd known, he would have made that trip down the mountain to get supplies. From now on, he'd do that.

Instead, he located the hardware section. He selected a twenty-ounce hammer and weighed out five pounds each of sixteen-penny nails for the porch and galvanized roofing nails from buckets lined up on the floor.

When he returned to the counter, he didn't try to hide his contempt for their unwillingness to help Roan. "I'm ready to pay." No matter what mistakes Roan had made, surely she didn't deserve this.

Inwardly, he sighed. He sure couldn't walk away from her now. He'd seen the .22 and the shotgun. He'd hunt her some meat— "Wait. Where's the salt you use to preserve meat?"

Noah's eyebrows rose. "You said you didn't have anything to hunt with."

Zane stood his ground, wondering if their enmity would extend so far as to harm her if they realized how poorly protected she was. Neither weapon was much good for self-defense except at close range. "I never said that. Where's the salt?"

"My advice to you is—" Frank began.

Zane wasn't grinning now. "When I want your advice, I'll be sure to ask for it." He turned back to Noah. "Salt?"

Grudgingly, Noah pointed to it.

Zane added it to his bundle, then said nothing else as Noah rang up the total. Zane counted out his bills and pondered the irony that he could buy out this whole town, no doubt, but he was running out of cash. Finding an ATM seemed a whole lot less than likely.

Neither man lifted a hand to help with his purchases, and that was just fine with Zane. If Roan didn't need the supplies so much, he'd have turned around and left without any of them.

WHEN ROAN AWOKE, he was gone.

And his quilts covered her now. The poor excuse for a pillow lay beneath her head.

He'd touched her, and she'd slept through all of it. She almost thought she could feel his warmth.

For a sinful second, she closed her eyes. Cozy for the first time all night, she pulled the covers tighter and snuggled deeper into the bed.

And breathed in the scent of him.

Hal. The name didn't seem to fit, but people didn't have a choice in what their parents named them. Her own came, she was told, from Roan Mountain not far away, famed for its display of rhododendrons in the spring. The name was uncommon, though, and she understood the cost of having a name other kids thought was weird.

He'd been kind, after all, more so than she deserved. More than she wanted. He couldn't realize how dangerous kindness was, how treacherous and deceptive, how it would weaken her to accept it.

How much she longed for it, as she craved still the siren song of her sweet little pills.

Today. This minute. Her teeth ached against the longing for surcease, for blessed relief, and Roan reminded herself that she only had to get through this minute. Just one.

Then the next. And then one more.

But she couldn't think past now, not yet. Though she knew that minutes added up to hours, hours made days, days became weeks, the knowledge didn't comfort. Only an addict understood that a minute seemed an endless desert, a barren span without respite, time that must be endured.

Ample for Roan to remember all that she wanted to forget.

Focus, damn it. She squeezed her eyes shut again. Clamped down. Shut out. Blocked every wayward thought but one.

Breathe, Roan. Deep and sure. Breathe and relax.

Picture the meadow, feel the breeze. Lift your face to the sunshine, let it warm your skin.

In. Out. You can do this. You can.

Behind her eyelids, Roan was there again, in the meadow just up the mountain, the place she'd been happiest, back when Gran had kept her during one of her mother's wanderings, a space of days, maybe weeks, when Roan was freed from her mother's demons and had a chance to be only a little girl.

Gran, can you hear me? I'm here. I'm home. I want to stay.

But I'm so scared, Gran. I'm not sure if there's enough of you left inside for me to make it. I want your strength. I want your grace. I want to be the woman you believed I could.

I lost my way. I'm sorry. I never thought I'd be in this place without you. Never again to see your face, to feel your hands on my hair. To lean against you, lay my head in your lap.

I need the minutes, Gran. I need the peace. Maybe I can't do this, but I have to try.

She gripped the rough iron bedstead where she'd spent the only safe nights of her life, and Roan pictured her grandmother sleeping beside her, warm and loving and wise.

She drew her fingers across the top quilt, a pattern called Grandma's Flower Garden. Gran had used old feed sacks and scraps of Mama's childhood dresses to make it years before Roan was born, stitching the tiny, colorful hexagonal pieces together by hand. Here and there, the fabric had worn thin, the muslin backing aged to dark cream, dappled with an occasional brown spot. Gran's hands had carried their own marks of time's passage, of long days spent carving a life out of thin mountain soil and longer nights watching over the sick and injured, fighting for their survival or easing them into the embrace of eternity.

Comforted by memories of the woman who'd been her true north, Roan slid once again into the silence and, just for an instant, felt the faint stroke of a workworn hand on her hair.

A THUD OUTSIDE jerked Roan awake. Full sunlight now blazed through the small window over the bed. A second thud had her on her feet, grabbing the fireplace poker and brandishing it.

Who was more surprised when the door opened was hard to tell.

Arms filled with freshly chopped wood, Hal stopped in midstep and grinned. "Sorry—dropped a couple. Should have made two trips.'' His smile widened. ''You any good with that thing?''

The slash of white teeth robbed her of thought. ''What thing?''

''Your lethal weapon there.'' He nodded toward the poker and continued into the room. ''I come in peace, *kemo sabe*. You can lay down your arms.''

Gratefully, she lowered the poker. ''What are you doing here? You were supposed to be gone.''

He glanced over his shoulder, one eyebrow lifted. ''I was. I bought a hammer and some nails. No fresh lumber, but I found some boards in an outbuilding that appear to be sound.''

''Why?''

''To fix this wreck of a porch and steps before you break your neck on them.''

''You're supposed to leave. It's morning.''

''Yeah, I noticed.'' His gaze shifted to the window. ''Late morning, actually. Nearly noon.''

She wanted to brush her teeth, drink some coffee. Attend to other necessities. ''You can't stay.''

He faced her. They stood less than a foot apart. ''I'm offering you help.''

''I didn't ask for it.''

''Maybe not, babe, but you damn sure need it. You'll never survive the winter without some serious work.''

''What are you after?''

Vivid green eyes scanned her from head to toe while Roan resisted the urge to comb fingers through her hair, to straighten the very wrinkled clothes in which she'd slept. If she'd ever felt less attractive in her life, she couldn't recall it. "Stop that."

"What?"

"Quit looking at me."

He grinned. "Why do I make you so nervous?"

Even white teeth gleamed beneath a dark swashbuckler's mustache. High cheekbones, square jaw and strong nose, wide, beautiful mouth…this was a man who knew his appeal, who understood how to use it.

He was too handsome for his own good.

But his eyes held shadows. Sorrow made a lie of his grin. She didn't understand the conflict, but something about him had her wishing—

Nothing. She could want nothing but for him to go.

"I'm not nervous," she said. "And I'll be just fine."

"I brought more chocolate."

"Why do you care what happens to me?" she demanded. "Why won't you just drive away?"

For a second, she could see his own confusion peer from behind the cocky smile. "Beats the hell out of me," he admitted. "But I've already got the nails, and I never leave a job undone." He headed for the door. "I wouldn't mind a cup of coffee, if you could see fit to make some. I'll bring in the groceries after I fix that hole. I'm tired of dodging it." With that, he was gone.

Roan stared at the spot where he'd just been. Groceries? He wanted coffee? She would march right outside and tell him—

What? She'd been very clear, and she might as well have saved her breath. The man wasn't listening.

He was right about the porch, one of the many items on her list. But he couldn't simply...

A nail screamed in protest as a board was pried up, then another. And he was whistling while he worked.

Roan glanced around her at all that remained to be done. She could use the help, yes, but at what price? What was a man in a luxury car doing replacing boards on her front porch? Where had he come from and where was he headed?

She jerked the door open. "I'll fix you something to eat, then you'll leave before dark, right?"

He spoke without looking up. "We'll see."

Roan slammed the door.

Then realized that she had no other path to get to the well or the privy. With as much dignity as she could muster, she grabbed a bucket and stalked past Hal, head held high.

SHE HAD TO get out of here, she thought later.

She couldn't stand looking at him one more second. He'd shed his shirt in the heat of the day, and his skin, rippling with every move of impressive muscles, glistened with sweat. She'd barricaded herself inside, cleaning with a vengeance, but the interior of the cabin was stifling, so she'd finally opened all the windows and the front door to catch the breeze that had kicked up not long ago.

But he seemed to be everywhere she turned. And she was sick of being inside.

Would he never leave?

Roan crossed to the door, intent on asking him exactly that, when she saw him stop at the well, let down the rope, then raise the heavy bucket as though it weighed nothing, take a long drink and upend the rest of the water over his head.

Liquid sluiced over gleaming flesh. He was, quite simply, gorgeous. Tall, muscled and virile. Every woman's dream.

Roan whirled and slammed the door. The last thing she needed in her screwed-up life was a fling with a stranger, no matter how decent he appeared.

Appearances could be deceiving—hadn't she learned that the hard way? First her husband, Ben; then Mick of the kind blue eyes. Ben had bought himself a raw girl he'd molded into a plastic doll until the life had bled out of her.

Mick, whom she'd met at one of Ben's rich friends' parties after Ben had moved her to Baltimore, had supplied her with sympathy and pills she'd eagerly accepted to escape the barren desert her life had become. She'd lost her way, never realizing the slippery slope she was descending down the path to other substances far more deadly—and when she'd gone out of control and Ben had shed himself of an embarrassment, Mick had offered a stone-broke, desperate woman a helping hand.

Not revealing until much later just how she'd have to repay him.

Gaze darting around the room, Roan seized upon a distraction. Gathering greens and herbs, checking the woods for signs of the largesse Gran had once shown her—that would get her away from Hal and his beautiful body.

First, though, she'd make him sandwiches and leave them on the porch. He'd expended a lot of energy already today, and she had no idea when—or if—he'd eaten breakfast. He'd fixed the porch and steps, had chopped more wood. His energy was endless, but surely he couldn't get by on only whatever he'd had that morning.

Peanut butter and jelly wasn't much to offer a man who drove a luxury car, but it was the most protein she could provide quickly. She still hadn't touched the supplies he'd brought inside. When she returned, she'd have to bake more bread; her funds wouldn't extend to buying from Noah's store anything she could produce.

Even if she could force herself to accept Hal's charity, soon she'd need to summon the will to take Gran's .22 and hunt, no matter how she quailed at the prospect. She had to reap nature's bounty in order to get through this winter. Gran would have shaken her head and reminded Roan that mountain folk had to be practical. Nourishment must be taken wherever it was found. Survivors couldn't afford pride or faint hearts or weak stomachs.

On that night she'd found herself in a stained, chipped bathtub in a seedy Baltimore motel, razor blades at the ready, Roan had made that first, stinging slice, and the pain had shocked her. Had yanked her out of the dun-gray haze in which she'd lived for so long. As she'd stared at the thin red ribbon of her own blood, she'd realized that, deserving or not, she wanted to survive.

She glanced down at her left wrist, at the scar still pink and fresh. With one finger, she traced it, then pressed hard, seeking the pain she'd avoided for so long.

I am a survivor. I'm making my stand.

Quickly, she covered the plate of sandwiches with a cloth, then took Gran's handmade willow gathering basket, long and oval and shallow, off its high shelf and hugged it to her chest. The mingled scents trapped in the ancient reeds brought Gran near once more.

She closed her eyes and let the past wash over her, precious memories of peace and love and strength coating the ragged edges of her terror that she'd fail again.

Roan drew in a deep, steadying breath. After a moment, she headed out the front door, sparing not one look for the man who'd invaded her refuge. Instead, she set the plate down where he could see it and tripped down the newly strong stairs, then nearly ran when she reached the corner of the house.

She didn't stop until she was well out of his sight.

ZANE WALKED OUT of the barn just in time to see Roan slipping into the woods. For a second, he considered whether he should follow, then caught a glimpse of the basket over her arm and shrugged. She wasn't exactly eager for his company.

Question was: why was he still here?

He removed his ball cap, ran one hand through damp hair and swiped an arm over his face to stop the sweat from dripping into his eyes. He rolled his neck around and heard a satisfying pop.

He was tired enough to drop to the ground and sleep where he fell.

Then he spied something on the porch railing, covered with a faded cloth. What looked like the edge of a plate poked from beneath, and he moved closer to investigate. Pulling one corner of the cloth to peer under it, he saw two sandwiches resting on one of the cracked, scarred plates they'd used last night.

PB&J. His favorite, though the sheer number of them he'd consumed in his early acting years should have cured him forever. He opened the cloth wide and grabbed one, then took a big bite. Making quick work of the sandwich, he picked up the plate and walked inside, then spotted the supplies he'd purchased still sitting on the kitchen table and floor.

And swore. She hadn't touched any of them, not one item.

Pride, pure and simple. The blasted woman was not going to accept any help he didn't force upon her, yet she'd dipped into her small store to feed him. Zane was too hungry and sick of junk food to refuse her offering, but as he gobbled up the sandwiches, he began to place the items he'd brought on the shelves, mixing them in with hers.

Just then, the tiny cell phone in his jeans pocket chirped. Zane jolted and fumbled to retrieve what had only a day ago been as natural an extension of him as his own arm but now seemed a beacon from a foreign world.

"Hello?"

Garbled sounds, mostly static. He'd tried a call when he'd reached his car, but the reception down there had been nonexistent. Same thing at the store.

He moved to flip the lid shut just as a voice crackled through.

"Where the hell are you?" his agent, Sal, asked. "I've been trying…reach…yesterday—"

Zane was more tempted than ever to simply hit the power button and turn the damn thing off.

"Upped their offer…won't wait long—"

"Sal, you're cutting out. I'm in a bad area. I'll call you tomorrow from the next stop."

"Wait…director wants to start casting…have to—"

"Can't hear you, Sal. Later." Zane disconnected

the call and turned his phone off. He could have put the pieces together, even with the static, but he didn't want to hear more about how his last release had out-performed even the high expectations of the studio or their expectations to have him do two sequels of the same schlock.

They were offering a hell of a lot of money, and he ought to have his head examined for not jumping on the deal with both feet. The funds could buy him the chance to make a little film he'd been thinking about for quite a while, something poles apart from his leading-man image. Risky as the devil, but the only thing that had gotten his juices going in a long time. A movie he and Kelly had talked about pro-ducing together during one of her good stretches, one of those increasingly rare blue-sky spans when she was the woman who'd first attracted him, fresh and sweet and whip-smart.

Now the film would be her memorial, and he just didn't know if he had the heart to continue.

Restless again, Zane cast off thoughts of the woman he hadn't been able to save and concentrated on what had given him major sore muscles but dis-tracted him from counting his sins.

The porch looked good. Ditto the steps. He'd chopped half a cord of wood already today and, long-ing for shade, had decided to inspect the barn.

The roof he'd save for tomorrow.

Tomorrow? What was he thinking, staying another day with a woman who longed to see him gone? And what would he do to get through another night on that floor?

The roof needed fixing, and that was that. Once he cut another couple of cords and patched the tin roof with scrap salvaged from the barn and shed, he'd leave for sure. Two days, three tops, then he'd be on his way home.

Home. On impulse, Zane walked to an open spot outside, flipped open his phone and hit On. He ignored the message waiting from Sal in favor of dialing a number he knew by heart, hoping it would connect.

"Hello?"

"Hey, brat," he said.

"Zane! Mom, it's Zane," his sister, Jenna, shrieked. "When are you getting here? Jesse's coming home next week, and he was psyched to hear you'd be home, too."

Zane smiled at the irrepressible cheer in his sister's voice. Six years younger than him, she'd been alternately doted on and driven crazy by four elder brothers even more determined than their father to guard her from life just as vigorously as she fought to experience it. Man, he missed her.

"That's great, Jen, but I might not be there for a few days."

"Why not?" she demanded. "Must be a woman." She fell silent. "Sorry, I didn't mean Kelly—"

"Forget it. And yes, there's a woman, but it's not what you think." Running one hand through his hair, he exhaled an exasperated sigh. "Listen, my reception is iffy here. Let me talk to Mom before I lose it again, okay?"

"Okay, but you'd better get here soon. Diego and Caroline's baby is due any day. You have a clue what Mom will do to you if you're not here to play uncle for the first grandchild?"

Zane smiled. His eldest brother had nearly died, but had fought his way back to a life forever changed by his injuries. He'd become a *curandero,* following in Mama Lalita's footsteps, only to encounter the biggest cynic ever—and married her. Now he and Caroline, a former cardiac surgeon, operated two clinics for the poor and traveled between Austin and La Paloma weekly, until Caroline had gotten too pregnant to travel. He could only imagine the chaos as Caroline's sisters, Ivy and Chloe, their husbands, her niece Amelia, and the entire town of La Paloma gathered to await the blessed event.

And he was risking missing it for the sake of a woman who wanted, more than anything, to see him gone.

"Zane, darling, how close are you?"

He cleared his throat. "Not that near, Mom. Thing is—" He frowned. "I'm still in North Carolina. There's this woman who's in real trouble. I'm going to stay a few days to help her back on her feet."

Silence. Then chuckles, fond and soft. "Oh, sweetheart, how like you to be riding to the rescue.

Always one to drag home strays, human or animal, since you could barely walk. So who is she?''

"She's not—there's nothing between us, just—" He paused. "I'm not sure why I'm here. She doesn't want me, has tried everything possible to make me leave, but—"

"She needs you."

"Not me, really, just…someone. She's all alone in this wreck of a cabin with no lights or running water—"

"How did you find her?"

He shook his head. "A guy was heckling her, and then she fainted on the side of the road and—"

"I love you so much, Zane." He could hear his mother's smile in her voice. "It's certainly not the first time you ever defended the weak. What does she think about having a movie star as her Prince Charming?"

"Well, see, she…actually, Mom, she doesn't realize who I am."

Outright laughter. "You've only got one of the most recognizable faces in the world. How has this come about?"

"To dodge the press, I dyed my hair, which is still shaggy after the last film, plus I grew a mustache and I haven't shaved in a week."

"You look that different?"

"I sure tried. Anyway, she doesn't seem to be someone who's up on the news. She's—Mom, she's hurting. A lot. I don't understand why, but there's a desperation about her, and she's too proud to ask anyone for assistance. But the cabin—she's never lived like this, I'd bet the farm, and winter's coming and—'' He broke off. ''I can't leave yet, Mom. I'm sorry. The baby's due any day, but—''

''Diego will understand better than anyone. After all the people he's helped, he's not going to be angry.''

''But you wanted everyone there when the baby came.''

''Should you be bringing her here? Could we do something for her?''

He smiled. He wasn't the only one in the family who took in lost lambs. Diego came by the penchant from both sides. ''Problem is, first I'd have to tell her who I am. I don't think she'd be favorably inclined.''

''Oh, dear. You've really boxed yourself in, haven't you? Who does she think you are?''

''Some guy named Hal. Short for Harold, of course.''

Grace MacAllister clucked her tongue. ''You're skirting a fine line, Zane Harold MacAllister. But your father will love the tribute.''

''How is he?'' As he asked, Zane fought a pang of homesickness. He wanted to hang out and work horses with his dad. Do a little fishing. He couldn't waste much more time here or he'd miss out altogether.

''He's just great. Eager to be a grandfather. Already made a fishing pole for the little one, boy or girl.''

Zane smiled. His dad thought there was nothing a little fishing time couldn't cure. His enthusiasm over a baby not actually related to him by blood said more than words could about how much he'd enfolded his wife's sons from her first marriage into his own heart.

"Give him a hug for me. Tell him to save me a cigar, okay?'' Zane paused, glancing around at the darkening skies. He cleared a thickened throat. "I want to be there with all of you, Mom. I was looking forward to—''

"I know, sweetheart. Please stop blaming yourself for Kelly. You did everything anyone could, but some people just can't be helped.''

"Blasted drugs.''

"I'm proud of you for rescuing this woman. What's her name?''

"Roan. Roan O'Hara.''

"Well, I hope Roan O'Hara is aware of how lucky she is.''

"I don't think she'd agree, Mom, but thanks. She'll probably tell me again tonight to get lost.''

"But you won't, will you, darling? Not until she's safe.''

He sighed. "She'd be safest if she'd leave this mountain. The people here don't like her, and she seems to be hanging on by her fingernails. I could give her the money to take care of everything, but..."

"Money can't solve some things, can it?"

He thought of everything he'd given Kelly, all the money he'd spent on doctors and rehab and shrinks and she'd still—

"No."

"I'll call you when the baby's born if you haven't made it by then."

Thunder rumbled in the distance. He shuffled his feet. "Thing is, I don't think I can let her know I have this phone. Sal's trying to reach me, and if she hears—" He faltered.

"Darling, you know secrets can be damaging. How is she going to feel when she discovers who you are?"

"She won't. I'm going to finish up here and be on my way with her none the wiser. She's so skittish she'd probably believe that I did it to embarrass her."

"All right. But stay in touch, will you? Keep me posted on how you are?"

"You bet. I love you, Mom. I'm sorry, but—"

"Shh, sweetheart. I understand. You're doing a good thing, and I'm proud of you. But you get home as soon as you can, you hear? I want all my chicks together, including my wandering superstar. Bye, darling."

"Mom—wait. This whole star thing—it might be

the reason Kelly—'' He hesitated. ''I'm just wondering…maybe I shouldn't…maybe this isn't—''

''You stop blaming yourself for Kelly. If you enjoy your career, then continue. If not, you'd better remember that we all adored you long before fame rode your way. Surely you're not going to insult us by suggesting we were less proud of you then than we are now.'' He could hear her gearing up. Grace MacAllister in high dudgeon was not for the faint of heart.

''No, ma'am. Can't imagine what I was thinking.''

She laughed. ''You're our beloved Zane, ditch digger or movie star. And you'd be helping that woman, no matter what your circumstances. Now, you get finished there and come home.''

''Yes, ma'am.''

''I love you.''

''I love you, too, Mom.''

He flipped the lid closed and held the phone tight and warm in his hand for a long time.

Then he stowed it in his car and went for his shirt, studying the gunmetal-gray clouds to the north. Roan had been gone a long time. He'd better check on her.

CHAPTER FIVE

THUNDER CRACKED in the rapidly darkening sky, its impact muffled by the canopy of trees, the verdant growth that tumbled and crept over the path Roan had once traveled with ease.

Drops of rain began to fall, fat and chilly on her uncovered head. She should turn back, she knew that, but she wanted to find the swing she and Gran had tied to the magnificent old oak that once served as her playhouse and shelter, refuge, just as Gran had been, from a childhood spent nursing her mother's hangovers and dodging the hands of the men who paraded through her mother's life.

The swing had to be here. With an urgency that increased by the minute, Roan tuned out the whip of the wind, the drops now a downpour. She couldn't be lost; once she'd been able to find her way to it with her eyes closed. She wanted badly to touch it, to sit on the rough wooden seat she'd cut herself with Gran's handsaw, to feel the rasp of the thick rope she'd shinnied up the trunk to tie far above.

She'd dreamed on that swing. Talked to the trees on that swing. Spent hours watching the kaleidoscope of bare branches and spring green, torpid summer heat and blazing fall glory.

Rain slid in runnels down her face. Her clothing stuck to her body, but still Roan searched, hoping to connect with the girl she'd once been, the one who'd dared to believe she'd escape becoming her mother.

That she had not was her deepest shame.

One tiny voice inside Roan had endured, however faint. Had stopped that gleaming blade, had shouted through the fog of drugs and despair until it was hoarse. Until finally, she had heard.

She would never go back to that existence. She must make it here. This was, in the most real way possible, Roan's last chance. If she couldn't survive and uncover the woman Gran had believed she could be, she would die as she had been dying by inches for years.

Now or never. Somehow, the swing held a key to finding her way back to the girl of hope.

"Roan—"

She shrugged off the voice as she would a pesky fly.

"What the hell are you doing out here?" Suddenly, there Hal was, big and soaking wet and furious. "I've been calling you for five minutes. Look at you—" He grabbed her arm.

She glanced down and saw that her white blouse was plastered to her body, her jeans gone darkest navy. Her breasts, small enough that she seldom bothered with a bra, were clearly visible, aureoles dark and nipples erect from the cold.

But none of that mattered. It couldn't. "Let me go." She turned away, trying to see through the downpour.

"Are you crazy?"

Slippery wet, she escaped him and plunged into the brush. "Go back. I'm not through here."

"There's nothing you need that can't wait." He grasped the tail of her shirt as she shouldered past. She heard stitches pop.

They both stopped in shock.

"I'm sorry. I didn't mean—" He frowned. "Can't you feel how the temperature's dropping?" He got a new hold on her and reeled her in.

She fought him. "You don't understand."

His eyes betrayed his confusion. "I don't want to hurt you, but you can't—" He grunted as her elbow connected with his rock-solid gut.

But for a second, his grip wavered.

She jerked loose, threw her basket at him and ran.

Wet branches slapped at her, vines whipped and slashed. Slick ground cost her balance; she landed hard. White bolts of pain shot up her arm.

But still she scrambled to her feet and ran, terror ratcheting as she heard his heavy steps behind her. Just as she feared he would catch her and glanced back to check, something hard smacked her shoulder. She whirled, barely missing the board careering toward her face.

Roan ducked. It hit him right in the chest.

"What the—" He knocked the obstacle away.

"No!" Roan leaped for it, realizing just then what it was. With both arms she drew it in, cradling it to her, pressing her face against the thick, weathered rope.

She looked around her, trying to uncover the place of her memory in this spot so overgrown that vines crept down the ropes and past, tangling with more vines on the ground.

And she smiled. Holding on for dear life.

He stood two feet away, staring at her. "What? What is it?"

She shook her head. "I can't explain. It's only that—" She scanned the area again, seeing a landmark. "This is mine. Gran and I made it."

Zane's rage drained away as puzzlement replaced it. The expression on her face…

"You were searching for this?" It was a swing the forest had entwined in a death grip, battered and buried, forgotten for how many years? "You risked catching your death of cold over an old swing?"

The wonder and hope disappeared behind embarrassment, and Zane wanted to cut out his tongue. "I'm sorry. It's important to you, isn't it?"

She chanced one glance at him, then down. She didn't speak, but her whole frame hunched in on itself. She gathered the swing closer as if for protection.

Zane felt shame enough to mask the sheer misery

of wet boots and soaked jeans. He thought about leaving her alone, but honest worry over her wouldn't let him. She was shivering with the cold now.

But he had to give her something. "There's this spring that my brother has on his land. It's special to him, and you can feel it when you're there, how it sort of soothes you. Calms you." He swiped at his hair to stem the water pouring down his face. "I always envied him, having that private spot."

Her eyes cut to his, then aside. For a moment, he thought she wouldn't speak.

Finally, she did. "My mother didn't like to stay in one town long. I lived in so many different apartments I lost track. Gran's cabin was my only home. Sometimes my mother would take off for months and leave me here. Gran said I needed my own special place, so…" Her voice died away.

Then she looked up. "I climbed that branch and tied the ropes myself because Gran couldn't."

Zane followed her gaze. "How old were you?"

"Nine."

"Pretty terrifying climb for a nine-year-old."

Her eyes were bleak. Haunted. "This was my safe place. Nothing could scare me here."

He wanted to ask her what she'd had to fear, but her teeth had started to chatter. "Think we can find our way back?" He kept his tone light.

A faint smile played about her lips. "Maybe."

Then she turned sad again. "I never thought I'd lose my way to this clearing."

"We could come back when the rain stops." He saw her stiffen. "You could, I mean."

Her grateful glance touched something inside him. "You're soaked. I'm sorry. You didn't have to come searching for me."

"Yeah," he said. "I did." And held out a hand. "Wish I'd left bread crumbs, though."

Tiny sparks of mischief danced in her eyes. "The birds would have gotten them if the vines hadn't covered them up." Slowly, almost stutter-step, she let her hand clasp his.

Zane felt the shock of it. One honest touch.

As he drew her forward, he kept a careful distance and tried to ignore how he could see the rounding of her breasts, the pucker of her nipples, the slim line of waist curving into hip. He'd been with so many women who were tucked and tanned, shaped by artifice where Nature hadn't granted Her bounty, yet this woman's nearly boyish body stirred him in a way he hadn't been in years. If ever.

And it wasn't simple lust. Something about her was so vulnerable. Exposed. She made him want to cradle her close and promise that nothing would ever hurt her again.

How badly he wanted to do it shook the hell out of him.

But she stood like a doe in the forest, poised to run. Sensing danger.

He understood now that she was fragile, not brittle. Worn, but not hard. He had a sense that he could tip the balance, push her over the edge to which she was barely clinging.

He wanted to encircle those bowed shoulders. Bring a smile to the sad eyes. Make her laugh, help her stand proud.

For now, though, he carefully kept himself apart from her, gesturing before him in a sweeping bow. "After you, madam."

The tiny quirk of her lips and the relief in her frame were his reward.

WITH TIME, they found their way back. Zane's sense of direction helped, honed by years of hunting and fishing with his father, exploring with his brothers, but it was Roan's eyes that spotted trees she remembered climbing, gullies she knew to cross.

The longer they walked, the more he saw in her a sense of belonging lacking in his daily life. L.A. was where he worked, but it would never be home, he realized. He knew many people there but had few true friends. It was the way of that world—temporary alliances, brief affairs, constant seeking for advantage. A career was a short-lived thing for most actors—those who endured were a rare lot.

It wore on you, the constant slipping in and out of skins. Someone without the firm grounding Zane's family had given him would lose any sense of a center, any compass that pointed to true north.

That was why he made a point of going home as often as possible, instead of taking the exotic vacations others did between films. He'd tried to treat his whole family to the luxuries he could now afford, all but a few they'd politely—but firmly—refused. Cade was always wandering somewhere, shooting roll after roll of the film that had established him as a real up-and-coming adventure photographer. Jesse was too busy chasing down criminals and making the world safe. Jenna loved baubles and was the easiest to pamper, but the thing Diego had needed most— his health—had been a struggle only he could fight.

Zane had been proud when his big brother had finally asked Zane to contribute start-up money for the indigent clinics he and Caroline wanted to establish. Zane had already set aside, without telling them, a college fund for their unborn child.

His mother had protested over the Christmas gift of perfectly matched pearls with the sapphire clasp echoing her eyes, but in the end, Zane had prevailed. His dad steadfastly declined to let Zane do more than buy the cigars Grace pretended she didn't know he smoked. Everything else, he insisted on Zane keeping for a rainy day.

Plenty of people would be happy to relieve Zane of any excess funds, but he was no man's sucker. He'd discovered a real knack for investing money and getting good returns, so as a result, he donated a lot to charity but still had a nice nest egg that would see him through quite a few years. Perhaps not the luxuries he had now, but plenty for what most people would consider a good life.

He could give the woman ahead of him, swaying on her feet, all she required to bring electricity and running water to this godforsaken place. He had the wherewithal to make sure she survived this winter in grand style.

But his gut told him more strongly than ever that it would be a mistake, not a mercy; that it would weaken her in some essential manner; that she would resent him, not thank him.

If only he understood why.

What made her so desperate? What haunted her eyes?

He had no right to ask her, not when he was lying to her with every breath.

Just then, she stumbled. Zane leaped to stop her fall, grasping her around the waist and hauling her against him in one swift move.

Wet and chilled, her body should have felt clammy and uncomfortable.

Instead, it felt good. Right.

For a second, she relaxed against him, her head bowed. Zane studied the part in her dark hair, the delicate pale skin. Slowly, he slid his hand beneath her chin and urged her face up. Lowered his mouth toward hers.

Blue eyes swirled with confusion, with longing and soft regret. Her lips parted slightly. ''No,'' she barely whispered.

He lifted his head but felt her shiver and enfolded her nearer, rubbing her back in a circle to comfort. "It's okay," he soothed.

Silent and tender, the moment spun out. Roan stood in his embrace, trembling, her fingers digging into her own arms.

Then cautiously, her fingers loosened. Grazed his chest.

Zane's body contracted painfully, his heart squeezed in an unfamiliar ache. He barely dared to breathe, waiting to see what she'd do.

She quivered with a wire-tight tension, her head bowed. Zane had never before experienced this sense of standing at a critical juncture, of just how intimate and fearful desire could be.

Her head rose, and the impulse to apologize was on the tip of his tongue. To move her, carefully and slowly as one would handle an injured animal, away from him. Toward safety.

To a man accustomed to the adoration of women, finding himself suddenly a danger was a shock, but he had the unmistakable sense that any wrong move could harm her beyond healing.

But he had no idea why. Or how she had come to such a crossroads, this woman who had never encouraged him, had done everything in her power to force him away.

Zane was still trying to find his footing through the treacherous ground of her vulnerability when suddenly, she rose to her tiptoes and brushed her lips against his cheek.

Had he touched a live wire, the shock could have been no greater. Something about that mouth, pressed to his skin so chastely, shook him as no woman's kiss had before. He disciplined himself, by an act of will greater than he'd demonstrated in his life, to remain still, to let her take the lead.

When what he wanted, against all wisdom, was to devour.

God. Zane loved women, yes, but he'd never been much of a romantic; yet somehow this woman's artless, terrified touch made him want to treat her like delicate crystal, surround her with flowers and silk and soft music. Lifted the idea of lovemaking to a new level.

One that scared him half to death.

Her breath drifted warm across his skin as a second kiss neared the corner of his mouth.

He waited…peered down at lacy dark lashes against cheeks hectic with scarlet. Agonizing seconds passed as he prayed for a glimpse of blue eyes, a clue—any clue—to what she was feeling. What she would do.

Closer she leaned, steadying for balance against his chest, her mouth just above his.

With a cry and a look of utter horror, she tore herself out of his arms and ran. Up the steps he'd repaired, across the porch he'd made safe, to slam the door behind her with a force that shook the whole house.

And Zane was left standing, needing to cool down a body so overheated he wanted to strip to the skin in the cold rain, doubting even that would work.

He wondered what the hell to do with a woman who stirred his sympathies and admiration, who was nothing like his usual taste in women but somehow could still set him on fire.

And who ran from him every chance she got.

ROAN STOOD inside the cabin, teeth chattering from fear as much as the chill. Never had she thought about responding like that to a man. She liked nothing about the sexual act; for her there had been no joy in it.

Frank Howard had capitalized on a girl's deep need for affection; as she'd settled into the humdrum existence of a job at the furniture factory, just like every other young woman her age who couldn't get away, she'd caught Frank's attention. Been the object of his single-minded pursuit, so flattering to someone who saw a dead-end road ahead, who knew that her only means of dodging her mother's fate would be the safety of these mountains, where nothing ever changed. She would grow old before her time, would bear too many children with not enough money to feed them.

Wild and bold, Frank had dizzied her, excited her by his drive to possess her that last crazy summer when she'd realized that she would never escape the blood that ran within her, never scale to heights of glory. Never win.

And in had walked Frank, whispering promises of Atlanta, maybe New York City and big cars and bigger houses.

She'd fallen like the proverbial ton of bricks. For three months, he'd blinded her with promises she understood now he'd never had a prayer of keeping. He'd wanted her body and had been rough in its handling, but she'd have done anything to please him.

It had required a pregnancy scare to wake her up. To set her straight, clear her vision to the cruelty behind the kisses, the obsession behind the smiles. She'd applied for a job in the office to get away from Frank, who'd slashed her tires and threatened worse.

And then she'd caught the boss's eye. The married boss, Ben Chambers, twenty years her senior, had come to her rescue and scared Frank away, only to decide that he wanted her himself. He'd bought a piece of clay he'd planned to mold into a trophy wife.

She hadn't understood that at first, of course. She'd seen only the mature man of resources who'd spotted her in his furniture factory and offered to take her away from the life she abhorred.

She'd still had fire then. Still had hope. But Ben hadn't wanted that fire once he'd claimed her; passion was for a mistress. A wife must be cool and above reproach. He'd moved her first to Charlotte, then an exclusive section of Baltimore, surrounding her with friends of his choosing, most of them much older than Roan and worlds apart in experience. Systematically, he'd shaped and honed her, subtle distaste here, sharper dismay there, until she'd become the woman of his dreams. Refined and cultivated, the perfect hostess, the wife in pearls and silk, as far from the seedy apartments and constant moves to dodge debts as it was possible to achieve.

And in the process, a young girl became an old woman overnight. Was it any wonder that her womb had proven unfit until Elise? Ben had wanted the image, not the messy reality of what Roan could only guess uninhibited sex might be. His version was all about silence and separate beds, about furtive trips in the night and lifted hems, about taking his own pleasure in grim silence on a body that had dried to dust.

With each miscarriage, he'd only become more intent, until Roan would have done almost anything to escape.

And did. The little pills her doctor prescribed to keep her calm became her best friends. Her only friends.

Until, at last, Elise. Somehow, she knew instantly that this one was different, that this would be the one she would carry to term. She threw away the little pills, did everything right, turned her focus on nurturing the life forming inside her. It was the happiest period of her existence. Colors were brighter, the air crisp, the sun warm with promise. Even Ben had responded to the glow that seemed to surround her.

She should have seen the warning signs when the doctor discovered she would have a girl instead of the son and heir Ben wanted. Day by day he withdrew from her, more caustic than ever, more demanding.

But she floated inside a dream, her only reality this baby she would love forever and who would love her. She performed her wifely role as expected—thanking the fates that her body did not attract him and she was thus spared that part. But through all of it, she was half-there, only concerned with getting done so that she could go back to playing music for her baby, stroking the skin that separated them, talking to her little girl for hours.

At the hospital, the nurses clucked about the father who showed up only once, but Roan was so enchanted by her little girl, so wrapped up in their shared world, that she paid no notice.

For five months, five glorious months, Roan was her strongest self, helplessly in love, thinking it would last forever.

But on that day when she checked on her baby, whose nap was taking so long, and discovered—

Roan dug her nails into her palms. So many days, so many endless, lost hours since that moment when everything good in her life had stopped. So many dark moments she could not bear to remember.

Little pills, more and more of them, to help her forget. To go on with a life that seemed pointless.

Her sterile marriage ended at the moment that Elise ceased to breathe, though the burial endured for many months until Ben could no longer disguise her spiral into self-destruction.

And the next time a man touched her, it was to demand payment for the drugs she needed, the surcease without which she could not live anymore.

Roan whirled away from the cabin door, shivery and hot and heartsick. The man on the other side of it was more dangerous than she could have imagined. His kindness was a lure, his body a threat.

For the first time since a young girl had succumbed to the man whom she thought would be her savior, Roan wanted to yield, wanted to seek the safe harbor she somehow knew Hal could be.

That seeking could be the first step down the path her mother had worn so deep. There were no safe harbors. There was no peace, not yet. But someday, if she remained strong and endured, if she made her stake in this place, there might be.

Roan would create her own refuge from now on.

She opened the door to tell Hal he had to leave today. Right now.

But when she peered through the pouring rain, he was nowhere in sight.

ZANE STOOD inside the barn, dodging leaks. Miserable in wet, chafing jeans, shivering against the wind sailing through the myriad cracks in the rotten wood.

His clothes were inside that cabin. At the moment, all he wanted to do was retrieve them, change and get the hell out of Dodge.

But to do that, he'd have to encounter that woman. The one who'd somehow managed to make a man adored by millions of women feel as if he'd suddenly become Attila the Hun.

Damn it, *she'd* responded to *him.* He was tired of dealing with a woman more skittish than any mare he'd ever tried to tame. He'd come on this drive to find peace, not to have life turn more complicated. The woman was trouble. Troubled. Big *T.* Don't go there. Run like hell in the opposite direction.

His fingers clenched in memory of the feel of her, mostly angles with only the occasional touch of soft, sweet flesh.

He could have nearly any woman he wanted at the crook of a finger. Recognizing how often women threw themselves at him wasn't ego. He had a whole staff to process fan mail that came complete with silk panties and G-strings.

But none of those women stirred him the way one difficult, choppy-haired, bundle-of-nerves wraith seemed to accomplish without trying.

Zane slammed a fist into a post, then grabbed his hand, cursing every vile epithet he could remember learning.

He slid his back down the post and crouched

down, staring at the dirt floor, the piles of junk littering most of the open space.

He couldn't escape the feeling that he owed her an apology. That he'd opened a dangerous door.

Zane couldn't remember the last time he'd begged a woman, but he'd been close to it with her. He still couldn't understand why. Or what held him here when he yearned so much to go home.

She'll probably tell me again tonight to get lost.

But you won't, will you, darling? Not until she's safe.

Zane dropped his head back against the post and sighed loudly to the still air. *No, Mom. I guess not.*

One fat drop splatted on his forehead and, frowning, he ducked the next one.

On his feet again, he examined the space to get a sense of what was required to make it habitable. The last thing he wanted to do was spend another night in that cabin with her.

Even if she'd let him inside. Which was, at the moment, highly doubtful.

He shivered again. He had to get clean, even if it meant standing naked in the rain to do so.

Then his gaze landed on a large metal object with curved edges. He moved nearer to investigate.

And smiled. A tub, galvanized tin and a tight fit for someone his size. In the gloom, Zane dragged it out and examined it for holes, finding none.

He wasn't much for baths, true, but women often

raised. The one she should admire but that at the moment, set her teeth on edge.

''I know you're in there. If you don't want the surprise, let me in anyway. I'm freezing. I need to get out of these wet clothes.''

A sudden vision of his naked chest assaulted her, and it was only too easy to expand that to the rest of him. She leaped to her feet. ''Come on in. I'll be in the kitchen. Call me when you're decent, then…''

Then what? The door began to open. She abandoned the room with all haste.

She heard more thumps and a dragging sound and almost went to investigate. But then everything fell silent, and she was tempted to let her imagination roam free.

So she concentrated on stirring up the fire on the woodstove and adding kindling, bringing the tea kettle back to one of the six eyes on top to get the water boiling for tea.

The front door opened again, then shut.

Roan frowned. That was quick.

But still she didn't investigate, and very soon, the door opened again. Something clanged, then she heard the sound of water pouring.

Then the door once more.

What in the…?

Suddenly, where she'd heard those sounds before hit her.

She raced around the corner.

Just as he reentered, two buckets in his hands.

"What are you doing?"

His eyebrows lifted. His gaze cut to the side. "Seems pretty obvious. I'm heating you a bath."

Roan focused then on the galvanized tub in which Gran had immersed her once a week, letting her make do with an old-fashioned sponge bath the rest of the time. "Where did you find that?"

"In the barn. It's still sound—rusty in spots, but no holes." A shiver shook him. "Any other kettles besides the one I'm using?"

Roan realized that he was still in the same very wet clothes in which he'd come to her rescue earlier. "Why are you doing this? Why won't you—"

"Leave?" he offered, completing the sentence for her, then shrugged. "I'm not finished with the chores I intend to do."

"Set those down," she snapped, knowing how heavy one bucket was, let alone two. "And for pity's sake, take these towels—" she threw two at him, which he caught with ease "—and dry yourself off."

Hal shook his head. "Not until I finish bringing in the water."

Fury shot to boiling. "You are the most—" Frustration choked her.

"Stubborn?" He grinned. "No one in my family would disagree." He nodded toward the kitchen. "Where's another kettle?"

Roan couldn't decide what to feel, what to do first. She wanted to throw something at the same moment his kind gesture engendered the urge to cry. "I don't understand you," she managed before heading for the kitchen.

But not before she saw his look turn grim. "That makes two of us," he muttered.

He said nothing more when she retrieved one of the wash-day kettles, merely strode across the floor to wrestle the heavy cast iron from her grasp. He lifted it without effort and placed it on the hearth. As if he'd done all this before, he stirred the fire higher, then emptied the buckets into the pot.

And went outside again.

Messy emotions tumbled inside her. Roan fought to find her way back to the dull, vacant safety of the days before this man had barged into her life.

But she couldn't find that comforting vacuum.

And it scared her to death.

She made her way back to the kitchen and, with shaking hands, lifted the steaming tea kettle, intent upon adding its contents to the tub. Thoughts disordered, attention distracted, she crossed the wooden floor.

A jutting splinter stabbed her bare sole. She jerked, and boiling water spilled, scalding her left arm. With a cry, she dropped the kettle.

The door burst open. He took in the situation at a glance, lowered the buckets down and was across the floor in seconds to kneel where she'd fallen. Steaming water soaked the floor, the pool spreading.

He picked her up as if she weighed nothing and

removed her from harm's way. "Let me see." Carefully, he pried her fingers away.

Instinct had her recoiling from him. His head lifted. "I just want to help you." Green eyes met hers, worried but strong and calm.

With a deep breath, she relented.

He probed her arm, and she cried out. "I'm sorry." He scanned the room. "Hold still." With quick steps, he crossed to the kitchen, then returned with a towel and dunked it in the cold well water.

He made his way to her and placed the cold cloth against the burn. Roan bit her lip again and tasted blood.

"I'm sorry. I know it hurts. We should get you to a doctor. Hold this, and I'll carry you to the car." He slid his arms beneath her.

She shook her head. "There isn't one."

He was already to the door, shouldering it open.

"I told you the closest hospital is a good hour away."

He stopped in midstride. "No doctors, either?"

"No." She tried to remember what Gran would do for a burn. "Let me down. I'll see if I can find something."

"You don't have a first-aid kit or anything?" At the shake of her head, he pursed his lips.

Then his eyes lit. "Wait here." He lowered her to the bed. "My car at home comes equipped with a first-aid kit. Maybe that one outside has something similar. I'll be right back."

Wild sarsaparilla was in the medicine box, she re-called, but the root had to be freshly dug to make an effective poultice. What else had Gran used? Roan rose, thinking to search.

Hal raced in, the familiar white box with the Red Cross logo peeking from beneath his arm. "Let's see what's here." He sat on the bed beside her and rifled the contents, then waved a small sheet of paper with a shout of triumph.

"Instructions—" He turned to her, face shining. "I knew I paid all that money for something." He read quickly. "'First degree burns…'" His voice trailed off, and he studied her arm. "'No blis-ters…not more than ten percent of the body burned…cool burns with water until burning or pain stops. Cover with dry sterile nonstick dressings and loosely bandage.'"

He poked into the kit, then emerged with bandages in hand. He hesitated. "This might hurt."

"It already does. Go ahead."

He filled a bucket, then brought it to her. Long, strong fingers held her arm gently, lowered it into the water. Roan did her best not to hiss at the sting.

Soon, though, blessed numbness stole over the pain. Her head drooped as she began to breathe more deeply.

He bandaged her arm, then removed the splinter from her foot. "Lie down," he urged. "What can I get you? How about a glass of water?" He pored through the kit. ''Here—aspirin. It'll help with the pain.''

''No pills.'' She didn't dare.

He frowned. ''Why not?'' Then his face cleared. ''Oh...my sister used to have trouble swallowing pills. I'll crush the aspirin in water for you the way my mother did.''

''No.'' She tensed. ''I can't.''

''You're allergic? Let's see if there's ibuprofen.''

''It's not that bad.'' She gritted her teeth against the lie. ''I'll be fine.''

''A hard case, huh?'' His face lit with approval. ''Good. I admire that. Where I come from, people swallow narcotics for a hangnail.'' His forehead creased.

She frowned. ''In west Texas?''

''No.'' Abruptly, he stood. ''Never mind. I'd better get you that glass of water.''

Disapproval rang out in his voice. What would he say if he became aware that she wasn't that stoic at all? That she'd done so much worse?

Her head was light. Exhausted from the day's emotions, she sank back against the bed. *I'll just rest for a minute. Then I'll get up and—*

ZANE HURRIED back into the room with a glass.

And stopped.

She lay on the ancient, worn bed, eyes closed. Sound asleep.

Zane took his time studying the woman whose

mystery seemed to deepen by the day. Many of the pinched lines of her face were relaxed now, and she appeared years younger. The white bandage on her arm; the badly cut hair; the ragged, still-wet jeans and threadbare top—she looked more like a refugee than a sleeping princess.

Refugee. That was it.

His strongest impression filtered to the surface: that of a woman on the run from something, surviving on nerves.

What? And why?

And what the hell was he going to do about it?

He sank to the floor, legs crossed, and watched her. Roan O'Hara was an enigma, all right. Today, in that clearing, clutching that decrepit swing to her breast, she'd become someone new. No longer a difficult woman, inexplicably stubborn and hostile, but someone who was once a child, both afraid and hopeful.

She'd been loved by her grandmother, that much was easy to see. And her grandmother, as a wisewoman, would have been treasured all around, just as Mama Lalita was an object of reverence and great affection in La Paloma.

Why, then, did the locals—if Noah could be believed—despise Roan? What had she done to earn their contempt?

Miss Hoity-toity…broke up a marriage to grab a man who could give her luxuries she thought she deserved.

Not that it was any concern of his—or shouldn't be. He was simply passing through.

But she, it had been made abundantly clear, was not.

The level of her desperation told him that she had nowhere else to go but this broken-down place of memories she apparently treasured as much as they tortured her. She'd done some wrong to her grandmother, that much was evident by the suffering in her eyes and the admission that she hadn't realized until much later that her grandmother was no longer living.

Grief and guilt, Zane knew firsthand, made a powerful combination.

He glanced away from her then, gazing into the fire as his thoughts played out. She obviously suffered from her actions in the past. He wouldn't pry into them—had no right—but he wondered what it would take to shed her of the pain that drove her to reject all help, even simple human contact.

Then the question flared—what would make him shed his own?

Zane exhaled softly. No telling. He couldn't imagine what could possibly release him from the responsibility only he could accept for Kelly's spiral into a place where she considered death the only option.

He had no right to be angry with her.

He was furious.

Violent emotion crashed around inside him. He

was mad as hell, by God— Suddenly, the room was too small, the cabin too confining. He needed action. Had to find a way to stem the rage building within him.

You didn't kill yourself, not when other people were still trying to help. He barely resisted slamming the door in his rush outside, down the steps and nearly to the barn before it even registered on him that the downpour had worsened.

With long, grim strides, he reached the barn and marched inside.

He barely resisted the urge to slam his fist into a post again.

Why, Kelly? She should have been stronger, should have been fixed by rehab, should have let him...

He exhaled, massaged his sore knuckles with the other hand. And stared at the packed-dirt floor.

Should have let him save her. He should have found the way to rescue her. His anger was at Kelly *and* himself.

He rubbed his forehead with his unhurt hand and struggled to talk himself back to the Zane everyone knew, the guy who had everything going his way. *Cielito sin nuves.* The one without a care.

God. Had he really once thought it important what kind of car he drove, whether he wore Armani or Klein? Just how far had he been seduced by a world in which he was adored?

Adored for now, that is. Only now. He could recount endless names in a list of yesterday's news, the has-beens who'd once occupied his shoes.

What the hell was a grown man doing playing make-believe in front of a camera, anyway?

His comfortable life had vanished the moment he'd heard about Kelly's death, and he couldn't seem to summon interest in finding his way back. So what did he do from here? And who on earth would feel sorry for him, given his bank account?

Zane looked around him, really looked. The dilapidated barn was filled with rusting junk, ancient dirt, rotting wood.

Yet someone, an old woman loved deeply by the woman injured and asleep inside, had made this her home. Had hung on through endless years in a place where survival was not guaranteed and never easy. Where a single injury and too many hours alone could be deadly.

He thought of Mama Lalita's house, tiny and weathered by time. With wood floors scrubbed endlessly over the years and furniture creased and worn from the imprint of bodies.

But much loved, always with flowers blooming outside, the air pungent with the healing plants of her herb garden. His elder brothers—or any of the rest of his family, for that matter—would gladly provide her with a new house or welcome her into their own as age took its toll, but for pride she maintained the home where she'd loved her husband and borne her son, and had welcomed every distressed soul for miles around. To rob her of that place, of that striving, would steal something essential from her.

Much as it would the woman sleeping in the cabin fifty yards from him.

Instead of dismissing the whole place as a firetrap, Zane forced himself to adopt a new perspective. He scanned the post that had stung his knuckles and viewed its fellow supports. They were solid, for the most part, as were the rafters, best he could tell from here. The roof wasn't hopeless, either. One thing about a tin roof—you could replace a panel at a time, as long as you could find one. The springhouse roof would have to stay, but there were two more outbuildings whose components could be cannibalized to repair both the cabin and this barn.

There was plenty of mud around, too, to rechink the log walls. With a sturdy roof and walls that didn't whistle at the mercy of a crisp wind, animals could be housed here and probably survive the winter.

Ditto the cabin and the woman determined to live within it.

Inside Zane, an unexpected excitement grew. How much better to focus on accomplishing something and quit resenting the delay. If he was clever, he could find ways to help her without harming her pride, and the challenge to his wits appealed to him.

Likewise the physical obstacles of making this place sound. His blisters had grown children, but the mounting stack of wood to the side of the cabin was a satisfying testament. He could afford to take a week or even two, if he'd give up on arriving home in time for Diego's baby to be born. If he'd forget all about Hollywood and agents and gossip and—

His mind swerved from Kelly's name.

Focusing on someone else would do him good. Too much of his life had become his career.

That ended now. Whatever path he took from here, he would grant himself two weeks in this place to do something worthwhile, to accomplish what mattered.

He would make Roan O'Hara safe.

If she didn't like it, tough. He'd sleep in the barn.

But maybe she would. The MacAllister charm had always worked in the past. Surely she wasn't completely immune.

He hoped not. He suspected he needed to do this as much as she could use the help. So he'd be the soul of patience and stay out of her way, focused only on the work to be done.

And if a niggling memory of soft lips and vulnerable curves wasn't so easy to ignore…

He wasn't a horny teenager. He'd control himself, get the job done and leave, his conscience clear.

With that settled, he strode to the car, the rain—hallelujah—finally abating. He grabbed his cell phone to deliver the news to the family who would understand.

And his agent, who would not.

CHAPTER SEVEN

ROAN WAS SWINGING, high in the air. Above her, lacy new spring-green leaves danced in the breeze. She arched back, thrust her toes out, trying to touch just one branch. One tiny leaf.

The swing ropes popped, jerked her out of the smooth arc.

"Careful there, Roanie girl. I have no medicine for a cracked head."

"I can do it, Gran. Just watch me." Fiercely, Roan concentrated, using all the power her thin legs could summon to go higher once more.

Gran chuckled. "Those leaves are a long ways up there, you know. You get high enough, that swing's liable to dump you right out on your pointy little noggin."

Roan giggled. "My head's not pointy." She squinted, wondering how much higher she'd have to kick to make it.

"You got a will on you, girl, I'll say that. You put that spunk to use, you hear? Don't let anyone hold you back. You can do anything you have a mind to do, if you just won't give up. Quitters don't win, and winners don't quit."

"I want to be a winner, Gran."

"Then you can be. What is it you want to win, child?"

Roan's gaze strayed to the leaves above, but she knew Gran meant something else. Something more important than touching a high branch.

She pondered all the things she wanted: a house where she and Mama could stay in one place, a puppy of her own, a bicycle and maybe even a pair of skates.

But there was one thing she wanted above all else, one wish she had no idea how to obtain.

"A daddy," she said, the swing slowing now, twisting from side to side as she turned to face Gran. "I want to get a daddy of my own, Gran. But I don't know how."

Gran looked a little sad then. "Sugar, that's not up to you. Your mama—"

Roan's chin jutted. "She says we're just fine without one." Her head cocked. "So why does she keep bringing those men who…?"

"What did you say, child?"

"Nothing." Roan had to protect Mama. Mama wasn't well, and when she was sick, she had to have her tonic. She depended on Roan to be there when she was so tired and sad. If Roan couldn't care for Mama well enough, people would try to take her away. Mama told her that.

Sometimes Roan wondered what it would be like to live with Gran all the time, but Mama had warned her that Gran was too old, that being responsible for a little girl would hurt her. That Gran might die.

Roan didn't want Gran to die. Gran's cabin was the only place Roan felt safe.

But she couldn't leave Mama, anyway. Who would get Mama her tonic? Who would protect her from...

Roan's mind skittered away from the thought of her mother's latest boyfriend, Al.

Suddenly, Roan knew it was time to return. "Gran, I have to go home. Mama might need me."

"Your mama—" Gran pursed her lips tight. "She'll be fine for now."

"No." Stubbornly, Roan shook her head. "You don't understand. I'm the one who—" She stopped, conscious that she couldn't talk about Mama's medicine to anyone, even Gran.

Gran's hands stilled the swing rope. Blue eyes much like her own studied Roan. "Sweetie, it's not your job to fix your mother. She has to do that for herself."

Roan's eyes widened. "No, you're wrong, Gran." She leaped from the high swing, the ground a hard jolt. "I'm her big girl, the only person she trusts."

Gran's hands closed around her arms and gently drew Roan up. Her eyes were solemn, her voice sad. "Would you like to stay here with me all the time, Roanie girl?"

Roan wanted that more than anything besides a daddy, but she remembered Mama's warning and shook her head. She would die herself if anything happened to Gran. "I can't."

Gran frowned. "Why not?"

Roan's stomach started hurting. She wrenched herself from Gran's arms. "I just can't—" she shouted.

Gran reached for her again, but Roan dodged her grasp. "I have to go home. Mama can't do without me. We'll go to Noah's store and call Mama to come get me. I've been gone too long." No matter how desperately she wanted to stay in this place where she didn't have to worry that Mama would run out of tonic or that some man like Al would...

"Roan O'Hara, stop your mind now," Gran ordered. "You get yourself under control, you hear me?" She clasped Roan's wrist firmly and shook her gently.

Caught in the terror that she'd been here too long and Gran would die if Roan didn't go back to take care of Mama, Roan struggled with all the strength of her ten-year-old body, now almost as tall as Gran's. "No! Leave me be, Gran," she pleaded. "I have to go back, don't you understand?"

Something sad and terrible rode in her grandmother's eyes. "Your mama is gone away, Roanie. You know that. You'll stay here with me now, and we'll do just fine."

"Then I'll find her." Roan jerked her wrist again. "I have to. I can't—" With a mighty yank, Roan broke Gran's grip.

Only to see Gran fall back and hit the ground hard. Frozen in horror, Roan screamed for help.

HER SCREAMS woke her up. Roan fought her way out of the paralyzing grasp of terror, stumbling from the bed, tripping over blankets. Barely catching herself before she tumbled to the floor, her chest heaving as she battled to remember that she'd been dreaming. That Gran had been unhurt, had nestled an inconsolable Roan in her arms. Had said she never doubted that Roan hadn't meant to hurt her.

Roan had been there for two or three more weeks, as best she could recall, but never once had she been able to relax again, her worst fears brought to life that she would be the reason she lost Gran forever. When Mama had returned minus Al, Roan had said goodbye to Gran once more with mingled relief and intense sorrow.

Gran would be safe. Mama would be safe. All Roan had to do was protect them both, and everything would be fine.

The old ache didn't recede with the light of day. Gran was gone for good now. Roan hadn't been able to prevent that, just as she hadn't been able to save her mother. Shaken by the hollow ache widening to encompass her entire chest, Roan clasped her arms around her middle, then gasped as pain struck. She looked down at her left arm and saw the bandage. Felt the sting in her foot. Rolled back through memories: the swing, Hal's kindness. The shelter he'd offered.

Her gaze drifted to the fire, long dead now. The ancient tub on the hearth. The bath he'd insisted on drawing for her.

She peered inside. The water level was higher. A kettle steamed on the hook over the fireplace.

Just then, the door opened and Hal stepped inside, bearing two more buckets of water. His eyebrows lifted. "Hey, how's the burn?"

She glanced down at the bandage. "It's better. I—" Her eyes shifted away, then back. "Thank you." She nodded toward the tub. "Is that for me?"

"For you? Yeah. I thought maybe…" He looked as unsure as she felt.

"It's so much trouble." She forced herself to face him. "Why?"

"You don't think you deserve it?"

What could she say? They stared at each other, and she wondered what was going on behind his eyes. Beautiful eyes. Beautiful man.

Desire swirled in the room, brushing their flesh like a cat twining around ankles, purring with pleasure.

Then he stirred. "Water's hot. I'll pour it in and then you can—" He frowned and turned away, busying himself pouring the water from the kettle into the tub, then testing the heat and adding cold water from the well.

A part of Roan squirmed, wanting to tell him to get out, to stop confusing her. To leave her alone so she could reconcile all these feelings rocketing around inside her.

But a part of her, a treacherous, unfamiliar landscape, wished that he would stay. Join her in that tub. Be her guide through territory she'd never crossed, the land where men and women met without power plays, freed from shame and duty....

"See what you think." He stepped back from the tub. "If it's too hot, I'll fetch more water from the well."

"I..." Roan was caught up in wondering. Remembering the feel of his body against hers, so hard, so warm. So strong and safe...but not safe at all.

She spun and gave him her back. "I'm sure it's fine." She was compelled to make the offer. "Why don't you use it first."

"Roan."

Her name. Only her name, but something in the timbre of his voice vibrated deep inside her. Slid past every shaky defense she'd been able to erect between her and the world.

"Look at me."

She shook her head. "No," she whispered. "I can't."

"Who hurt you, Roan?"

The gentleness nearly undid her. "No one. It's all my fault." And if he asked her for details, she was terrified that she'd spill every one.

Instead, he said nothing. One minute he was by the fire, a safe distance away. The next, he stood right behind her, the heat of him sliding over her back, warming her. Protecting her.

"Don't." Her voice was a broken murmur. "Don't be nice to me."

"I think you've had too little kindness in your life," he said. "Let me take care of you tonight, Roan." His hands curled around her shoulders.

She knew she should resist. If he had any idea what kind of person she really was…

But oh, how desperately she wanted to yield. "You don't understand who I am. What I've done." She tried one more time to warn him.

A faint laugh shook him. "I'm the last person to judge you." His breath wafted over her nape. "It's just a bath, Roan." His fingers tightened, then eased. Suddenly, cool air replaced his warmth. "Okay. I'll wait outside."

No. She nearly cried out, sensing the loss of something rare and precious.

Time and experience, though, had taught her to ask for nothing. If she let herself want, she would head back into that terrifying cycle of cravings that could never be fulfilled.

So Roan stood with her back to the door, head bowed, legs trembling. Hands fisted around the buttons of her shirt to keep from begging him to stay.

The cold air swept inside. The door clicked softly.

Biting her lip against the overpowering sense of loss, Roan focused only on one button at a time. *One minute. Just survive the next minute. That's all you have to do.*

Once stripped of all clothing, she climbed into the water, hissing at the heat of it, then settled down and let her head fall onto her bent knees as the warmth of it seeped beneath her skin.

But the warmth couldn't reach into the cold, empty heart of her.

He could. Somehow, he could. She didn't understand why. She only knew that she wanted... needed...

More than she could afford to take.

Roan settled into the tub, relaxing inch by inch. Muscle by muscle. With a deep sigh, she concentrated on forgetting what she had just passed up.

ZANE BRACED his arms against the porch railing, reviling himself, his upbringing, his frustration level, too much of which was decidedly sexual.

What was it with him? How could he want a woman like her, a skinny, overwrought bundle of nerves and God knows what other baggage?

She played against type, though, something that had always held an inordinate appeal for Zane. It was cousin to the urge that had him considering the small movie over the surefire blockbuster, the antihero role when he'd been so clearly typecast as the hero. The All-American Zane MacAllister.

Zane snorted. There was nothing all-American

about the urge he had to breach that doorway. Climb inside that tub, naked as the day he was born.

And cuddle a creature so wounded he'd probably scare her half to death.

Lots of women had stirred his libido. This one hit too close to his heart.

Damn it all to hell.

Zane hung his head and laughed without mirth. *A fine fix you've got yourself in, hotshot. What the devil were you thinking?*

A chill shook him. Why hadn't he brought a jacket outside? He backed up against the cabin wall, closing his arms against the brisk wind. He'd just have to wait. How long could it take?

Then he recalled the hour-long showers that were part of Kelly's normal routine.

But Kelly was all girl, self-centered and self-indulgent. The woman inside…

Roan O'Hara hadn't pampered herself in a long time, if ever, he'd bet anything.

Zane shivered and tucked his arms closer to his body. The rain was gone, but the wind had picked up, slicing right through the thin fabric of his T-shirt.

Okay. He'd go inside, avert his eyes. Be in there only long enough to grab the jacket in his bag.

Right? his conscience demanded.

He frowned. Then sighed.

Right.

He raised his hand and knocked on the door.

ROAN JERKED at the sound of his knuckles rapping. She'd nearly fallen asleep, lulled by the warmth. "What is it?"

"It's getting cold. I need my jacket."

"Oh." She huddled in the water. "All right. Come in."

The door opened, letting in the draft. "Sorry." Long strides crossed the room.

Carefully, Roan studied the fire, waiting for him to leave.

But he didn't. Ponderous silence was broken only by the popping of sparks.

She buried her face against her knees.

"You okay?"

Head down, she nodded. She lowered her arms to clasp her legs close. "Oh—" She hissed against the sting of the burn.

"What's wrong?" Instantly, he was right there beside her.

She jerked her arm out. Shook her head. "Nothing."

Disapproval colored his voice. "You've gotten the bandage wet. I'll fix it."

"No." She lifted her face.

She saw hunger, rich and ripe. No one had ever looked at her that way. "Don't..." But she couldn't break the lock of his gaze on hers.

"I want to take care of you, Roan." His eyes mesmerized her. In the firelight, they glowed golden. Crackled with more than reflected flames.

"You've barely met me," she whispered.

"You're right." He nodded as he knelt beside the tub. Drew closer. "It doesn't seem to matter."

His expression reflected her own confusion. "I don't know what to do. You shouldn't be here," she protested.

A wry smile curved his lips. "You ain't just whistlin' Dixie." Voice gone husky, he averted his gaze and lifted her arm, then peeled the bandage away with care. "Try to think of me as a nurse." A quick, wry grin. "I'll try, too."

He rose. "Stay right there."

In moments he was back, towel and first-aid kit in hand. Forehead screwed up, he focused on a thorough job of bandaging.

"There." A smile of triumph as he finished. "All done. Let's get you out."

"No, don't."

"Just a nurse, remember?" He lifted her from the cooling water and set her on her feet. With infinite care, he picked up the towel and wrapped it around her with the caution of one who had handled a baby.

His simple presence was overpowering, as much due to his compassion as his sheer male magnetism. She longed to tell him to hurry. She itched to undulate against him. Begging for a touch she'd never experienced except for those brief, explosive moments when he'd held her.

He stilled, the heat of his body surrounding her.

His face was only inches from hers, his mouth a heartbeat away.

Roan couldn't move.

He leaned forward, nearly closed the gap. His breath washed her face. "Just a taste, Roan." He lowered his head. "Only one." He touched his mouth to hers with a still, hushed reverence.

When she whimpered, he shushed her softly. "I won't hurt you, baby. I promise I won't." He pressed a soft kiss to one corner of her mouth, then the other.

Roan shuttered her eyes. When he paused, she caught her bottom lip in her teeth and sighed. Her tongue wet her mouth.

"Sweet mother—" His voice went low with an edge of naked hunger.

"Please," she murmured. "Show me. No one…"

Suddenly, the heat of him vanished.

Her eyes popped open.

"I can't." He dodged her gaze.

Shame chilled the terrible longing. Could he sense who she really was, what she'd done? She tightened her grasp on the towel. "Please go now."

"Listen, I don't want—" He muttered his frustration.

"It doesn't matter." She gave him her back.

He spun her around. "I'm attempting to do the right thing. Don't you get that?"

"Don't lie to me. Of course a man like you wouldn't be interested. You don't have to spell it out."

"I'm not interested?" He shook his head. "I'm driving myself nuts trying to keep my hands off you, and you think…" He raked his fingers through his hair.

"Why?" she asked.

"What?"

"Why would you want me?"

"Beats the hell out of me." He laughed.

His laughter was more than she could bear. "Please leave while I dress." Her voice shook. She gripped the towel and struggled for composure. "I know it's cold outside. I'll hurry and then you can—"

He didn't let her finish. "Wait a minute. You don't believe me?" His mouth descended to hers, his kiss hot and hungry, but gentling even as the tension in him conveyed itself to her. The sweetness of it brought tears to her eyes.

Head down, Roan shoved at his chest. "Don't."

Long fingers slid into her hair. "You said show me. Tell me why."

"I didn't mean it. I don't like sex." There, it was out.

He uttered a bark of laughter. "Yeah, right." Then he stared. "You're serious." A rumble issued. "Who was he? What did he do to you?"

"I don't want to talk about it." She drew away, even as she craved to move closer.

"That's your privilege." His fingers tightened, the towel a thin barrier between them. "But know this,

Roan O'Hara. You're wrong." His eyes locked on hers. "There's passion in you, and it runs deep and hot."

He let her go. Put distance between them. "One day the right man will show you just how wrong you are."

His words stirred the cold ashes of abandoned hopes. Within her, one tiny ember flickered. She spun, putting her back to him.

Zane saw the tiny knobs of her spine, the ribs that showed too prominently beneath her skin as she hunched to cover herself.

Hell. If he behaved as he should and walked away from her, she would blame not him but herself.

But if he remained and did as he craved so badly to do, she might never forgive him, once his identity was revealed. Without knowing who he was, she was already preparing herself for him to cast her aside. How much worse would it be once she knew?

And she would have to find out, sooner or later, unless he left now.

Caught on the horns of his dilemma, he studied Roan. If ever a woman's body language said two different things, hers did.

So Zane ignored what his own needs demanded and did what was right. With only a little regret, he swept her up in his arms and strode to the bed.

She tensed to resist, but he laid her down with care and slid her beneath the aged quilts. With more self-control than he'd ever practiced in his life, Zane leaned over and placed a kiss on her forehead. "Go to sleep. I'll wash outside."

"It's cold out there."

He paused at the door but didn't look back. "I'm counting on that."

THE NEXT MORNING, they moved about the cabin in stiff silence. Hal insisted on cooking breakfast despite her protests. Roan busied herself tidying up, wishing he would leave.

She wasn't hungry, but he brought her a full bowl of oatmeal. She paid little attention, scooping up the first spoonful and sticking it in her mouth, planning to dawdle until he went back outside to work.

Flavor exploded on her tongue. Apple. Cinnamon. For the first time that morning, she looked into his face. "Where did you get them?"

Mischief rose from his smile to his eyes. Somehow, it was natural on him. For a second, she thought again that she'd seen that cocky grin before.

"Found an apple tree out back, fruit just starting to ripen. A miracle it could grow anything, the way the vines were trying to take over."

"Gran's apple tree." Roan was thrust back years, remembering the scent of apple butter simmering on the cook stove. Nothing went to waste in Gran's world. *No reason to throw them away,* she would explain. *The peelings are as tasty as the flesh.*

With relief at the easing of tension, she expanded. "The days we'd make preserves and apple butter, this cabin would get so hot I'd want to jump into the spring to cool off.''

''Did you?'' His voice held none of the unbearable tension of the previous night.

A little bit, she mourned that. A whole lot more, she thanked fate or lucky stars or his common sense.

Relief made her smile. ''Are you kidding? She'd have tanned my backside. The spring was her refrigerator, not my swimming hole.''

He laughed. ''Any willows around here? Nothing worse than a willow switch. My mother would make us pick our own just to ratchet up the torture.''

''You can laugh about it?'' Gran had meted out physical punishment sparingly, but the memory was indelible.

''If you ever met my mother, you'd understand. She needed whips and chairs to deal with the four of us boys. Diego was always more serious, but Jesse…he was wild. And Cade? He'd dare anything physical, try any stunt. The more dangerous the better.'' His eyes were fond. ''Hasn't changed that much. I wasn't a lot of trouble, but only because I was too little. But Mom had her work cut out for her, and she was never a woman to use Dad as a threat. If we earned punishment, which we often did, she didn't use the old 'wait till your father gets home'. She took care of business, all five foot two of her, maybe a hundred pounds dripping wet.''

Roan tried to imagine a woman faced with this big

man and three equally large brothers. The affection flowed through his every word. "You admire her."

He paused, mouth full. "Of course." He swallowed. "Mom's the best." He chuckled. "She'd still send any of us to the woodshed if she thought we needed it. Don't get me wrong. Dad's a big guy and a definite authority figure, but Mom…" His grin was huge. "Mom's scary."

He didn't seem the tiniest bit frightened. What he did appear to be was a man who admired his mother deeply and knew himself to be wholly loved.

Roan glanced down and realized she'd eaten every bite. The atmosphere in the room had turned comfortable and warm as he painted a picture of life worlds apart from her own experiences. She gobbled it up as she'd devoured the meal.

"Here." Hal rose, held out a hand. "I'll do the dishes."

"Why are you being so nice?"

One eyebrow arched. "You can't get your bandage wet. I haven't seen any rubber gloves handy, so it seems it's up to me."

"You don't have to do that."

"I don't think a little case of dishpan hands will kill me." That quick, devastating grin again. "You can dry. Then I'll change the bandage."

They passed an oddly companionable silence broken only by the sound of water sluicing back into the dishpan, the creak of their footsteps across the ancient, cracked linoleum floor, the birdsong outside in the trees.

Later, as he concentrated on peeling away the adhesive tape, she was still intensely aware of him physically. He filled up the tiny cabin with his big body and larger personality. Part of Roan gravitated toward him as a plant stretched to meet the sun, and part of her closed inward for protection, sensing that when he left, the cabin would be forever marked by his absence.

But somehow, there was peace in this moment, and Roan craved peace more than she needed air to breathe. She tried very hard not to waste this respite.

"Gran could draw out fire," Roan said a few minutes later, half to herself.

"She could do what?" He glanced up from the bandages.

"Nothing...only a mountain superstition." But Roan had witnessed it herself once, and denying what Gran—and many others—believed made shame swell in her chest. With the heel of her right hand, she rubbed a spot just over her heart.

The interest in his eyes warmed her. "Tell me what that means."

"It's silly."

"Tell me anyway. Mama Lalita loves to hear about other healing traditions."

She shrugged. "Some of the older people around here believe that certain healers can call the fire out of a burn and heal it that way."

"With some sort of incantation?"

She searched his expression for signs of contempt but saw none. "I don't know what they say. The words are secret. She would lean over the burned part and blow on it while passing her hand over it three times in a motion like brushing it away from the body." She paused. "Gran said she'd teach me one day when I was ready...." Roan stared into the past, wondering how different life would have been if she hadn't gone in search of more.

But she had.

"What else did she do?"

"You can't really be curious about this."

Both eyebrows rose. "I'm curious about almost everything." He chuckled. "When I was a kid, I always had my nose buried in a book, trying to find out about this or that, whatever grabbed me at the moment."

This big, gorgeous male, so vital and physical? "I can't picture it."

Faint color stained his cheeks. "I get sick of being judged by my looks. I'm tall now, but I was a skinny little runt with thick glasses until late in high school. I know what it's like to be invisible. There are times when I wish—" He stopped. Glanced away for a second. When he looked back at her, everything personal and private had been wiped away in favor of polite interest. "So...what else did she do?"

The warm interlude had evaporated. "It doesn't matter."

"Not everything that heals is logical, Roan. That doesn't make it invalid."

"You don't believe that."

"You don't know what I believe," he said, head down as he focused.

A part of her hoped he would argue. Wanted some evidence that there really was an answer beyond what could stand the test of science.

She'd failed the standard remedies, both physical and psychological. If Gran had been alive, she would have produced the magic Roan was so desperate to find.

But Gran was gone. Only this place was left, faint traces of her inside each log and floorboard she'd tended, every blade and tree and bush she'd nurtured and cherished.

If Roan touched enough of them, dug them from beneath the debris of time and neglect, could she replenish the missing parts of herself and find the woman Gran had once seen in her?

All of a sudden, Roan wanted to be alone. She couldn't concentrate with him around. He was too alive, too vivid. The comfort and peace were an illusion. He called her out of herself when she desperately needed to burrow in to listen…to probe for answers, to hear whatever wisdom remained as echoes of Gran.

"Thank you for the bandaging." Voice crisp, she pulled away and rose, smoothing the edges of the tape. "And for breakfast and the dishes."

He frowned at her. "What did I say?"

Roan called upon every bit of decorum she'd learned as the wife of a head of industry. "Nothing. I simply have work to do."

He stared at her. It was all she could manage not to squirm under the scrutiny.

"Yeah, okay." He spent far too long repacking the first-aid kit. "I've got plenty myself."

"You don't have to—"

He held up one palm to stop her. "Don't say it again, Roan. I'm not leaving yet." His gaze met hers, and the green eyes were as sharp as the emeralds they resembled just then. "I can move my things into the barn if that would make you feel better."

The nights were getting colder. He drove a luxury car and had the smooth polish of a well-fed creature, yet he'd accepted the primitive conditions without complaint and now he would move into even less welcoming quarters if that was what it took for her to let him stay.

She was ashamed of herself and knew Gran would be, too. No matter how set on self-reliance Gran had been, she would never have made a stranger feel so unwelcome. Roan forced herself to unbend, though it felt far too dangerous.

"I'm sorry. I—" She couldn't quite meet his gaze. "It's rude of me not to be better at accepting your help. I don't understand why you're doing it, but—" She forced herself to confront him head-on. "I thank you for all you've done." She sucked in a deep breath. "And I don't want you to sleep in the barn."

His eyes were oddly tender, as if he understood the cost to her. "I won't hurt you, Roan." Then he turned away and left.

"Yes, you will," she whispered.

CHAPTER EIGHT

ZANE STOPPED at the car on the way to the barn. He glanced over his shoulder to be sure she was still inside, then grabbed his cell phone. With long strides, he covered ground, headed to a clear spot out of sight.

Time to check messages, in case his mother had called.

Four from Sal, each one increasingly frantic. Zane stifled his impatience; Sal was only doing what he'd been hired for, protecting Zane's interests and advancing his career. That Zane's career seemed so distant and unimportant these days wasn't Sal's fault.

So you're ready to throw it all away? He could hear Sal's nasal voice challenge him. *Everything we've worked so hard to create?*

Zane's hand holding the phone banged against his thigh as he stared out across the suffocating, wild tangle of green. *What's your problem, buddy?* he asked himself.

But he had no answer. Only a vague, unnamed itch. A burr beneath his skin that made him restless and uneasy with a sense of something missing.

It was just this whole uproar with Kelly, probably.

An unholy mess, indeed, one he'd only too gladly dropped into the laps of his staffers, primarily Annie, while he took off to figure out how the hell to deal with how angry he was at a dead woman.

Oh, yeah. His folks would be so proud.

Shaking his head, Zane lifted the phone again and finished his messages. Annie's forced a grimace. His dad's made him smile.

"Son," Hal MacAllister's voice boomed. "Your mama is worried about you. You know I don't like your mama worried. I'm proud of you for helping that little lady, but we're ready to see you at home. I just got the prettiest filly you ever laid eyes on. Bring the lady with you. Nothing much a good dose of working horses won't help."

Zane chuckled at the same moment his heart twisted with longing to do just that—go home.

He took a deep breath and dialed. Sal first, then Annie. *Face the music, you jerk.*

Then he'd reward himself with a call to his dad.

Sal still wasn't happy about Zane's decision to stay here for a couple of weeks. *What could you possibly find interesting, surrounded by hillbillies?* Zane could visualize Sal's shudder. Anything between New York and L.A. was the wasteland to his agent. Sure, somebody out there bought movie tickets, but box-office numbers were all Sal wanted to know about them. Nothing else mattered.

Zane forced himself to tune back in.

"For chrissake don't get yourself snakebit or any-

thing while you're there. No hiking, nothing strenuous—remember the insurance policy. Think about
camera angles. No scars, you hear me, Zane? You
sit on a goddamn porch and look out at the sunset
or whatever the hell people do when there's no civilization, but you just remember that in five more
weeks, that director's gonna want your bare ass looking prime. *Capisce?*"

Zane glanced down at his scraped knuckles and
blisters and barely stemmed a laugh. "Got it, Sal.
Now, go chew on your cigar and leave me alone."

"You drive me freakin' nuts, ya know that, kid?"

"I love you, too, Sal." Zane gave in to his chuckles then. He could still hear Sal's good-natured cursing as he disconnected the call.

One down. He dialed Annie's cell. He wasn't sure
why she bothered with having an office; she was
never still long enough to sit at a desk.

"Where the hell are you?" She didn't bother with
preliminaries. In the background, he could hear
voices and clatter overlaying what sounded like the
hiss of an espresso machine.

Annie sucked down coffee the way a vampire
gorged on fresh blood. If her veins were pricked,
she'd bleed dark brown.

"Hi, Annie." He was overcome with nostalgia for
a life that seemed beyond his reach in more ways
than simple distance. Only a few weeks ago, his biggest worry had been which scripts to accept. "How
are you?"

Instantly, her voice warmed. "I'm good. Worried about you, though. Talk to me, Zane." He knew that it was more than business with Annie, that if she were in the same room, she'd be clasping his arm, and her elfin face, with its horn-rimmed black glasses, would be screwed up in concern.

They'd flirted briefly with the idea of an affair. Annie was several years older than him, but that wouldn't have mattered. She was an interesting woman.

Instead, they'd decided to be friends. Annie had a soft spot for all her clients, but he thought she had a special one for him.

Right now, he couldn't let himself tap it. "Press hounds gotten tired of me yet?"

"Are you kidding? Disappearing only whetted their appetites. They're straining at the leashes, sniffing the ground for the slightest clue."

"I'm sorry. It's rough on you."

She snorted. "Get real. This stuff sets my juices running. Makes me feel kinda hot and bothered."

Zane laughed out loud. "You're priceless, Annie."

"All in a day's work, my boy." Then her voice sobered. "How are you, honestly, Zane? Not the press release but the real deal. What's going on?"

"I'm just hanging out…" He glanced around him. "You know I can't handle the city life for months on end without going nuts."

"I do, but I'm talking about Kelly. Tell me you've

accepted that there was nothing else you could do for her.''

''Wasn't there? I got so fed up with her antics, and I—'' He closed his eyes. ''She called me last, Annie. Me. A cry for help, and I hung up on her.''

''Zane, listen to me. She played mind games with you. She used you, used your fame and your money as crutches to keep from looking at who she really was. She was weak, damn it, and no one could fix that but Kelly. Didn't I help you clean up after her for two years while she did everything possible to make your life hell? All along, she counted on the fact that big-hearted sap that you are, you'd turn yourself inside out for her. I could kill her myself for contacting you.''

''Whoa, Annie. Stop. Maybe that's true. Perhaps she was like the others and mostly what she wanted was to be seen with Zane MacAllister the film star. But that doesn't change the fact that inside her was a sweet, mixed-up girl who got lost in the Hollywood lifestyle, and it killed her. She wanted too much, and I gave it to her because I was too caught up in all of it to see what was happening to the innocent girl I first met. I killed her, Annie, as much as those pills did.'' Nothing anyone could say would change his responsibility.

''Zane, you need to talk to someone. You're dead wrong. What does your family tell you? If you won't come back to the real world and get some counseling, why aren't you in Texas with Mama Lalita, letting her do her magic?''

One drunken night by the pool, he'd talked to Annie about his family in a detail he shared with no one else in the life that had never seemed fully real. ''It's not magic. And I don't want to take this home to them. I'll figure it out myself.''

''You need your family, Zane. What the hell are you waiting for?''

Not in a million years would he tell anyone from his Hollywood life about Roan O'Hara, even if he thought they'd understand.

''I'll be on my way soon.'' Chagrin swept over him. ''Annie, if it's getting too crazy, dealing with the media, I can come back.''

''Are you trying to insult me now? I can handle these bozos with both arms tied behind my back.'' She paused. ''Go home, Zane.''

He glanced in the direction of the cabin he couldn't see from here. ''Soon, I promise.''

''You're a good guy, one of the few real people in movieland. Maybe too real.''

Zane had to swallow hard. ''Annie…''

''Listen, tiger, my macchiato is getting cold. You know how that pisses me off.'' Affection and worry colored her tone.

''Heaven forbid.'' He tried for a chuckle and didn't quite make it. ''You're the best, Annie.''

''Don't you forget it.'' Her voice softened. ''Take care, cowboy. You're in the wrong mountains. Get the hell back home. The clock is ticking.'' Without further fanfare, she was gone.

Tick, tock. No one understood that better than he.

Zane closed the cover of his phone and leaned back against a tree. He wanted to talk to his dad in the worst way now, but for once in his life, Zane wasn't confident that his acting skills were up to the task.

His dad would only worry. This should be a happy time for all of them.

And Zane had a list of tasks to complete before he could go, no matter that he'd generated the list himself and no one would be the wiser if he didn't complete it.

He made his way back to his car to drop off the phone. He'd go inside, have a talk with Roan about what should be accomplished before he could leave in good conscience. If he put his energy into work instead of lusting after a woman who wasn't asking for anything from him, maybe the list wouldn't take too long to finish.

He'd call his dad later, when he had a better sense of the time involved.

Good. All right. He had a plan. He headed back to get it started.

ROAN OPENED the ancient wooden quilt chest made for Gran by the grandfather Roan had never met. *A travelin' man,* Gran had called him, a wanderer with a restless heart and itchy feet. *I knew the price, child,*

Gran had answered Mama's easily cast blame once, when neither knew Roan was awake. *'Course I did. Didn't matter. If I'd turned that man away, somethin' in me would have died forever.*

What about me? Mama had screamed. *Didn't I deserve better? I was a bastard, an unwanted child.*

Gran's voice had held a fury Roan had never heard before. *That is a lie and you know it, Clary. I wanted you. You were all I'd ever have of him.*

To hell with him, Mama had lashed out. *To hell with you, too. You're just as selfish as he was, to bring a child into the world as some kind of goddamn souvenir.*

Instead of as an afterthought? Gran had asked. *At least I loved your daddy. I knew who he was.*

And that was how Roan had discovered that she was an accident, a bastard child of a man her mother couldn't have picked out from the jumble of careless nights if her life had depended upon it.

A pretty pair, aren't we, Mama?

On that last visit, she'd told Gran that she'd been aware of the circumstances of her birth for years. Gran had been too wise to try any pretty stories or make excuses. *O'Hara women don't need a man,* Gran had said. *We are warrior queens. All that comes down in your blood, Roanie girl.*

Roan had thought differently. *I love you, Gran, but I can't be like you,* she'd confessed. *I don't even want to. I have a man now, and I'm going to be the*

*one who breaks free. I'm leaving this mountain to
make something of myself.*

Roan lifted one last quilt and leaned into the chest,
peering through the shadows, almost afraid to see.
To breathe.

There. Hands clenched on the wooden lip darkened and worn to satin by decades of human touch,
she stared. Deep in the shadowed corner, its brass
hasp dulled with age. Roan would have recognized
it anywhere, though she hadn't laid eyes on it in
twenty years.

Gran's book, the one she'd scratched in late at
night by candlelight, using one of the turkey quills
she'd sharpen with the wicked little knife that was
never far from her hand.

Roan extended an arm, then yanked it back as
though the book would burn her. *You can be one of
us, Roanie girl. Your mama doesn't have the knack,
but you do. All that's required is that you accept the
sacred duty, the stewardship of this mountain and all
the souls who live upon it.*

But Roan, who'd borne responsibility for her
mother since childhood, had not wanted any more.
She'd craved freedom from it. To be rich, to travel,
to be the one cared for, instead.

Everything she'd left this mountain to obtain had
turned to dust in her hands.

And Roan was only too aware that having nowhere else to go was no substitute for the calling that
Gran had intended.

Hal's whistling stirred Roan from her contemplation, had her drawing back her hand from the leather cover she could not yet summon the courage to touch.

His heavy steps mounted the stairs. Crossed the porch.

Roan grabbed a stack of quilts and dropped them back inside as she would smother a deadly fire. Gran was wrong. She was an O'Hara in name only. Never a queen, though she'd once aspired to rise in the eyes of the world. Not a healer like Gran, certainly not a wisewoman.

But a warrior…somehow, facing the battle of her life, Roan must find that warrior inside herself.

She'd barely closed the lid when the cabin door opened. She wheeled around, hands hidden behind her.

"Roan, I have to talk to you." He stopped. "You okay?"

She straightened. Moved away. "Sure." Busied herself smoothing the quilts on the bed. "What did you want?"

He drew his questioning gaze from the chest. "I'd like to make a list of the things that should be done before winter."

"Why?"

His voice was still a stranger's. "So I know how much longer I need to stay."

She matched his tone. "You can leave now. I thought I made that clear."

His brows snapped together, but he continued as though she'd said nothing. "I'll have the barn roof finished today, and I can have the logs on both it and the cabin chinked by the end of tomorrow, I think. Then you'll be able to get a cow for milk and maybe a couple of hogs to breed and raise for meat. There are volunteer tomato plants buried in the garden. No telling what else is underneath the weeds. It's too late to plant for this year, but I can get the soil turned under—"

"Who asked you?" Temper pushed her past the desire for distance. She poked a finger into his chest. "Who died and made you God so you could figure out my life for me?"

"So what are you planning, huh? Or do you even have any plans? Have you given a second's thought to how much wood it will take to get through a winter? Who's going to chop it if I don't? You don't have the muscles or the money to hire it done. Think Frank or Noah or anyone else is going to come chop it for you free?"

The name stopped her cold. "Frank?"

"Yeah. Remember him, the guy who still believes he has a claim on you?"

"What? How do you—When—" She began pacing. Her skin buzzed with nerves. "Who are you to be talking to anyone about me? Have you ever heard the word *privacy?*" She spun on one heel. "Did I ask you to get involved? No." Her mind rocketed

OFFICIAL OPINION POLL

ANSWER 3 QUESTIONS AND WE'LL SEND YOU
2 FREE BOOKS AND A FREE GIFT!

0074823 IIIIIIIIIIIIIIIIIIIIIIIIIIIIIIIIIIIIIIII   **FREE GIFT CLAIM #** | 3953 |

YOUR OPINION COUNTS!

Please check TRUE or FALSE below to express your opinion about the following statements:

Q1 Do you believe in "true love"?

"TRUE LOVE HAPPENS ONLY ONCE IN A LIFETIME."
○ TRUE
○ FALSE

Q2 Do you think marriage has any value in today's world?

"YOU CAN BE TOTALLY COMMITTED TO SOMEONE WITHOUT BEING MARRIED."
○ TRUE
○ FALSE

Q3 What kind of books do you enjoy?

"A GREAT NOVEL MUST HAVE A HAPPY ENDING."
○ TRUE
○ FALSE

YES, I have scratched the area below.

Please send me the 2 **FREE BOOKS** and **FREE GIFT** for which I qualify. I understand I am under no obligation to purchase any books, as explained on the back of this card.

336 HDL DZ36   135 HDL DZ4M

FIRST NAME   LAST NAME

ADDRESS

APT.#   CITY

STATE/PROV.   ZIP/POSTAL CODE

www.eHarlequin.com

(H-SR-03/04)

The Harlequin Reader Service® — Here's how it works:

Accepting your 2 free books and gift places you under no obligation to buy anything. You may keep the books and gift and return the shipping statement marked "cancel." If you do not cancel, about a month later we'll send you 6 additional books and bill you just $4.47 each in the U.S., or $4.99 each in Canada, plus 25¢ shipping & handling per book and applicable taxes if any.* That's the complete price and — compared to cover prices of $5.25 each in the U.S. and $6.25 each in Canada — it's quite a bargain! You may cancel at any time, but if you choose to continue, every month we'll send you 6 more books, which you may either purchase at the discount price or return to us and cancel your subscription.

*Terms and prices subject to change without notice. Sales tax applicable in N.Y. Canadian residents will be charged applicable provincial taxes and GST.

If offer card is missing write to: The Harlequin Reader Service, 3010 Walden Ave., P.O. Box 1867, Buffalo, NY 14240-1867

BUSINESS REPLY MAIL
FIRST-CLASS MAIL   PERMIT NO. 717-003   BUFFALO, NY

POSTAGE WILL BE PAID BY ADDRESSEE

HARLEQUIN READER SERVICE
3010 WALDEN AVE
PO BOX 1867
BUFFALO NY 14240-9952

NO POSTAGE
NECESSARY
IF MAILED
IN THE
UNITED STATES

back to a day long distant, an angry young man with tears in his eyes. "What have you done?"

"I met him at the store. He doesn't like you much, Roan. Stay clear of him."

"I intend to. I only want to be left alone." She glared at Hal. "Forget your list. I'll do it myself."

"Goddamn it, Roan, you could die here!" he roared. "How the hell can you claim to know this place and not understand the risk you're running? Personally, I expect you'll be gone before Thanksgiving. It doesn't take a genius to see that you're not even vaguely prepared to survive a winter alone. Stop kidding yourself, why don't you?"

Every word, every question, was battery acid poured over her skin. Into her heart, opening it up to the terror that never left her.

No one was more aware than Roan of just how unfit she was. No one. She could very well not survive here, and she knew it. She'd come back to this place understanding that she was dead if she stayed out in that world, that sooner or later she'd fall back into the life that would burn out like a Roman candle…or merely fizzle into the outer reaches of purgatory.

Maybe she wouldn't make it through the first winter, but at least she would die in the only place she'd ever truly been alive.

Somehow, that insight steadied her, and an odd thing happened.

Roan found the first hint of the warrior within her.

With no one to live for and nothing left to lose, she had little to fear but loneliness, and loneliness was an intimate acquaintance. It had been her most reliable companion for most of her life.

Along with the warrior came its sidekick, pragmatism. There was a strong, healthy man right in front of her who, for whatever incomprehensible reasons, felt bound to help her. With his efforts, for however long he'd stay, she could accomplish more than twice as much as by herself.

There was a time for independence, but there was never an excuse for stupidity.

"All right." She had herself in hand now. Understood the path. "Let's make that list."

"What?" He goggled at her as if she'd grown an extra head.

She shrugged. "You've got some misguided Galahad complex and a strong back. I'm determined to make it through the winter after getting a late start. You want to help, and I'm saying yes. Let's get to it." Amazingly enough, she found that accepting his help made her feel better, not worse. Not weaker.

She was the one doing the choosing.

Meanwhile, Hal looked poleaxed. "I don't get it."

"I'm not crazy." She smiled. "Not that crazy, anyway. Stubborn, yes, and maybe too proud, but since I can't seem to get rid of you, I might as well be practical."

"So you want me to stay."

"Not really, but...yes."

"You don't want my money."

"Forget it. No more charity. I can't afford to pay you now, but I'll figure out a way if you can be patient. We'll keep track of your hours, and I'll sign a note with you to repay every cent you spend and every hour you work, if it takes me a lifetime."

He appeared ready to argue, but he stilled the protest unvoiced, and she saw a glimmer of something that just might be respect rise in his eyes. He held out a hand for a shake. "Agreed."

She slid her own into it, smiling back with a lightness inside her that she hadn't felt in more years than she could count.

He got an odd expression on his face. "What about the, uh, the physical attraction? How do we handle that?"

"It won't be a problem." She wouldn't let it. "I told you I don't like sex."

He grinned then, that smile that was wide and white and would make any normal woman's heart flutter. He burst out laughing. "You are so wrong about that, and maybe if you're lucky, I'll be the one to show you why."

Her heart wasn't fluttering, damn it. She wouldn't let it. "You wish." She turned away, hunting for paper and pencil.

His chuckles trailed along behind her. "You know, babe, I think I just might."

Roan pretended she hadn't heard him.

AND SO THEY PASSED the next few days in an odd companionship, busy outdoors from sunrise to sunset, working in the evenings by firelight and lantern until their weary bodies screamed for sleep.

He refused to consider swapping places on alternate nights, insisting—falsely, she thought—that the floor was better for his back. She dug into Gran's chest for more quilts to pad his pallet. They took turns on kitchen duties, and each day, Roan remembered more that she'd seen Gran do.

Finally, Roan decided the time had come to be practical about Gran's book. She would never be capable of taking Gran's place with the people of the valley, even if they'd accept her, but she'd better be prepared to care for herself. Until she could get a complete system for food and warmth up and running, what meager funds she had would be stretched too thin for doctor visits if she was injured or ill.

Tomorrow, she would get out the book. Today, she would tackle the garden. Hal had repaired the barn roof, chinked the logs on both it and the cabin and had oiled and sharpened tools he'd found. This morning he was using a scythe to mow the waist-high growth and clear paths between the cabin, barn, springhouse and garden.

Roan had done her best not to watch the play of muscles in his back and arms as he cut wide, powerful swaths, pausing only long enough to yank the T-shirt hanging from his waistband and wipe sweat from his face.

They'd done their best since the truce to act as merely agreeable strangers. They'd both worked hard, and Roan had hoped the exhaustion of a body unaccustomed to such strenuous effort would lull her into instant sleep when her head hit the pillow.

It wasn't working for her. Sneaked peeks beneath folded arms showed her that slumber didn't come quickly for him, either.

Buried under their careful truce and silence, desire was a steady hum. He was a beautiful man, but strangely enough, his allure came from sources beyond the physical: his powerful determination to help her, his quick mind, his easy humor. And dancing in the shadows, an explicable sorrow only visible when he didn't know she was watching.

More and more often, she had a sense that she was missing out on something special, that he might be the one man who was different, who could initiate her into a secret world where sex was more than physical and extracted no price, where a woman could afford to relax her vigilance. Where a man might be more than animal or tyrant.

Just then, Hal paused and looked around as if he sensed her contemplation.

Roan snapped out of her reverie, rushing to the well to fill a bucket of water, then took it to him.

"Thanks." He dipped the cup she proffered and drank deep and long.

She watched the muscles of his throat move, followed the path of one drop of sweat as it rolled down his neck and over his chest, headed toward his hard, ridged belly.

When he grasped the bucket and brushed her hands, she jolted and lost her grip on the wood.

He caught it easily and grinned as though he knew what she was thinking.

She surveyed the paths he'd cleared. "You've made a lot of progress."

He didn't respond until she met his gaze. His mouth was curved, but his eyes were snapping, answering sparks of heat. "You forgot your hat."

"It's cool today."

He glanced upward. "Sun's still strong, and your skin's too fair. You'll burn."

Gran had worked hard outdoors virtually every day of her life, but she'd never gone without a hat and sleeves and had religiously applied a balm she made herself. As a result, her skin at eighty had appeared decades younger.

Roan had tried to like wearing hats but had been too much the tomboy as a girl and later, under Ben's direction, had felt imprisoned, slathered with expensive creams day and night. She'd tried wearing Gran's old straw hat here. "It won't stay on."

"That's why it's got a strap."

"I don't like it rubbing under my chin."

"You won't like skin cancer, either."

"Yes, Daddy." She stuck out her tongue.

He swooped in and slicked his own tongue down the length of hers.

Roan went rigid, stunned by the flash fire inside her. Her mouth softened, lips parting. Her eyes drifted closed. Ready. Waiting.

Something tightened around her head, and she blinked. The bill of his cap shaded her face.

His look scorched her down to the toes. "I'm not your daddy." He upended the water over his head, then picked up the scythe and strode to the well to drop off the bucket.

Without another word, he went back to work.

Roan stared at him for a long minute, her insides like fresh custard, warm and quivering.

She touched the brim of his cap, smoothing her fingertips across it, aware of every thread, every valley between them.

Then, breath escaping in a whoosh, she headed for the garden.

Once there, Roan doffed her gloves, needing a tactile connection to something that would remain once the overwhelming male yards away left. She knelt and forced herself to focus.

Tomato plants, yes. She spotted three—no, four— their fruit withered, much of it plopped on the ground, once-red skin crisped brown by the sun and popped open, spilling seeds that would mean new plants next spring.

Roan pulled weeds around them, clearing the dense growth and recalling how Gran would turn over the soil with a pitchfork, working into it dried, powdery chicken manure and cast-off hay from the stall where her cow spent the night.

In that instant, Roan could feel the press of coarse hair against her cheek where she'd leaned into Boadicea's side, fingers curled around the warm, rubbery teats as milk zinged into the bucket. The sharp, crisp scent of fresh hay mingled with the earthy, pungent cow dung, overlaid with the aroma of rich, buttery milk.

She smiled. Of course Gran would name a homely, placid, cud-chewing cow after a Celtic warrior queen renowned for defeating Roman legions.

Come to think of it, Boadicea the cow hadn't been all that placid, either. More than once, Roan had danced to avoid hooves ready to crush her toes.

Carefully, Roan plucked three still-gooey tomatoes and set them aside to harvest the seed. Then she pulled a whole plant, lifted its creeping, hairy roots to her nose and sniffed the dirt clinging to them, smiling at the displaced earthworms wiggling in panic.

Burrow down, she thought. *Seek shelter from the coming winter. I'll feed you better next spring.*

Hope stirred within her. From a stony mountainside, Gran had created loam so rich it had repaid all the backbreaking effort by producing, year after year, bounty that had fed Gran over each harsh winter.

That soil hadn't died with her grandmother. It slept beneath the tangle, waiting for Roan to assume Gran's place as its guardian and caretaker. Symbiosis between unlike creatures who needed each other to survive.

Roan sat back on her heels and surveyed the garden and the fruit trees beyond it, visualizing not the tumult and overgrowth, not the threat posed by vines and grasses waiting to devour, to return all of this to the reign of ancient species and hard, cold rock. Instead, she saw this place as it had once been and could be again, coexisting in a harmony only obtained by constant vigilance. Respect for nature side by side with simple needs, taking only what was necessary to survive while returning to Mother Earth any excess so that she might rest, well-sated.

To make a life in these mountains would be hard and lonely and unsafe, but Roan had lived through all that already, in a world where there were no good memories. Surely she could live here, maybe even prosper.

Prosper might be too strong a word just now. Roan would settle for surviving the first winter.

Tonight, she would retrieve Gran's book and study the lessons in it. Tomorrow, she would continue, step by slow, measured step, the process of claiming this place as hers. Of carving out a new life. A new Roan O'Hara. Not the Roan Gran had envisioned, perhaps, but certainly not the Roan who'd been inches away from the gutter. From a self-loathing so deep she'd have sought anything to mute it.

From a shiny, sharp blade streaming scarlet with her blood.

Roan brought earth-coated fingers to her nose and

inhaled deeply, banishing the coppery scent that still lured her.

Hal would leave soon. She would be completely alone. Still afraid, still uncertain. Perhaps not worthy.

But alive. That was something.

Maybe even enough.

ZANE DRAGGED himself up the steps in the growing darkness. In a few minutes, after he sat down and rested, he'd start hauling bathwater as he had each night since he first discovered the tub.

At the moment, though, he could barely lift his arms. The mere thought of buckets filled with water made his muscles want to weep.

When he got back to L.A. he'd tell his trainer, Chuck, he was going about things all wrong. Forget fancy equipment—just move his clients to the back of beyond for a few weeks. They'd wind up fit, he grinned, or dead.

At the door, he paused, not sure he could summon the strength to turn the knob. Amazing how all these camera-ready muscles still weren't enough. He'd spent too little time on real work the past few years, doing films back to back.

One good thing about this level of exhaustion, though: he was nearly too tired to think about jumping Roan O'Hara's bones.

Okay, so the spirit was still willing. The flesh was definitely too weak.

Zane was still smiling as he pushed open the door. His eyes popped wide at the sight that greeted him.

The tub sat before the fire in its usual spot.

But it was full. And steaming.

Across the room, Roan's head rose from her study of a big leather book. "Hi. You want to eat first or soak?"

"Me?" He'd been the gentleman, avoiding temptation by using cold water from the well instead of enjoying the welcoming warmth of the tub.

"You've worked even harder today than before. It's the least I could do."

"You are a goddess. If I thought I wouldn't fall flat on my face crossing the floor, I'd kiss your feet."

She laughed, and it struck him once again how young she looked at times like this, so rare for her. He'd spilled his guts about all sorts of family stories, but he still knew very little of her past, except for the clear impression gained without words that life had not been kind to her.

"You've got a great smile," he said.

She ducked her head, fair skin blooming rosy. But he thought she looked pleased as she got to her feet. "How about having your cake and eating it, too? Climb in and I'll bring your food to you, then I'll wait on the porch. You can eat while you soak."

"I'm too tired to eat right now, unless it can't hold."

She shook her head. "It's stew. Time only improves it." She glanced around her for a sweater. "I'll just go, then."

"The wind's picking up, coming from the north." Telling her to stay was on the tip of his tongue. He'd never been all that modest and his naked backside had been viewed by millions, but Zane found himself strangely hesitant to strip down in front of her.

She was nearly to the door.

"Wait." He hadn't felt this tongue-tied since he was fourteen.

She didn't glance up.

"Listen…it's cold out there. Just…turn your back until I get in. No need for you to be outside freezing."

Dead silence.

He started stripping. "Suit yourself. I'll be quick."

You don't understand, Roan wanted to say, but didn't.

One thing she was certain of, though, was that he deserved to soak and he wouldn't do it now, not if she went outside as he'd been doing for her every night. Too much the gentleman, but he'd worked like a slave all day.

She waited where she was until she heard the water slosh.

And he groaned, deep and heartfelt. Then sighed.

"Take your time," she said, scuttling past him and averting her eyes. "I'll just—" She fluttered her hands. "I'll face the other way."

Which she tried to do, settling herself in the opposite chair and attempting to read Gran's spidery handwriting.

Until he sighed again.

And she just had to peek.

Oh, God. Limned in firelight, eyes closed, profile

noble, he was the picture of an exhausted warrior fresh from battle. During the barren, emotionless years of her marriage, she'd devoured historical romances on the sly, losing herself in tales of medieval knights and feisty maidens.

He'd make the perfect hero, muscled and fierce, nobly self-sacrificing, lusty and—

Looking at her.

She gasped and averted her face.

Zane didn't even try to stifle his smile. "Have mercy for a poor wretch and wash my back?"

She hunched over and shook her head.

"Sure?"

Vigorous nodding.

Zane chuckled. "I'll be finished soon. Your turn next."

"No." She actually squeaked. "Don't rush. I'm clean."

Then she jumped up and zipped into the kitchen.

Zane was caught between amusement and pure frustration as he glanced down at his eager body. He wanted her hands on him so badly he could barely see. Wanted his own on her even worse.

And she'd been staring at him as though he were made of pure chocolate and she hadn't eaten in years.

Yet here they were, pretending to be only allies in crossing items off a list. Just co-workers, purely platonic.

What crap.

If only it were that simple. If her gaze had been

mere physical interest, he knew he could have her beneath him in no time flat.

But he'd seen more, and it scared him to death. Not the starstruck awe for a wealthy film star to which he was so accustomed, but honest admiration. True respect.

As if he was worthy of either. If she only knew...

Past relaxation now, Zane stood abruptly...

Just as Roan came through the door clutching a bowl in her hands.

Silence. Pulsating. Breathing, though neither of them could.

Roan's eyes moved over him, so slowly, so greedily, that his sorely tempted body responded in a way neither of them could ignore.

He'd never felt this naked in his life.

Roan blinked, then shot her glance up to his. In it, Zane saw unbearable temptation...and cold, stark fear. She closed her eyes and swallowed hard. When she opened them again, he read only apology and shame.

"I'm sorry," she whispered. "I just can't." With extreme care, she set down the bowl on the table, grabbed a quilt off the bed and walked outside.

Zane grasped for the towel like a man gone blind.

CHAPTER NINE

ROAN AWOKE, surprised that she'd slept at all. She'd stayed outside, huddled in the quilt, for a very long time. That Hal hadn't come after her had surprised her a little, but she was grateful for his restraint. Perhaps he'd accepted the truth that he couldn't protect her much longer, that once he left, there would be nothing between her and this harsh mountain.

He was up and gone already this morning, she was sure. The cabin felt different when he was absent. She dawdled, though, before checking to see if his things were still there. She wouldn't blame him if he'd chosen to depart before the list was finished. Not after her reaction last night.

The memory still had the power to nearly stop her heart, melodramatic as that sounded. She'd considered him gorgeous fully clothed, but naked...he was honestly too beautiful to be true. Men probably didn't welcome being called beautiful, but in his case, no other word was sufficient.

He was, without question, the most stunning man she'd ever seen.

And he'd wanted her.

Oh, probably not her, Roan O'Hara, certainly not

the sordid reality. But he would have taken her if she'd let him, that much she knew. Perhaps it was only that she was female and available, but she believed he would have been careful with her, would have demonstrated a side of sex she'd never encountered. He was too much the gentleman, too genuinely nice a person not to make sure she found satisfaction.

But in those charged moments when he'd stood before her naked, what had sent her running was the look in his eyes.

Incredibly enough, she thought he'd been scared, too. Aroused and powerful and gorgeous, but... vulnerable. Afraid...of himself...and of her. Of this unlikely and impossible thing that was growing between them.

I could love him, she'd thought in that instant.

But her weaknesses were poison-tipped arrows. He deserved to be protected from the taint of them.

So she'd let him believe that she was frightened of him when in truth, she was far more frightened of herself.

Roan sat up in the bed to look for his duffel in the corner where he kept it. When she spotted it, she took her first full breath of the morning.

You should go, Hal.

Please don't go yet.

Her mind and heart battled while Roan readied herself to face the day. She felt restless and itchy, the kind of gnawing that once she'd have pacified with a pill.

Her gaze darted toward the kitchen, where the moonshine jug still sat. Hunger and heartache opened the door for despair, and before Roan realized it, she'd crossed the room, hand outstretched.

Maybe she should just reveal to him who she really was. Give him a demonstration he'd never forget.

He'd leave then, surely.

But she remembered how it had felt, lying in his lap, half-dazed from hunger and grief. Thought about a man who refused to leave a total stranger, who could probably afford to hire people to suffer the blisters and sore muscles he'd endured the past few days.

She had to save him from himself, from his own chivalry. He'd only leave if he believed she was strong enough to make it.

Roan snatched back her hand from the jug handle and put distance between herself and the container as fast as she could. She sat on the bed and rocked, arms clasped tightly around her middle as she sought comfort from within, a well still dry as a bone. She cast about in her mind for refuge....

Her swing. Roan's fingers dug into her sides as she drew in a jagged breath.

For a few moments in that clearing, clutching the swing to her breast, Roan had touched her childhood hopes.

A child's refuge would never work for an adult. Would it?

You're crazy to go to that mountain alone, the hospital social worker had insisted. *No support group, no meetings, no sponsor. You'll be back using in a matter of weeks, if not days.*

Maybe the swing wouldn't help. But perhaps it could.

Roan grabbed for clothes, not caring if anything matched, fevered with the need to reclaim the one place that she'd ever found peace.

An hour later, she'd cleared the vines from the swing and a small area beneath it. Her head was light because she hadn't bothered with breakfast, had barely noticed that Hal was nowhere in sight, so intent had she been on finding her way back to the clearing. She'd grabbed gloves and a sharp knife and the scythe, that was all.

But as each tangled vine fell away, she could breathe a little more easily. She'd go back in a bit, get some food, then return.

"Hey, babe."

Roan whirled. And nearly screamed. "Frank."

"I heard you were back. Wanted to welcome you."

That wasn't welcome she heard in his voice. She remembered the day she'd told him she was marrying Ben, how his face had gone dark red, how he'd left bruises on her arms as he argued that she was making a big mistake. That an old man could never keep a hot piece like her happy.

"Nothin' to say?" He shrugged. "We do better

not talkin', anyway, don't we, girl? Seems to me I recall you wiggling like a cat in heat beneath me—you remember that, Roanie? We could take up right where we left off.''

Shame washed over her. She'd been a fool with Frank Howard. He'd sworn vengeance, and it appeared he hadn't forgotten anything.

''I saw your new fella at Noah's store. Funny how you go for the ones with money, ain't it? I can hurt him, Roanie—you know I can. What's it worth to keep him safe?''

Oh, no. Hal. Where was he? Roan tried to calm herself as she thought frantically. ''Frank,'' she managed to say. ''What a nice surprise. How are you?''

''Don't pretend you care. Always land on your feet, don't you, darlin'?'' Fixed and grim, his smile had the cheer of cardboard. ''Interesting thing, though. He don't seem to know too much about you. Think he might change his mind if he understood what a whore you are?''

''I have no idea who you're talking about,'' she said.

''Don't lie to me.'' He advanced on her. ''Not ever again. I've had enough of that, you hear me?''

Roan forced herself to stand her ground. ''I never misled you.''

''Oh, yes, you did. Everytime you let me inside you, while all along you'd set your sights on someone bigger.'' His laughter raked over raw nerves. ''Bet ole Ben wasn't really bigger, though, was he?''

His eyes were small and vicious as he drew closer. "Remember how you liked it, how you couldn't get enough?"

He'd been the one who couldn't get enough. Roan held the swing before her like a shield.

"What are you doing with that?" he sneered. He was only four feet away now.

Roan dropped it and stepped aside to deflect his interest. If he thought she cared about it...

Too late. "Damn thing musta been here for years." He grabbed the seat. "Yours, Roanie girl?"

"Don't." She bit her lip to stem more words.

"Or what?"

"It's just an old swing." She seized on another topic. "So what have you been up to, Frank?" She tried for flirtation but fell miserably short.

His laughter was ugly. "Like you give a shit." He clamped a hand around the rope. "Junkie whore." He spat on the ground.

Roan closed her eyes and bore it, hoping he'd expend his fury in words.

The snick of a stiletto jerked her eyes open.

Frank smiled. Fingered the gleaming blade. Assessed the rope.

"No, Frank." She despised herself for adding, "Please." It was only a child's swing. She shouldn't care so much.

"What's it worth to you?" His eyes glittered diamond-hard. He lifted the knife toward the rope.

Something inside Roan snapped. She'd only

wanted to be left alone on this mountain to try to make something of the wreck of her life. She'd destroyed so much. Lost so much.

Enough. She launched herself at Frank, fighting back against all the cops, all the social workers, the lowlifes from the street. Against Ben Chambers and his social straitjacket, her mother and her weak will—

And Frank. Cunning, vicious Frank, who wanted her on her knees.

Frank advanced, his face alight with anticipation, and roared out a challenge, the knife blade gleaming in the cool, green glade.

ZANE WHISTLED as he walked through the woods with a coil of thick rope over one shoulder. Noah might lack social graces, but his store held a surprising array of treasures. This rope, for instance, which Zane intended to use to replace the rotting ones holding up that ancient, decrepit swing that meant so much to Roan.

It wasn't an item on their list, but it suited him for two reasons: one, she had so little luxury in her life and this was a gift he could give her on the sly; and two, he wasn't eager to see her again after last night. The list contained only items that required him to be around the cabin, much too close to memories of—

Unfamiliar sounds halted him.

Then he realized what they were. A man's shout. A woman's scream.

Roan.

He ran full-tilt toward the commotion. At the edge of the clearing, he spotted Roan, nose bleeding, blouse torn, her eyes filled with both terror and rage, facing a man holding a knife.

Frank.

"Let her go." Zane charged, grabbing the man's shoulder and yanking him away from her.

Eyes wild, cheeks raw with jagged red trails, Frank latched on to Roan's arm, brandishing the knife. "What's it to you, city boy? You think you got a claim? Don't you know she likes to spread it around? Hot little piece, this one." His smile was vicious. "She'll cheat on you, though. Gotta watch that." He shrugged. "A good time, 'long as you recognize that she's a slut."

With effort, Zane ignored the barbs, keeping one eye on Frank as he did a quick check on Roan. She'd lost all color, frozen in place. "Pick on someone your own size, coward."

Frank's eyes glittered with malice, but he let her go, shoving her so hard that she fell to the ground.

Zane wanted badly to beat the living hell out of Frank.

But not until Roan was safely out of range of that knife. "Move away from him, honey," he said gently.

Roan's eyes were dull as she looked at him, but she complied, scooting backward into the shelter of a big tree. She huddled into a ball of sheer misery.

"Okay, buddy. I'm all yours. Bring it on."

"No!" Roan cried out. "Hal, you don't know what he's like."

Frank cocked one eyebrow, fingers beckoning. "What'll it be, boy? Gonna come out from behind her skirts?" He snickered. "Not that her skirts ain't most often found flipped over her head."

That did it. One swift kick at Frank's wrist dislodged the knife, then Zane waded into Frank with both fists.

Frank knocked Zane's head back with an uppercut to the chin.

Zane charged again, lowering his head to catch Frank square in the midriff, sending them both flying.

Frank fought back, and he fought dirty. Zane blessed every stunt fight, every brawl with three elder brothers as he struggled to block and counter the heavier man. Rage fueled him as he recalled Roan being terrorized by this brute. Grimly, he sought to punish Frank, suffering his own share of blows.

Frank staggered back, chest heaving. He laughed with no trace of mirth. "Your pretty boy here, he thinks he can take me." He stared at Zane but spoke to Roan. "But you ain't gonna be around forever, are you, city boy? Roanie here, she's a fickle woman. You might keep her naked and willing for a little while longer, but ain't no one satisfied her yet." He looked at Roan over his shoulder. "'Course, maybe he'll find out just what you are, and he'll get wise like Ben did. What you think, Roan honey? Want me to tell him all about the shame you brought on your grandma?''

Zane glanced at her stricken face. "Shut up."

"Huh, sugar? Want lover boy here to know?"

"Enough." Taking advantage of Frank's focus on Roan, he slipped up beside Frank and twisted his arm, finding a pressure point he'd learned from a martial arts advisor on his last film. He dug fingers into the tender spot. Hard.

Frank gasped. Sweat broke out on his forehead.

"I just might be the city boy you think—" Zane ratcheted up the pressure. "But even city boys understand a thing or two about bullies. I don't much care for bullies, Frank." He tightened his grip.

Frank gagged.

"You and me, we don't have to like each other, but we can come to an agreement, see. As long as you stay away from Roan, I'll be glad to let you go your way and I'll go mine." He relaxed his grip.

Frank wheezed out his relief.

Zane smiled. Then hit another pressure point.

And brought Frank to his knees on the ground before him. "One thing about having money is that even if I'm not here, I can hire men who aren't much on bullies, either. Maybe I won't be here long—probably won't. But you'll never be sure if Roan's guarded or not." He increased the pressure. "Best to assume she is, Frank. Good idea to head on down the road and let her be."

He released Frank and stepped back. "Bye, now. Nice meeting you."

Frank rose unsteadily, his color gray, his breathing hard.

His eyes filled with hate. "She's not worth it, boy. And we ain't through."

"Fine by me. As long as you leave the lady alone, I'll be glad to oblige you anytime. You say the word." Then, in a move calculated to enrage, Zane gave his back to Frank, as if he posed no threat, and began to walk toward Roan.

"This ain't the end, boy," Frank shouted, but his voice was already receding, and Zane knew he had won.

This round, anyway.

He spared no more time for Frank, focusing instead on the woman before him, her eyes dark and vacant.

He stopped two feet away and knelt beside her. "Roan," he said quietly.

She didn't answer.

"Let me hold you, Roan." Slowly and carefully, he extended his arms.

She recoiled.

"He won't come back," Zane said. "And I'll protect you."

One faint flicker. "You can't. Nobody can."

"I'm sorry I wasn't around when you needed me." He wasn't batting too well on that score lately.

"But I'm here now." Gently, he clasped her arms to draw her close.

One pale shoulder lay exposed by the torn shirt. Her whole body shuddered hard enough to rattle bones. "No man...not ever again," she whispered. "No touch...I can't let—"

She stumbled to her feet and bolted from the clearing.

He tore off after her. "Roan, stop. You can't see where you're going."

But she was beyond comprehension, guttural sobs punctuating her headlong race through whipping branches...

Until something tripped her. She broke her fall with her arms and bent double, shuddering.

Zane crouched beside her. Tentatively, he placed one hand on her slender back, feeling every rib.

"Don't." She recoiled. "Go away."

He removed his hand but remained there. "I'm not leaving."

She curled up in a sitting position, everything about her shouting the urge to protect herself. "No."

"Don't say you don't need me, Roan. I'm not buying it." He caught a glimpse of her face then, a portrait of misery.

But not fear, he didn't think. "I won't harm you."

She tucked her head into her legs. "Of course not."

Relief coursed through him. "I'm going to pick you up now and carry you back to the cabin."

"No." She flinched. Then took a deep breath. "I can walk."

He had his doubts, but she had a right to her pride. "Okay. Let me help you up, though." He extended a hand.

After a moment, she accepted it and let him lift her to standing. She glanced down at herself, at the torn shirt. With a gasp, she turned away and tried without success to straighten it, but half the buttons were gone. Her shoulders rounded protectively.

Zane's hands clenched with the need to help her out, to restore her to the prickly woman she'd been. This vulnerability terrified him. Quickly, he stripped off his T-shirt. "Here," he offered, handing it over her shoulder. You can put this on to…you know. Cover yourself."

"You'll get cold." She took it, looked at it for a minute. Clutched it against her breast.

"I'm worried about you, not me."

"You were incredible." Finally, she met his gaze. "I can't remember the last time anyone stood up for me."

"He didn't—" Zane left the question unfinished.

"No." Her gaze darted away. "Thanks to you."

"He hit you." Fury rose again as he studied her face. "You should be examined."

She shook her head. "No."

"I could force you."

She met his eyes. "But you won't, will you?"

He exhaled in defeat. "I want to be sure you're okay."

Her mouth tightened as memory darkened her eyes. "I'll be fine."

He decided the moment could use some lightening. "How about two wounded warriors lean on each other on the walk back?"

A smile flitted across her lips as she glanced at him in wary gratitude. After a long pause, she answered, "All right."

He placed an arm around her shoulders. She hesitated, then slid hers around his waist. Slowly, they made their way back to the cabin.

SLUT. WE'RE NOT FINISHED. Frank's voice boomed inside Roan's head as she entered the cabin. Saw in her mind's eye the blade, the contempt in Frank's eyes.

She slipped from Hal's grasp. How could she stay here, understanding how deep the hatred went? Realizing now that her neighbors would never accept her, that her mistakes would follow her forever?

But where could she go?

"Hey," Hal said, coming up beside her. "Why don't you sit down. Rest a minute."

"No." She shoved away from that broad, muscular chest. Looked around for escape.

"Sit." With firm pressure, he urged her shoulders down. "You're pale as milk."

"I don't want to." She eluded him, but the walls

of the cabin were shrinking in on her. Panic rose. She would never make it. She wanted a drink. Wanted more, but a drink would help.

Blindly, she raced for the doorway.

He caught her first. "Hey, take it easy. He's gone." Hal pulled her close.

She struggled against his far greater strength. He wasn't budging. "Let me go," she whispered.

"Not until you're calmer." He wrapped her in his arms and cradled her head in one big hand. "Let me be your friend, Roan." His voice was everything soothing, everything safe and warm and kind.

Was it so wrong to want his comfort? Roan stood stiffly in his arms, her fingers flexing as she tried to resist the lure of all that he offered, how it would weaken her if she said yes.

But the terrible yearning for oblivion had faded when he embraced her.

Replaced by a craving that could be just as habit-forming.

As long as you recognize she's a slut.

Roan jerked.

Hal held on. "Take a deep breath. Just relax. Let all of it go." His chest rose with his own inhalation.

"No. He was right. Frank." She curled her fingers against Hal's chest. "I've done...terrible things."

"Shh," he murmured, spreading his legs and rocking her side to side. "I don't believe that. We all make mistakes."

She heard aching regret in his voice. Was this where the shadows came from?

"Not like mine. You have no idea…"

"It doesn't matter. You're safe now."

Oh, God. How she wished… His words aroused a craving she'd fought all her life, but time and hard knocks had demonstrated how futile it was to think that hunger could ever be met and mastered.

There was no safe place, not even here in the only spot she'd ever experienced it, however temporary. For the moment, though, if she kept her sights low, her expectations minimal, she could have this respite, fleeting though it would be.

And so Roan let herself relax against him, a man she barely knew, a hero faced with a woman who'd forgotten how to believe in them.

"That's right," he crooned, his arms so strong and reassuring that she let her own close around his waist, his bare skin a banquet for flesh that had been so long deprived of caring human touch.

His heartbeat thudded against her ear, its rhythm slow and deep. A remnant of fear shuddered down her body as she relaxed a little more. Endless moments formed a chain of contentment she didn't dare trust, but oh…how good this felt to her. She snuggled against him.

A quick gasp…the tightening of his arms…the press of him against her belly…

He quickly put space between them. "I'm sorry. I

don't want to scare you." His cheeks were actually red.

"I'm not that weak." She clenched her hands. She wouldn't be, damn it.

"Of course you're not. You may be the strongest woman I've ever met, and given the women in my family, that's saying something."

Why, now, were tears pricking her eyes? Her head dropped as she tried to find her voice. "I'm going to make it."

"I think you can, but Roan..." He paused. "Are you set on this?" There was an odd note in his voice. "I have friends, contacts. I could help you settle somewhere else or hire someone to..."

Did she want to remain, after what had happened? Honestly? No. She wanted to run far and fast.

Help me, Gran. Help me discover that strong woman this man thinks he can see. She was too aware of just how weak she truly was, how close to the edge. How easy it would be to slip over.

Her throat filled. She cleared it. "No. But don't worry about me. I understand that you need to leave soon. You never lied to me."

He moved away, looking anywhere but at her. "There are things you don't know about me," he finally answered.

"Same here, but we won't see each other again, so it doesn't matter." *At least, it won't if you never find out.* "You're free to leave whenever. I'll be fine."

He studied her for a very long time, his brow wrinkled. "The list isn't finished. I'm going nowhere yet."

She could only stare back.

Then he smiled. "It's your turn now."

She blinked. "What?"

"I'm going to heat you a bath. Take care of you."

"You're hurt. You should lie down."

He laughed. "After a few lousy punches? Get real." He headed for the door. "Sit. Take a load off. You've been through a lot. I'm going to fix you a bath, then you'll have a nap."

Once on the porch alone, Zane dropped his head and exhaled loudly. He wanted to take care of her. Images of Frank assaulted him.

What in the world was he doing?

Then he thought about the woman inside.

You never lied to me. Zane pinched the bridge of his nose between finger and thumb. What was the greater kindness—to continue the charade or to shatter her illusions? He had to go soon. What in the hell had he done, getting involved with her?

His fingers curled in memory of how she'd felt in his arms. How much he'd wanted to step out of that tub last night and lose himself in her. To exalt her, pamper her, show her that she could indeed relish the act of making love.

He clenched his teeth, trying to stem the need that was eating him alive.

She was wounded. Frank's slurs were still etched into his memory. *Slut.*

Sometimes, Zane hated his own kind. He reached the well, brutally yanking the bucket upward and replacing it. Men hurt women. Battered them into submission for the sake of satisfying their base urges.

Frank was such a man, and within Zane grew a drive he'd never imagined.

He could kill Frank, he thought. With little remorse.

The darker impulses heretofore had played no role in Zane's life, yet suddenly he was assaulted by them. From someone known to be kind and easygoing, he'd turned into the most primitive sort of male, pawing at the ground, ready to defend his...

Mate. Oh, no. Uh-uh. No matter how much Roan O'Hara aroused protective instincts in him, getting more involved here made absolutely no sense in the grand scheme of things.

Zane MacAllister was destined for greatness. Everyone was sure of that. His star was hot and rising higher. He just had to get past this situation with Kelly and—

How could he leave Roan? The realization hit him right between the eyes that he couldn't.

He had to find a way to make her go with him to Texas. Once there, he'd figure out something. He would never forgive himself if he left her behind, aware of how much Frank—and others—despised her.

What the hell had she done to them? More than simply marrying a rich guy, that was for sure.

I don't like sex.

Hot little piece, this one.

The voices battered him as he made trips in and out of the cabin, carefully ignoring the woman huddled in her grandmother's rocking chair, pale and still. Throughout the process of heating the water and testing it, he averted his gaze from her. Fought to be invisible, a simple human servant. Only a caretaker.

While the primitive aftermath of fighting for her roared through his veins.

The tub was full, the water hot. "It's ready." Was that his voice, a croak?

Then from beside him, when he'd never heard her move.

"Show me."

"What?"

"You said I was capable of passion. That I just hadn't met the right man." Those blue eyes were merciless in their focus. "Maybe I have."

Zane sucked in air through his nostrils. Yanked his gaze away. "No."

Her hand covered his forearm.

He clenched his jaw. "Get in the tub, Roan."

"I wanted you last night. You're beautiful. Such...so much man."

He squeezed his eyes shut, remembering.

Responding. Ready to drive within her.

"Get in the tub, Roan," he repeated.

She shrank into herself; he saw it from the corner of his eye. Once more she was the damaged woman he'd met, and he wanted to throw something.

"I'm trying to do right by you, don't you get that? I won't be here long."

Blue eyes blazed. "Screw you." Defiantly, she stripped off the torn blouse. Unsnapped her jeans, drew the remainder of her clothing down those long, smooth legs, then stepped slowly into the tub, daring him not to look.

He wasn't gentleman enough to comply.

But when she sank into the water, he breathed a sigh of relief and turned away to give her privacy.

Every sound tormented him, each splash, every slide of water over flesh he ached to touch. He couldn't stand it anymore and spun around to go outside.

Until he saw the expression on her face as she lay there, eyes closed, so sad and hurt.

Caretaker. Remember that.

He stepped up behind her and tried not to focus on the slender pale limbs he could see too clearly beneath the water. He picked up the pitcher she used to wash her hair and filled it.

Roan didn't move.

Carefully, he poured it over her hair, then reached for the shampoo. Fingers that itched to trace over her body slipped into her hair instead, massaging her scalp.

Her breathy whimper nearly undid him.

Long, painful minutes passed, punctuated by tiny moans. Silvery sighs. Zane was surprised that despite the gnawing urge to slip his hands down her neck and over her shoulders to the cool rounds of her breasts, he could somehow content himself with the way her hair slid like coarse silk between his fingers, how the curves of her skull felt as fragile as an eggshell in his big hands.

Until she arched her back and undulated, bringing those small, tender breasts out of the water.

"Show me." Her voice went low and throaty. Blue eyes popped open to pin him. "Please."

"Roan..."

"I'll never know if you don't. I'll never believe that sex can be anything but misery." Her stare was merciless. "I'll live alone here the rest of my life and no one will ever touch me."

Roan held her breath as she refused to relinquish his gaze. "I understand that you're leaving. I'm not asking you to stay. I only want this." Amazed at her daring, she clasped one of his hands and brought it down to cover her breast.

And gasped at the feel of it tightening on her flesh. *More,* was all she could think. *Now.*

"Close your eyes." His voice was tight.

She glanced up. His face was hard.

"I have to rinse your hair first." A muscle in his jaw jumped. "Do it, Roan," he warned.

Exhilaration rose within her, right alongside nerves. She shut her eyes. Released his hand. Luxuriated in the warm water cascading over her heated flesh.

She brushed the water from her eyes, then opened them to see him staring into the fire. "Hal—"

"Don't." He faced her then. Fierce. Furious.

But also, she thought, a little sad. She started to speak.

He stopped her with a raised hand, studying her until she had to look away. "Forget it," she said.

"No." His voice was rough at first, then turned gentle. "Lie back, Roan. Give me…" For the first time, she heard uncertainty in him. "Just…give me a second."

Roan obeyed, but beneath her skin, humiliation burned. She should have kept quiet. He didn't want her, and she—

Without warning, he scooped her from the water. Set her on her feet before the fire. Wrapped her in a towel he'd warmed, trapping her arms inside.

He pulled her close and rested his head against the top of hers. She could hear his heart thudding.

Then, with a deep, shuddering inhalation, he stepped back, bringing the towel with him.

And simply looked at her.

His silence cast Roan into an agony of awareness. She was too thin, too ruined…too old in a way that had nothing to do with years. The crystalline rim of her daring shattered on the knife-edge of fear, and she lifted her arms to cover a body shorn of illusion. Drained by false hope.

"Roan..." Too carefully, he covered her once more.

"Don't." She gripped the towel and ducked her head, eyes stinging. "Don't pity me."

Zane caught her shoulders and cursed himself. Refused to let her slide past. "You misunderstand."

It hurt to see her, so fragile beneath the bravado, her skin not all that was bruised. With her head bowed, she was once again the woman he'd first met, made small by despair.

She was trying so hard, and even now he had no idea what her demons were, and thought he shouldn't ask because theirs were separate paths, crossing only this once, never again to meet.

But he couldn't do this the way she wanted. Couldn't simply demonstrate his much-admired skills with women, and then go.

He crooked one finger beneath her chin and lifted her face to his. "Judge the truth for yourself. It isn't pity. It's fear."

Her eyes widened. "You're afraid? Why?"

"There's a sorrow in you that I want to heal, and I'm not..." His gaze shifted, then returned. "I'm not the right man. I couldn't live with myself if I hurt you, instead."

Roan forced herself not to shrink away. Not to run, though everything in her quivered to do just that. For too much of her life, she'd sought escapes of one kind or another. All of them had failed.

From somewhere within her, she found a tiny

scrap of the iron she would need to forge the woman she wanted to become and stood straight. "I'll survive you. I'll survive all of this."

Within green eyes turned gold by firelight, she thought she saw respect stir, crowded as it was by worry.

But when he would have spoken, she covered his lips with her hand. "Don't talk anymore. Words are too complicated." Her voice slid low. "I don't need your healing. I only want to know how passion feels."

The fire crackled, and sparks danced high in the air. Desire and nerves, hunger and longing leaped between them. His lips pressed against her hand, soft yet firm, while his gaze searched deep inside her.

And Roan shivered, sensing that she'd won. Half-fear, half-anticipation.

His hands, long and lean and so masculine, rose to lift the towel from fingers gone abruptly weak. Slowly, he drew it from her shoulders, the tiny cotton loops gently abrading skin suddenly sensitive to the slightest touch.

With his eyes still locked on hers, he blotted the moisture from her hair, then leaned to trace his lips over a drop escaping down her temple and over her cheek. His breath warmed her skin as his mouth drifted to hers.

He hovered there, not making contact yet, until her eyelids fluttered closed. Until she felt the heat of him all along the front of her body, her respirations adjusting to his, sounding unnaturally loud in her ears.

Every inch of her flesh strained toward him, every beat of her heart seeking, striving…she rose to tiptoe, her fingers flexed outward like a cat's paws, nails stretching…retracting…

Teasing…

Longing…

When his mouth skimmed hers, shock sliced through her body like the crack of a whip. She grabbed his biceps, fingers clenched in his shirt to drag him against her, seeking to muffle the near-painful bite of primal need.

A quick graze of lips. Then his heat vanished.

Roan gasped. Blinked.

Stared down at the top of his head as he knelt before her like some knight pledging fealty.

Her own Prince Charming, for Roan indeed felt as if he were awakening her from years lost.

''Hold on to me,'' he said, lifting her foot onto his hard, muscled thigh. Head bent, he focused on drying her with agonizingly slow, measured strokes. She bit back the pleas for him to hurry, to get to it because she was off balance, she couldn't stand this.

He drew his middle fingernail up the sole of her foot.

And Roan nearly screamed.

He chuckled and looked up at her, eyes both intense and alight with mischief.

Then, as if he hadn't set her hair on fire, he returned to his task, so thorough yet neutral that he could have been a mere caretaker.

Except his hair brushed her thigh. His breath whispered over the parting of her legs...

A kiss skated over the inside of her knee, and Roan's legs buckled.

He caught her to him, strong arms closing about her, his cheek to her navel, his hair tickling the lower curve of one breast.

Roan wanted to clasp him to her and never let go.

It frightened her so much that she tried to back away.

Zane tightened his grip, sensing that this might be the most important act of his life. "Shh," he soothed, rising to his feet and cradling her, sweeping his hands over her back in unhurried, lazy arcs.

When she stilled again, he nibbled at her distress with soft, easy kisses, forehead to eyes, eyes to cheeks, cheeks to the racing pulse points at her throat. "Let me show you how beautiful you are," he murmured.

Once again she tensed, shaking her head. "I'm not. No lies, Hal. No sweet words. I don't need them."

Hal. Zane squeezed his eyes shut, torn once again. She needed sweet words and so much more. If he stopped now and revealed his identity, even if she understood how he'd stepped into this trap without malice or intent, she would never let him back this close again. She thought she was ugly, believed herself without appeal. If he showed her with his body, if he made her see her own beauty, her courage and strength, then when he did explain, wouldn't she be hard-pressed to believe he'd meant to hurt her?

Please. Let me do this right. He'd never been more uncertain in his life.

"No words," he agreed. "I'll let my body convince you, instead."

He began an assault on her senses unlike anything Roan had ever known. Tender kisses to unexpected places, the inside of her wrist...her ankle...the underside of an arm, tickled, made her nipples tighten. Tongue sliding the length of her collarbone, ending with a nip of teeth that shot arrows straight to her middle.

Hot, excruciatingly patient strokes turning suddenly so urgent that he pulled away. Let her go.

Zane dragged in one pained breath, then another. Too fast. Too crazed, he was. Too hungry, no matter that she was nothing like the women he'd preferred.

That was the problem. She was outside his experience, a woman he couldn't dally with, comfortable that it wasn't serious for either of them, that both would walk away whole. Kelly had been his one mistake, but there'd been no cracks in her veneer for him to recognize. Her fault lines had been deep but well hidden. She'd gone into it with the same light heart he had...at least at first.

But Roan was different. Right from the beginning, he'd known that everything about her was serious.

There was no play in this woman, however desperately she needed fun.

She was porcelain, her finish crazed and yellowed, her insides hollowed out, her shell frighteningly thin, yet there were moments when he thought he could see a slender framework of pure steel.

The risk of guessing wrong, as he had with Kelly, broke him out in a cold sweat.

But he'd made her a promise, and promises were sacred to Zane.

So just as he saw her coming out of the spell he'd painstakingly woven, emerging into the unforgiving light of her own doubts, Zane lifted her into his arms and carried her to the ancient, too-small bed where he would do his best to teach her to believe in herself again.

HAD SHE EVER fancied it possible to feel this way? Had she even dreamed that she could release her vigilance, that she'd have no choice but to drift along the current and trust that there would be a hand beneath her back as she floated, that she could afford to let arms loosen, legs part…her whole body glide, weightless?

Trust. A small word, yes, but pregnant with meaning and menace and, oh, the relief of it after so many years alone. Roan's deepest self unfurled from the tiny, terrified creature who'd sought to hide so long ago, lashed almost beyond surviving by all the wrong choices, the promises not kept, the myriad failures.

As he held her close and let the sunlight of hope kiss her hair, taste her breasts, stroke her inner flesh, Roan felt herself expanding into someone she'd glimpsed only in passing, the faintest of possibilities.

And that burgeoning created room for something big and bold and prowling, a woman Roan had never even imagined. Passive acceptance shattered, swallowed up by avid seeking. Fevered craving.

By greedy demand. Her soul alight, her body humming, Roan turned the tables on the man who had brought her to the pinnacle of the mountain.

But even as he wondered about the next move, Roan decided for him. With one simple stroke of her tongue across his lips, she flayed him open, down to the bone.

That one hot, wet slide of flesh against his mouth staggered Zane. In an instant, he lost all power of thought, of speech, of hearing. He forgot about tenderness, cast away caution as she shattered any notion he had of restraint. Female called to male. Heat called to heat. She became woman, elemental and basic. Irresistible, unmanageable… He dove in and took it all.

Sweet mercy, was all Zane could think as she rose, quick as a cat, from beneath him and bent her efforts to pleasing him. Tantalizing him as no woman had done before, her moves a fragrant, mouthwatering concoction of spices not fully ripe, not quite at peak but oh, dear, sweet hell….

Zane reared upward to mate with this creature, this

goddess who roused the animal in him, the primal male whose world had narrowed to one woman. His woman.

Gasps. Moans. Clawing needs. Heights never scaled, depths untouched.

Recognition. Two halves become whole.

Zane now had her beneath him, poised to slake the thirst parching both of them, the near-furious demand that would not be denied.

Suddenly, her dazzled eyes flared with panic. "No. You can't risk…"

With a shock, Zane realized that for the first time in his life, he'd been so consumed by a woman that he'd forgotten all about protection.

Brutal need balked. *I'm not a risk,* he nearly snapped.

But women had another concern. "I'm sorry," he barely managed to say, launching himself off the bed in search of his bag, his movements clumsy and frantic.

Roan plummeted to earth.

But in seconds, he was back with her, catching her in freefall, his eyes dark, uneasy with yearning she could almost taste, apology she could nearly touch.

Roan perched on a razor's edge, ready to topple into self-loathing at the slightest push, but instead of forcing her with his potent skills, he did, again, the unexpected.

He held her. Only held her, letting her chilled soul soak up his warmth.

And when he quivered as if lashed by fear strong as her own, Roan found herself the one to comfort, the one who could grant ease.

The one with the intoxicating, wholly new power to choose.

She chose life and hope. Survival and strength.

Then it became Roan's hands that stroked, Roan's mouth that kissed, that gave them both the freedom to fly.

With a heart-deep sigh, he met her. Matched her. Drew her with him to the heights until they were no longer two but one, a being quicksilver and beautiful…and exquisite.

Complete.

And at last, Roan understood why it was called lovemaking. Why poets waxed eloquent and men died for it.

There was passion in her after all, just as he'd said, with the right man.

This man.

Beautiful…unattainable…impossible dream that he was.

St Joseph
as we
the near

DIAPSE —

CHAPTER TEN

ROAN LAY WIDE-EYED from terror.

Scenes played out, so many of them she could barely breathe. The man of her dreams, the prince of every girl's imagination, reposed beside her, his body curved protectively around hers as if, even sleeping, he understood her fears and would soothe them.

Her whole body, still singing from the exquisite pleasure of his lovemaking, went stiff and miserable as the facts of her life reemerged.

Though she'd had herself tested for disease and passed muster, no official verdict could cleanse the stain from her soul. Only time—please God—could do that. She had a lot to prove, and brushing against this man's kind heart had both soothed the ragged edges of her heart and made her more aware than ever of the chasm between her and him.

He'd called her beautiful, and she couldn't stand for him to find out just how wrong he was. If she thought about that moment when he'd poised over her, his body bare to hers as though he could trust…

She wanted a pill, just one. Or a drink. Roan had known the safest route was to pour out the jug of moonshine, but she'd kept it as a test for herself, a gambit whose danger she'd thought she'd assessed.

The trials, it seemed, were just beginning.

You should be proud of yourself.

He wouldn't say that if he knew everything she'd done.

She thought of all the lovely pills she'd flushed down the toilet that night when she'd hit bottom.

Her little friends. With them, she'd feel strong, not afraid to be here. Calm instead of doomed. Brave enough to stay, to be alone again after Hal left.

This minute. This one minute is all you have to get through.

More than ever, she was afraid she couldn't manage. The slide back down that cliff she'd crawled up with bleeding fingers pulled at her, cajoled her, the precipice so near and hypnotic. One instant of inattention…

She had a flash of Mick's hand strapping the rubber strip above her elbow, tapping the veins. Telling her that bliss was only a needle away.

The rush of it, the warmth. Ecstasy had raced through her like molten gold. She'd been powerful, invincible…

Calm, for a change.

Then senseless, lost in the beauty of oblivion.

Until she'd awakened to the man who wanted her body as payment. In one instant of understanding, she'd seen her future. Her failure.

She'd become her mother after all.

Roan jerked. Hal grunted in protest.

Before his arms could tighten around her again, she slipped from the bed.

She crossed to the fire and stoked it with slow, careful movements, focusing only on the logs, the poker…even as her heart turned to ashes at what she knew she must do for him.

His list—their list—had to be abandoned. She had to find the strength to make him leave.

Before she gave in and begged him to stay.

For right now, however, fatigue dragged at her. Her entire body ached from Frank's beating. She forced herself up from the chair and began to quietly gather Hal's belongings, trying not to think about the fact that Hal's threats notwithstanding, Frank could still be out there somewhere, lurking. Vengeance simmering.

He'd always been more about brute force than brains. She'd found the danger of him attractive, back when he'd been whipcord-lean and edgy. Before she'd understood that edgy could mean unbalanced and deadly.

The unconscious man sprawled all over Gran's bed would soon be gone, anyway. There was no reason for Frank to believe that tale about hiring bodyguards when Roan herself didn't buy it.

They were strangers, she and this city boy who had the skills to hunt and repair porches. Intimate though their last hours had been, he didn't have the most fundamental facts about her and wouldn't like them if he did.

While she, Roan realized, stopping dead in the center of the room, hadn't even asked his last name.

Good Lord. How could it be that they'd shared so much, yet so little that mattered?

Except that he'd made her laugh, the way she hadn't laughed since childhood, if even then. He'd chopped wood for her, replaced a roof, cleared brush, worked like a slave—

Charged into danger to rescue her.

Taught her what love was and how badly she wanted it.

And she only knew that his name was Hal-short-for-Harold.

Slowly, she turned and studied his still form.

He was kind, though; she was certain of that. Strong and funny and oddly modest for someone so handsome.

He loved his family and was adored by them, too, she understood without ever meeting them. He had the confidence of someone who'd never doubted that he was cherished, never been abandoned. Never threatened by those who were supposed to nurture.

He hadn't ever really been challenged, either, she'd bet. He could be judgmental about weakness because he possessed none. Hadn't experienced coming up short.

Roan understood all about failing challenges. She

sank against the rough log wall. *One minute. Only one.*

She could not fall short this time. She would make that trip down the mountain for supplies and among them would be a sturdy lock for the door and ammunition for the weapons Gran had left. When she was alone again after Hal's departure, Frank would come; she never doubted that. Only if she gave him a reason to fear her would he let her be. Even if there had been a sheriff living right next door to her instead of miles and miles away, courts and cops would prove no barrier to a man steeped in mountain justice.

The ancient codes still ruled here. Eye for an eye. Take the law into your own hands. Might makes right.

Hal moaned and rolled to his side, his face set in lines of strain. "No." His voice was hoarse and anguished. "No. She can't be dead. Why wouldn't she let me…"

Dead? Who was dead? Roan struggled out of the cobwebs. "Hal?"

He tossed violently, shoving the covers off.

Roan touched him in an attempt to settle him, making a concerted effort not to ogle the body that had given her such incredible pleasure.

But her fingers registered the layers of hard muscle, the breadth of his shoulders. She traced fingertips down his arm, powerful yet capable of being so gentle. He tossed and tried to roll away. She placed her free hand on his shoulder, murmuring reassurance until he stilled. Finally, he slid completely under again.

Roan rubbed her eyes and mourned. Sleep called to her, but she couldn't rest until he was gone, until she'd cut the cord that bound them before it was too late.

But he'd need his sleep to continue his trip safely. Roan finished packing his belongings, then settled onto the floor. A little more time she gave herself to watch him, to savor memories she'd have to lock away soon or go mad longing for them once he was gone.

ZANE BATTLED the nightmare. A coffin unseen. A funeral not attended. A pull he couldn't fight. Down the dark hallway of his grief, he approached a circle of light, a rim over which he'd see Kelly's face, so still and lifeless. Heart nearly ripped from his chest, he forced himself to face the responsibility he'd abandoned, the woman he hadn't been able to save.

Oh, God. *Roan.* Zane shuddered and fell to his knees.

The woman in the casket was Roan, fragile and lost and—

Zane bolted up in the bed, unable to comprehend for a minute where he was.

When he saw Roan sitting by the fire, something inside him leaped. Alive. She was alive. Thank God. He buried his face in arms crossed over his knees and fought to steady his breathing. As he did so, he became aware of silence, utter and complete but for the crackle of the fire. Filled with foreboding. All his joy fled.

Zane lifted his head. And knew.

In the faint light of dawn, the soft, singing, shining warrior woman had vanished. A cold, closed-in stranger had taken her place. His duffel lay at her feet, filled and zippered. His clothes were arranged neatly at the foot of the bed.

He didn't have to ask why. He shouldn't have protested, but he would anyway, damn it. "The list isn't finished."

One second. One tiny flicker.

Gone in an instant. "Enough is done," she said in a voice he'd never heard. "It's time for you to go."

He was being shown the door. He, Zane MacAllister, Sexiest Man Alive. The Prince of Hollywood. Fury shoved him to his feet, naked. Daring her to notice. Challenging her to ignore him. "What if I'm not ready?"

She stood, fingers clenched. "Then you're no different from Frank, refusing to let a woman say no."

A cold, terrible wind blew through him, freezing his ability to think past the outrage. There was no trace left of the woman to whom he'd made love so tenderly. Who'd given him a sacred trust he'd held precious.

"What the hell's wrong with you?" he demanded.

"Listen, I'm grateful for last night. You were

right.'' Her smile mocked him. ''I owe you for en-
lightening me.'' She turned away. Busied herself
with the poker, her voice breezy. ''You're very talented. I'm sure you'll have no trouble getting any
woman you want.''

As long as it's not me. She might as well have said
the words out loud.

Zane hadn't gotten a brush-off from a woman
since he was fifteen years old. The effrontery of
Roan's actions nearly shocked a laugh from him, except that he was insulted and mad as hell.

He shook off the growing rage and focused on
grabbing clothing and donning it, consumed by a
sense that he'd stripped his soul naked, too, only to
have her reject him at his most honest.

And that concept was a laugh in and of itself, since
every time she'd moaned and called his name, it had
compounded his lies.

She was right. He could talk to Noah, force the
old guy to accept money to arrange for the needed
repairs still not crossed off his list. He'd pay a pre-
mium and she'd be off his conscience.

Dressed now, Zane had already hefted his duffel
over his shoulder when he cast one last, angry look
at her…

And saw the bow of her shoulders, so reminiscent
of the day they'd met. Spotted the white knuckles at
her sides.

''Roan—'' He had to try one last time to reach
her. Bare himself once more. ''Talk to me,'' he

urged. "Tell me why you're doing this. Last night was…" He didn't have the words to express what he'd thought they'd shared.

But when her head rose and she turned to face him, he saw that he'd been wrong. No uncertainty lurked in her. No special understanding, no soft remembrance.

Only a smile that cut him to the bone. "It was terrific," she agreed briskly. "Now I need your address so I know where to send the payments. Do you think ten dollars an hour is fair for the work you did, or should it be more?"

Stunned, Zane froze to the spot, unable to believe what he was hearing. He stared hard at her, refusing to let the hurt of it inside, while wondering where his vaunted instincts about women had fled if he could be this wrong about her.

She stared right back, but the fire cast her features into shadow and he couldn't be certain of anything.

That he was nearly ready to beg shook him worse than anything had in a long time. Zane MacAllister didn't have to beg women, ever. He wouldn't start now.

"Forget the money," he growled, and headed for the door.

"I won't do that. I can't. Tell me how to reach you. I pay my debts."

"Screw your debts. Consider your bill paid last night." He slapped her with words, blinded by pain he shouldn't feel, confusion he didn't need, sorrow he didn't want.

Then he jerked the door open and charged down the steps as if the devil himself followed.

CHAPTER ELEVEN

ROAN HUDDLED on the floor, staring into the weak morning light through the old, wavy glass. The fire faltered, nearly as weak as her dying heart.

But she'd done the right thing for both herself and Hal. If she could explain, he'd understand that and be glad.

And someday, she'd forget the pain of their parting after all the joy he'd brought into her life. Oh, please, please…let the agony ebb soon, before she died of it.

She heard the sound of a motor, faint at first, then growing louder. Her treacherous heart leaped.

Had Hal come back? Why? And how would she explain—

A loud knock on the door. "Roanie? Where are you, girl?"

She froze. Not Hal. *Frank.*

"I know he's gone. I've been watching, see. We got some business to finish, you and me."

And she hadn't had time to get that lock.

"Roan!" he shouted. "You hear me?"

Roan stared at the door as if snakes writhed on the other side of it, ready to slither in.

"Don't make me mad, darlin'. Come on out where we can talk. Or maybe we'll talk later, after." He laughed, the sound of it harsh and grating. "Get out here, or I'm gonna be forced to come in after you."

Roan kept herself beneath window level, scooting across the floor toward the corner where Gran's shotgun stood.

The door burst open. Roan screamed and scrambled.

Frank caught her arm and jerked her against him, his smile widening, his eyes cold and flat. "Hey there, sugar," he crooned. "Where you goin' in such a hurry? Didn't you hear what I said?"

Roan couldn't let herself flinch. Frank's temper was a dangerous thing, coiled to strike when you least expected it. "I wasn't going anywhere." She swallowed hard. Forced a smile past the nausea, seeking her long-unused hostess smile. "How are you, Frank?"

He went still, those predator's eyes fixed on her.

Then he smiled back.

And slapped her hard.

Roan tasted copper where her teeth cut the inside of her mouth. She shook her head to clear the dizziness and forced herself not to react.

"What's wrong, baby?" he sniggered. "Waiting for that bodyguard?"

"No." The worst thing she could do was show her fear.

He let go of her arm suddenly, and the release made her light-headed. She wavered for a second.

He pounced. "I own you, Roanie. You never understood that." He grabbed her head and ground his mouth against her, brutally forced her lips apart to thrust his thick tongue inside.

Roan gagged. Shoved at him.

Frank gripped the neck of her shirt, twisting it in one meaty fist, then ripped it open. "I told you I'd be waiting, you bitch. You goddamn slut." He jerked at her waistband while the other hand worked at his belt, unsnapped his jeans.

Though she knew she couldn't win, Roan fought him, using nails and teeth, kicking and gouging for his eyes.

Frank bellowed and knocked her to the floor, yanking his pants open as he followed her down.

BEFORE HE REACHED Ladyville, Zane's head cleared enough for him to see what was off about Roan's behavior. He reversed directions, kicking himself for being too hurt, too stunned by the about-face she'd pulled right on the heels of his nightmare, to think straight.

Only an idiot wouldn't remember that a wounded animal would fight when cornered, would defend itself by going on the offense. Roan, with her inexplicable self-loathing, had laid herself as bare as he had the night before. If he, who had boundless self-confidence, had felt vulnerable, how much more would Roan feel stripped naked and defenseless?

Cielito, he could almost hear Mama Lalita say, *she is in need of healing, the* pobrecita. *Bring her home.*

He'd do his best. He hadn't the faintest idea how to convince her, but he had to try.

When he neared Roan's cabin, though, his heart stuttered as he saw an unfamiliar pickup abandoned just down the road from it. A flash of memory recalled that same pickup at Noah's store the day he'd bought all the supplies.

Frank.

Zane abandoned his car, bounded toward the cabin.

And heard Roan scream.

He burst through the door and took in the scene in a split second.

Breasts bared, jeans yanked down, Roan choked against the fist gripping her throat, her eyes filled with terror.

"Get off her!" Zane roared.

Frank twisted to face him, pants open, body poised to drive inside her, his face a distorted mask of lust and the rage to punish.

Zane dove at him, knocking Frank aside, both of them hitting the wood hard.

Vicious eyes intent on Roan, Frank dislodged Zane with inhuman strength, already reaching to trap Roan beneath him again.

Zane lost his mind then, casting off everything civilized, wild and blind with man's primitive need to protect his woman. He leaped on Frank's back, yanked him around and smashed his fist into Frank's face. Bloodlust ran high as he pounded again and again, barely feeling the blows he took in return.

Roan's warning scream snapped him out of it, just as he felt the agonizing slice into his side.

He put a hand down and it came away glistening red.

Frank unbalanced him, kicking his head as Zane stumbled. Frank smiled through his battered mouth, deadly as a raptor, and brandished the bloody stiletto.

Reeling, Zane thought about what Frank would do to Roan if he got hold of her again. He charged Frank once more, dodging and weaving around the blade, ignoring the burn in his side.

But his movements were slower now, his coordination less as he battled the ringing in his head and the loss of blood.

Cunning and feral, Frank watched. Seized a moment of inattention and swept Zane's feet from beneath him. He loomed over Zane with the knife, coiled to strike.

A blast rang out. "Don't do it, Frank."

Zane squinted through his swimming vision to see Roan brandishing her grandmother's shotgun.

Movement in the corner of his eye drew him back. Frank's arm rose again in a deadly arc.

"Frank!" Roan shouted. "I promise you the next one won't be aimed high."

Frank froze, chest heaving, the light in his eyes savage. He started laughing, and the sound of it lifted the hair on Zane's neck.

"She'll drive you crazy, boy. I promise you'll regret the day you dipped your wick in her. She'll chew through you and spit you out like you were nothin'."

Zane squeezed his eyes to narrow slits, trying to steady his vision. His head was light, and his side felt as if someone had poured battery acid in it, but he gritted his teeth and made it to his feet. He glanced at Roan's stricken face, her knuckles white on the gun.

Frank wiped at his bleeding nose. "You won't shoot me, Roanie." He stalked toward her, every step filled with menace. "Go ahead. Prove me wrong."

"Drop the knife, Frank." Oddly steady now, aware that Hal's life depended on her, Roan pressed the butt of the shotgun into her shoulder. "I can't miss at this range."

Slowly, Frank studied her, his eyes mocking. "You may be a whore, but I don't believe you're a killer."

She stood her ground. "You have no idea what I'm capable of."

His head cocked. "Oh, I know plenty about you, girl. You bet I do. Want to discuss it in front of lover boy here?" He took a step closer.

Roan watched him coming and shuddered. She

flicked a glance at Hal, his shirt rapidly staining red at his waist. She forced herself to focus on Frank. Both of them realized that she had only one shell left, and he still had the knife in his hand, well within reach of Hal.

Then Hal surprised them both. Face twisted in pain, swaying on his feet, somehow he found the strength to make one swift strike at Frank's wrist.

The knife went flying, and Frank spun to retrieve it.

Roan covered the distance between them and pressed the shotgun into the back of Frank's neck first. "You're right that I don't want to kill you, Frank, but you're wrong if you think I won't. You have one more chance to leave before we see who's drawn the winning hand."

She saw his neck flush mottled red with his rage, but he didn't move toward the knife. She held her breath, aware that snakes were deadliest up close, but filled with an urgency to deal with Hal's wound. Her last glimpse of him had revealed his golden skin turning pasty white. She couldn't imagine how he'd remained on his feet this long.

"I don't forget, Roan O'Hara. You better run far and fast once I go." Frank's voice was low and dangerous.

But she'd won. For now, at least.

It was all she could do not to sag in relief. She was staying, but this was not the time to discuss it.

He bent to pick up his knife.

"Leave it there." She tightened nearly numb fingers on the trigger.

He straightened slowly and faced her. In his eyes she saw a trace of respect mingled with the dregs of a yearning that had festered into hatred. He locked his gaze on hers and held it for endless seconds.

At last, however, he left, his unspoken threat still ringing in the air.

She stayed right where she was, her arms quivering from holding the shotgun, her hands clasped like claws.

Then Hal was beside her. "Roan," he said quietly.

She couldn't speak. Couldn't think.

"Let me take the shotgun, sweetheart." His voice slurred.

Roan blinked. Lowered the weapon. Looked at Hal.

"Ohmigod," she gasped. "Sit down. Let me see."

He clasped her forearm and swayed, but his eyes were intent. "Forget me. Are you... Roan, did he…"

She glanced down at herself, at the torn shirt, the jeans barely clinging to her hips. With a gasp, she turned away to fasten them.

"Roan, talk to me."

She covered her mouth with one hand, struggling against the nausea. Remembering Frank's thick fingers and hairy thighs, the weight of him as she fought for a breath and tried to escape.

Roan shoved away the nightmare vision. Hal was

hurt, and she didn't know how badly. His needs had to come first.

"I'm okay." She kept most of the tremor out of her voice. "Please…" She grasped his arm and steered him toward the bed, her mind racing.

The last two steps, he leaned much of his weight on her. As gently as possible, she eased him to the mattress. With shaking fingers, she pulled his blood-soaked shirt away. *Oh, God.* She bit her lip to keep from saying it out loud. Gran always said keeping a patient calm was important.

"You're going to be all right." The wound was to the left side of his waist and about an inch or so long, but she couldn't tell how deep, only that it was leaking a steady stream of his life's blood. "I'll be right back." She hurried to grab something with which to staunch the flow.

When she returned, his eyes were shut and he was still. For a second, her heart stuttered. Then she saw his chest rise again.

Calm yourself, Roan. You'll be no use to him otherwise.

She dragged in a breath and folded the first cloth, then pressed it hard to his side.

He hissed.

"I'm sorry, but it's bleeding a lot." She folded another cloth with her free hand, then laid it atop the first. "Can you hold these while I find something to bind them?"

He placed his hand on top of hers and squeezed.

"I'll be fine." He tried for a grin and didn't make it. "You were brave as hell, Roan. You kicked his ass."

Tears burned then. "You're the one who charged to my rescue." She blinked and pressed harder.

He gasped.

"It's not slowing down, Hal. I have to get you to a hospital."

He frowned. "Not…good idea. Don't want anyone—" His eyes closed.

"Hal." She leaned over him. "Hal, don't go to sleep."

He was silent too long.

"Hal!"

With effort, he lifted his eyelids. "Roan, there's something…have to tell…"

"Don't talk. Save your strength. I'll need your help getting you outside." She bent to her efforts, removing the first bloodstained cloth and replacing it with two more. She tore strips from a sheet and wrapped them tightly around his middle to secure the pads.

Keys. Where were his keys? She scrubbed her face, yanked at her hair to steady herself. His car was essential—her pickup, even if it didn't break down, would be miserably uncomfortable. She could make a pallet, and he'd be able to lie down the entire trip in the back of his SUV.

"It's all right," she soothed, even as her hands trembled. "You're going to be okay. I'll take care of you.'' When she touched his face, he quieted, his breath escaping in a slow, tortured exhalation. ''I'll get you help.''

Gingerly, she stuck her fingers into one of his pockets, then the others, aware of every minute's passage.

No keys. She glanced out the window and saw his car door hanging open. Maybe he'd left them in the ignition in his rush to get to her.

Tears threatened again. Why had he come back?

But thank God he had.

''Hal, are your keys in the car?''

Silence. Then finally, ''Yeah...think so.''

Relief swept over her at the sound of his voice. ''Stay with me. I'll be right back.'' She headed for the door, thinking fast. He was much too heavy, but if she got the car right up to the steps and folded the back down, all she had to manage was the distance from the bed to the last step.

Oh, yeah. No big deal. Only two hundred pounds or so of dead-weight muscle and bone.

Roan raced to the car, and was relieved to see the keys hanging in the ignition. She stepped up into the plush leather seat and familiarized herself with the setup.

Expensive sunglasses hung from the visor. When she turned the key, the engine purred like a well-fed lion, throaty and masculine. The console tray held a pack of chewing gum and a map. The CD played Martina McBride.

Roan snapped off the music. She liked Martina a lot, but she could afford no distractions.

Carefully, she pressed the accelerator. The big car shot forward. Roan grabbed the wheel with both hands and eased the vehicle around, then backed up to the porch. Leaving the motor running with the heater on full-blast, she opened the passenger doors and fumbled with various levers until she lowered the seats to flat. She rounded to the rear and lifted the hatch.

Okay. Next, blankets and the pillow. Then Hal.

When she walked back inside, her heart nearly stopped. He was sitting up in the bed, attempting to rise.

"What are you doing?"

His eyes were glassy. "You were gone. I thought…" He lowered his head, his body sinking backward.

"No!" Roan leaped forward. He'd done half her work; she had to keep him upright, then get him to his feet. "I need you to stand up."

"Uh-uh," he mumbled. "Tired. Cold."

"I know. I'm going to get you a doctor." She managed to sling his arm around her neck and grab one belt loop in front and back. "Stand up, please. Try."

"Don't want…" A violent shiver shook him. "Go 'way."

"You can lie down in a minute. Right now, come with me. On the count of three, help me get you on your feet." She leaned into his body. "One, two, three—" She shoved to standing, gritting her teeth.

A load of bricks would be easier to lift, but she threw her legs into the task. "Hal—please."

"Dad's not here," he muttered.

Roan ignored his ramblings. "Stand up," she ordered. "Now!"

"All right, all right." He straightened his legs at last. "Bossy woman won't leave me in peace."

"You can yell at me when we're in your car."

"Where we goin'?" he slurred. "Wanna go home. Diego's baby…Mom…" He sagged against her again.

Roan propelled them toward the door through sheer will, then struggled across the porch with him, sweating despite the chill air. Finally, they got to the SUV. She eased him around so that his back faced the bumper. "Okay. Sit down."

He sank to the edge.

"Wait a minute."

Too late. He collapsed backward. Groaned.

As she worked him farther into the vehicle, Roan cast an anxious glance at the widening red stain at his side. She zipped up the porch steps, grabbed her purse, quilts and the pillow, then raced back. Fearing that moving him on top of the bedding would tear the wound worse, instead she placed the pillow beneath his head, layered more cloths on his side and secured them again. Then she covered him up, closed the hatch and ran to the front.

Once inside, she shifted the car into gear and took off, praying, as she listened to him groan each time she hit a rut, that she could remember her way to the hospital, that soon he would be in good hands.

And that, if her unskilled care hadn't killed him, one day he would be able to forgive her for what had happened when he'd come to her rescue.

A real hero. A champion for a woman who'd done nothing to deserve one.

AN HOUR LATER, Roan roared to a screeching halt at the emergency entrance to the hospital in Asheville. She charged inside, her heart pounding.

"I need help, quick." She grabbed the first person in scrubs. "I have a man in the back of the car. He's been stabbed."

Chaos erupted then, swallowing her up. In the first minutes, she couldn't see the organized ballet of it, pelted by rapid-fire questions from people swarming the car.

She tried to reach Hal, to comfort him. Instead, she found herself pushed aside as the whirlwind descended on him and she was left behind.

"Ma'am? Would you come with me? I need you to fill out some paperwork on your husband."

Roan faced a woman, round and middle-aged. "He's not my husband."

The woman shrugged. "Boyfriend, then. Do you have his insurance card?"

"He's not my—" Roan went blank. Insurance

card? Did he even have insurance? She'd gone without for so long that the possibility hadn't occurred to
her, but surely someone who drove a car like that
would be covered. "I...don't know. I'll have to
check." She tried to peer past the woman's shoulder,
seeking Hal's location. "Tell me what they're doing.
Will he make it?"

So much blood. *Please let him be all right.*

The woman placed one comforting hand on her
arm. "He's in good hands now, don't you worry."

The warmth of it brought a rush of tears to her
eyes.

Roan blinked them back.

"My name is Sarabeth," the woman said. "You
want to sit down for a minute before you move your
car?" She smiled gently. "This is the emergency entrance, so we can't be blocking it for long."

"Oh..." Roan's gaze swiveled to the door. "I'm
sorry, I just..."

Sarabeth patted her. "Don't fret over it. You're
scared. I understand that. Why don't you come over
here and rest for a minute." She nodded toward the
entrance, where a security guard was frowning.
"You hold your horses, Eldred. This girl is shook
up."

"No." This woman's kindness was something
new to her. Except for Hal, no one had been kind in
so long. She swallowed hard. "I'll go move it and
see if..."

"You sure, sugar? Eldred could do it for you."

Roan found a small smile. "No. Thank you." Now that Hal was in competent hands, her legs had somehow gone shaky. "I'll be back."

"Okay." But Sarabeth's forehead wrinkled. "Somebody oughta check you over, too."

Roan glanced down. She'd thrown on a shirt to replace the one Frank had savaged but had changed nothing else. She touched the forgotten bruise on her face. "I'm fine." She turned away, covering the distance to the door with measured steps.

"The police will be here soon." Eldred nodded as she passed but looked concerned, too. "You can park it right over there." He pointed.

Police. Roan stumbled.

"Positive you don't want any help?"

She shook her head. "No." She walked away fast.

Once at the car, she saw the jumbled, bloodstained quilts, and fear seized her again. How was he? What were they doing? He'd gotten so quiet the last few miles.

She took a deep breath. His fate was out of her hands now. She closed the hatch, pressing her hands flat against it, forehead against the glass as she murmured a silent plea. *He's a good man. Please.*

Then she straightened and rounded to the driver's seat. The engine was still running, she realized. In a big city, his expensive car would already have been stolen, security or not.

With care, Roan pulled away and entered the lot Eldred had indicated, then slid the big vehicle into the first space she found. She shut off the engine and collapsed against the soft leather. How could she talk to the police with her history?

Yet how could she leave until she knew if Hal would make it?

Suddenly, the adrenaline that had kept her going through Frank's attack and the long, terrifying trip drained away. She longed to fall asleep right here.

Roan tightened her knuckles on the steering wheel. She could make it a little while longer before...

Before what? How could she hang around? She had only a few dollars in her purse and no credit cards.

It didn't matter. Leaving wasn't an option. He had no one else there who cared about him.

Cared, maybe even...loved. If only he hadn't been so kind to her. That compassion called to her nearly as much as his strength. How badly she wanted to rest, to quit fighting...to lean on that broad chest and feel the safety of his arms. The intensity of her longing terrified her.

He'd lost so much blood. Fear sent her scrambling. She had to get back inside.

Insurance card, Sarabeth wanted. Roan had seen no wallet in the bag she'd packed for him, felt none in his pockets. Maybe it was in the car somewhere. She flipped open the shallow top section of the console.

A cell phone. Roan stared at it.

He'd had a cell phone all this time? Why hadn't he—

Never mind. Not now. She flipped on the dome light again. Headset, phone charger…no wallet. She fumbled for a latch to open the bottom compartment.

CDs, more maps, trail mix…Roan felt odd, rifling through someone else's belongings, but she had no choice. Next would be the glove compartment.

Her hand touched leather, rounded corners—

She brought the object to the light.

A golden brown, glove-soft leather wallet. Her fingers traced to the center, preparing to open it—

The act felt too intimate. She'd barely met the man, yet she and he had been through so much together. Despite the distance she'd tried to keep, he'd gotten closer to her than anyone had in years.

Even though she still didn't know his last name. Good grief. How could that be? Her fingers tensed again, but somehow she couldn't make herself open it. Maybe she should let Sarabeth…

Roan slid from the seat, grabbed her purse and the keys, then locked the doors.

No, she wouldn't relinquish her responsibility to a perfect stranger, however considerate. She'd face the police, answer their questions. That Hal had gotten involved was her fault; it was up to her to see the process through. As soon as she reached the entrance where the light was better, she'd look for his insurance card herself.

She nodded to Eldred as she passed through the

electric doors, then heard them swish shut behind her. Inside the lobby, a shiver shook her as the warmth chased away the outside chill.

Roan stuffed her purse under one arm and opened Hal's wallet, barely glancing at the California driver's license—

California? She peered closer at the picture, even as her mind struggled to comprehend.

She'd seen that face before. Where?

A glimpse of the name in black print.

She blinked. Squinted, unable to believe what she read.

"You found it. Good." Sarabeth approached.

But Roan could barely hear her for the roaring in her ears. Mutely, she held out the wallet to the woman, shaking her head.

"What's wrong, sugar?" Sarabeth cast a glance at the license.

And gasped. Her gaze flew to Roan's. "You're kidding me. I'd never have recognized him." She shot a look over her shoulder at the door where they'd taken him. "Eldred, you got any idea who we got in there? Lord have mercy, child, why didn't you say something?"

Eldred neared, but Roan's knees were shaking with a stunned mix of anger and humiliation.

Sarabeth grabbed her. "What?" She frowned. "You didn't know?"

Roan shook her head.

"Know what?" Eldred demanded.

"We got us a movie star in there, that's what." Sarabeth smiled. "Zane MacAllister, Mr. Sexiest Man Alive himself. Been in the news lately, too, 'cause that girlfriend of his had drug problems, 'member that? Poor man. Not like he couldn't have any woman he wanted. A pity what happened to her."

"What…" Roan could barely find her voice. She hadn't read a newspaper or seen TV in weeks. "What do you mean?"

"She killed herself, didn't you hear? Her last call was to him, then she did herself in." Sarabeth focused on Roan. "You don't look so hot, honey." She turned to Eldred. "Put her in that chair over there while I grab someone to take a peek at her."

As soon as Sarabeth disappeared through the swinging doors, still clutching Hal's—

Not Hal. *Zane.*

Oh, God. Her knees buckled.

"Miss, you come on now and sit down."

Roan could only shake her head as she tried to absorb the magnitude of what he'd done.

Lied to her. Made a fool of her.

Made love to her, probably laughing inside the whole time at the pathetic, stick-thin woman who'd begged: *Show me.*

She had to get out of here. She owed him nothing now, not when he'd…

Untrue. She owed him everything. If not for him, Frank would have…

"Ma'am, you seem peaked. Here now, lean on me."

"No." She resisted Eldred's grasp. "I have to go." She swiveled her head back and forth, desperate to be where she could think.

She was furious with him. Horrified. So many images zipped through her mind. *I don't want your food or your money or your body. I'm not that desperate.*

Of course not. Women around the world would prostrate themselves at his feet for a glance, a kiss.

His kiss. Roan could still taste him, feel him inside her.

Show me.

Oh, God. She buried her face in her hands. She'd pleaded with Zane MacAllister to make love to her.

And he had. Oh, dear sweet heaven, how he had.

But he'd done so much more. Images of him tumbled inside her. Chopping her wood. Bathing her, comforting her. Sleeping on the floor of Gran's cabin.

My mother would… He'd been raised to be a gentleman.

But a gentleman didn't lie with every breath.

Judge the truth for yourself. It isn't pity.

I'm not the right man. I couldn't live with myself if I hurt you, instead.

She had to escape. Had to make it back to Gran's. Had to think.

Or not think. She wasn't sure she could bear to

spend another second on memories of the man she'd known as Hal.

Anyway, there was no reason to stay, now that everyone would realize who he was. He didn't need her; that was for sure. They'd take special care with someone like him.

Been all over the news lately.

The police will be here soon.

If her past came to light as a result of her part in this fiasco, the press would have a field day.

No matter that he'd deceived her, he'd done so much for her. The least she could do to repay that debt was to take herself out of the equation to avoid causing him further trouble.

"Ma'am?"

She spotted a rest room across the way and nodded toward it. "I have to…"

Eldred seemed embarrassed. "Oh. Sure." He peered closer. "You make it on your own?"

Roan swallowed a building nausea and clutched her purse. "Yeah. You go back to your post. I'll manage."

He hesitated, but just then, an ambulance siren sounded. He hurried back to the entrance.

Roan hid inside the rest room, resisting the urge to be very, very sick. Instead, she watched through a crack in the doorway until the new emergency began its own ballet.

What could she do for someone like Zane MacAllister, anyway? He could buy anything he wanted, have anyone he wished at the snap of a finger.

Where was he now? Had he awakened? Was he afraid or lonely?

Two female hospital employees dressed like clerks made a beeline for Eldred. "Is it true Zane Mac-Allister is here?" At Eldred's nod, one of them squealed. "Ohmigod—is he as gorgeous in real life as he is on the screen?" Excited chatter rose.

Three more joined them. "Where's the woman who brought him in? One woman kills herself over him, and he's already got her replacement lined up? Who is she?"

Roan held her breath.

Eldred shot a worried glance in her direction. "Don't know. Now, get on back to work. We've got injured folks needing attention, and you're in the way."

The group didn't disperse, though. Instead, others in the waiting room joined them, voices rising as news spread. Two of them spoke into cell phones. The excitement was palpable.

Roan jammed the door closed, heart beating double-time.

That girlfriend of his had drug problems. Killed herself.

His anguished cry. *She can't be dead.*

His contempt. *Where I come from, people swallow narcotics for a hangnail.*

Now another woman with a fondness for pills had

endangered his life. Complicated it. He'd be grateful, no doubt, to see the last of her.

She took a deep breath and opened the door a tiny bit. The lobby was filling with crying relatives and chattering bystanders craning for a look into the emergency room.

In the midst of the chaos, Roan slipped away.

CHAPTER TWELVE

THE ODORS HIT HIM FIRST, pungent and biting. Acrid antiseptic. Overcooked food.

Around him, Zane heard hushed conversation. Muffled laughter. The squeak of shoe soles on waxed floors.

He opened his eyes. Piercing brightness flooded in. He squeezed them shut.

Groaned.

"I told them my little brother was too ornery to die." Beyond the amusement, worry was the bass note.

Zane squinted at the brother who was as dark as Zane was fair. "Jesse? What the hell are you doing here? Where am I?"

"In a hospital in Asheville. You've got a stab wound and a light concussion, along with a lot of bruising, but the doctors told us you're going to be fine. Want to explain what the hell happened to you?"

Out of the flood of memories, Zane picked out one word. "Us? Roan—is she okay?" He tried to rise, but Jesse restrained him.

"Is Roan the woman who brought you in?"

Zane could barely recall the trip, lost in a haze of dizzy, pounding headache and the burning in his side. One image stood out, though—the feel of her thin body supporting his. "Yeah. She was hurt, too. Has she been looked at?"

Then it hit him. "Oh, hell. If you're here, then…" He closed his eyes. "She must know who I am."

Jesse was saved from answering when a nurse bustled through the door. "Well, our star is awake. I'll notify your doctor. How are you feeling, Mr. MacAllister?" The woman slipped a sleeve over the thermometer, crisp and efficient, but her eyes sparkled with female interest. "I'll bet you've got quite a headache."

Zane shrugged. "I'll live."

"Millions of women will be happy to hear that."

"Where is—"

She slid the thermometer into his mouth before he could finish.

He jerked it back out. "Where is she?"

"We need to take your temperature, please."

"Not until you tell me where she is."

"Who?" But she cast an odd glance at Jesse.

"The woman who brought me in. Has she been examined?"

"Please don't get excited, Mr. MacAllister. I'll see what I can find out."

"Jesse?" His brother's solemn expression wasn't unusual. A smiling Jesse was.

"Let her do her job," Jesse said. "Then we'll talk."

Zane gripped the thermometer. "Tell me what's wrong. If she's badly hurt—if that bastard—"

Jesse crossed his arms over his chest, every inch the federal agent, the inscrutable big brother calling the shots. "She's not. Now, let the woman finish."

Zane glared at his brother. "Damn it, Jesse…" His brother had been a hostage negotiator for years. He couldn't be manipulated; he'd talk when he was ready and not before.

So Zane suffered through the checking of vital signs and the notations on the chart, but through the partly opened door, he could see several people just standing around, glancing inside. Every word he said, every move he made, would be reported to the press. He read the woman's name from her ID card and summoned a smile. "Thank you, Verna. I appreciate your help."

A faint blush stained her cheeks. "You're very welcome. Is there anything I could do to make you more comfortable?"

He turned on the charm that had always worked—until Roan O'Hara. "Your smiling face is plenty. Thanks."

If anything, she brightened. "I'll be back in a little bit. You must be glad your brother was able to make it so quickly."

Zane nodded. "I sure am. Having family here is a real comfort."

"We'll make sure that the rest of them are brought right in when they arrive." With that, she left, closing the door behind her.

"The rest of them?" Zane's eyes whipped to his brother's. "Tell me Mom's not on her way here."

Jesse's somber gaze lit. "You think anyone could stop her?"

"You could, if you wanted. There's no reason for her to make the trip, and Diego's baby—" He started to sit up, then gasped and sagged back to the mattress.

Jesse looked worried and studied him. Finally, he spoke. "They're not on a plane yet. I got them to agree to wait until I could talk to the doctors. I called them an hour ago."

"And?"

At last, Jesse smiled. "Caroline went into labor two hours earlier. Mom was torn, but I told her to stay until the baby was born, and I'd remain with you."

"Oh, wow. Diego's really gonna be a daddy. Imagine that."

"It's not hard. He's great with kids. But I didn't know if he'd ever get that chance after he was injured."

"Yeah." Zane went silent, too, pondering the months when their eldest brother's hold on life had been so precarious, then the many months more when it appeared he'd never walk again. "I'm glad for him. First finding Caroline, then the clinics and now the family he always wanted. He's been through so much. He deserves all this and more.''

Jesse's eyes were far away, and Zane was reminded that his second brother had seen more than his share of woes. "I'm sorry you're not there. You don't have to hang around. I'll be fine."

Jesse rolled his eyes. "You're kidding, right? Mom would kill me if I left. Anyway, I'm here to guard the gates until your staff arrive."

Zane groaned, and physical pain was the least of it. "Hell. How bad is it out there?"

"Could be worse." Jesse shrugged. "There's talk of a candlelight vigil, but at the moment only about five hundred people are gathered outside the front door of the hospital—most of them with cameras. One satellite truck so far."

"Shit. Annie will have a cow." Zane scrubbed his face and hit a bandage on his forehead, instantly reminded of Roan. "Where is she, Jesse? Swear to God she's all right?"

No matter how he might want to avoid it, his brother could be counted on to tell the unvarnished truth. "I don't know."

"Why not?" Zane bolted up again, grabbing his side. "You said she wasn't badly hurt."

"Settle back first, and I'll tell you what I can."

Woozy and aching, Zane complied.

Jesse took a deep breath. "She's gone."

"Where?"

Jesse held up his hand. "No idea. She wouldn't

let anyone examine her, but the admissions clerk and the security guard who talked to her said she seemed very tired and upset over you but that she left under her own steam.'' He frowned. ''She was battered, though. You gonna explain what happened to you two? I'm holding off the local cops, but I can't do it forever.''

''In a minute. Tell me she took my car.''

''She didn't.''

''What?'' Zane's hand clenched on the bed rail. ''She doesn't have any money, and there's damn sure no taxi service to that mountain.'' He started to lever himself up again. ''I have to find her.''

''Forget it,'' Jesse snapped.

''I can't.'' Zane shoved against Jesse's hand, but he was ridiculously weak.

''If I have to kick your ass, I will, Zane.'' Jesse opened the drawer of the bedside table and pulled out a brown envelope, which Zane recognized. He'd thrown it into the car. It contained the mail he'd brought from his loft. ''Look in here. Maybe there's a clue.''

Zane's protest died. On the front, the previous address had been scratched out. Just above it, feminine handwriting said simply *Zane MacAllister*. The already torn flap had been folded down several times.

He paused for a minute. ''How did she find out?''

''The clerk wanted insurance information. It wasn't on you. Roan searched your vehicle and found your wallet.''

"How did she handle the news?"

"Not well." Jesse's terse response said volumes. "The clerk got all excited and ran off to tell everyone. The security guard said Roan seemed as though someone had knocked the stuffing out of her. He was waiting with her for the clerk to get someone to look at her when another emergency rolled in."

Zane could only imagine her distress. She'd already been stretched to her limits. "So no one examined her?"

"She said she was going to the rest room. Next thing he knew, she was gone. That—" he pointed to the envelope "—showed up on the admissions desk."

Zane peered inside. Car keys and cell phone. He shook it out, hoping for a note.

No such luck. "Jesse, she's not safe up there."

"Tell me where the cabin is, and I'll start a search." Jesse paused. "Mom explained why you didn't reveal who you were, but…" His piercing dark gaze showed his disapproval.

Zane clutched the envelope. "I thought I'd find the right time or—"

Jesse's eyebrows lifted. "Or?"

"I'd be gone and she'd never have to know."

"Nice, easy package, huh? You'd wave your magic wand and make everything better, then be on your way?"

"There's nothing easy about Roan O'Hara." He stared at his feet. "Hell, I don't know what I thought.

This whole thing with Kelly, and then…I just wanted to go home. Find a little peace.''

His brother's hand came to rest on his shoulder. ''I understand.''

Zane met Jesse's eyes, so often haunted by shadows of what he'd seen in his work. ''She really is in trouble up there, Jess. The guy who stabbed me will go back after her. He hates her guts, and she humiliated him. I can't just desert her.'' Futility combined with exhaustion, and he exhaled sharply. ''I don't have a clue what to do for her, but she's got no one else, and she's in that rickety cabin, planning to spend the winter.'' Zane struggled to part the heavy drapes of fatigue and pain, but weariness overcame him. Against his will, his eyes began to close. ''Got to…''

''Rest now, little brother. I'll stand guard until you wake up again. Then you can tell me where to look.''

Zane attempted to answer, but sleep wouldn't let him.

ROAN WALKED for hours on the dark streets and tried not to think. She just wanted someplace to lie down and forget everything. Dull fatigue had settled into her very bones, and the effort to get back to Gran's seemed like climbing Mount Everest.

There was no one to call, no one who would help. No one who gave a damn what happened to her.

He might. Like a dandelion's puff, the thought drifted.

Roan shook her head. The man she'd met as Hal…maybe. Out of pity, no matter what he'd said.

But Zane MacAllister, Greek god of Hollywood?

He'd forget her in an instant. Or hate her for throwing him right back into the glare of scandal.

Either way, he was better off without her, and she was better off without him. She'd known how dangerous was the allure of the knight in shining armor.

Hadn't life taught her there were no fairy tales?

So tired. She couldn't even summon up the energy to be angry anymore. She had no idea how she'd find her way home.

Or if home was just a mirage she'd conjured up in a dingy, bloodstained tub.

A door opened in front of her, and a man walked out, nearly toppling her. "'Scuse me," he said. "Going in?"

Roan's caught the yeasty scent of beer, the acrid smell of cigarettes. Heard the pool balls clacking, the juke box playing, the voices a bee's drone in the semidarkness.

The man held the door. "Miss?"

She glanced at the dirty, night-dark street, the murky future stretching out ahead of her. Thought of the effort it would take to get back to the mountain, when oblivion was right here at hand.

"Yes," she answered.

And stepped over the threshold into a world where she could hide, just for a bit.

"WELL, BIG GUY, you sure know how to keep a girl challenged." His publicist Annie's eyes sparkled with grim humor.

"Glad to oblige." Zane hit the button to raise the head of his bed.

"Doctor didn't say you could sit up yet."

"The doctor can bite my ass." Zane blinked to clear his vision. "Tell me what's going on." He looked around. "Where's Jesse?"

"In the hall. Pacing. Talking on his phone about putting out an APB on your girlfriend."

"He can't do that." Zane jerked back the covers. "He doesn't understand how she is. He'll scare the devil out of her."

"Whoa there, cowboy." Annie grabbed his arm. "You're not going anywhere." She nodded toward the IV stand. "You're a little tied up."

Zane cursed. "Get him for me, Annie. Please."

"Who is she, Zane? There are three twenty-four-hour cable satellite trucks in the parking lot, and the hospital switchboard shut down from the volume of calls. I've had to turn off my cell phone so Sal and your director will stop calling and screaming at me. Your brother is barely keeping the local cops at bay, and a clam has looser lips than his. Whatever you've told him, he's not sharing with anyone." Lines around her mouth deepened. "I love you, Zane baby, but how in the hell do you expect me to put any kind of lid on this when I have no information?"

Zane grasped her hand. "I'm sorry, Annie." He

blew out a breath. "After all you had to juggle because of Kelly, you don't deserve this." He squeezed her fingers. "Listen, I promise I'll give you all the details you want if you'll just please go get my brother and bring him to me before he does something all of us will regret."

Annie frowned, but she complied. She returned with a scowling Jesse.

"Zane, the guy who did this to you has to be caught. This woman is an accessory—"

"Sweet mother of—" Zane didn't try to muffle his curses. "Jesse, he was going to rape her. He'll kill her next time. Don't you dare make her out to be some kind of criminal." Exhaustion forced him to lie back.

Jesse only looked more worried. "An APB is the quickest way to get her located. If what you say is right and she needs help, that's how I can best give it to her."

Zane's gut told him that he hadn't been the only one hiding secrets. How much would it scare her to be stopped by the police?

But how was she going to get back to the cabin without his car? The prospect of Roan, injured and upset, hitchhiking, made his gut clench with fear.

He opened his mouth to respond to Jesse just as Jesse's phone rang. His brother turned away and participated in an intense conversation.

"When you left L.A., you only wanted to be alone and not talk to a soul." Annie's eyes were fond. "I might have guessed you couldn't resist playing the savior, but who is this mystery woman and where did you find her? What do you know about her?''

''Not enough.'' Jesse spoke first, snapping his phone shut. ''And neither of you is going to like what I just learned.''

ROAN STOPPED next to a stool and gripped the tired wooden curve of the bar.

The man behind it, grizzled and sallow in the dirty yellow half-light, nodded. ''What'll you have?''

She stared at him without comprehension, a world-weary traveler cast onto shores unknown.

The man frowned. ''You staying or going?''

Roan sucked down a lungful of smoke, breathing in the scents of her childhood, caught in an undertow of yearning for firm ground.

''I believe she ain't sure, Melvin,'' said a nearby patron. ''You there, girl. Pull up a stool and set a spell.''

Roan blinked. Saw the attention focused on her and nearly ran. Tightened her fingers on the only solid thing in her world.

Where will you go, Roan O'Hara? Even if you make it back to the mountain, you'll never belong. They don't want you there. The only one who did is dead, and you broke her heart.

You know this world. Know this life to your marrow.

Stay. Give in. Let's stop fighting.

Roan dragged her vision up from the scarred floor. "Southern Comfort," she said. "Straight."

"Yes, ma'am," answered the bartender. "Comin' right up."

She hiked a leg and settled on the barstool.

The man two stools down chuckled and lit another cigarette.

"SHE WHAT?" Annie's head drooped.

"She's got a record," Jesse said. "Drug charges." He kept his gaze on Zane. "Seems your lady friend had a nice little Valium habit that grew up into something really nasty, and—"

"And what?" Zane wasn't at all sure he wanted to know.

"She got into a bathtub with razor blades six months ago."

"Oh, hell." He closed his eyes. Kelly all over again. Christ.

It all made sense now, how thin she was, the air of desperation that clung to her like a second skin. How she held on to herself so hard as though she didn't dare relax...

No pills. Zane straightened. "She's not using now, Jesse. I'd swear to that. She's—God, she's trying so hard to make it."

"Zane, no," Annie urged. "Don't even think about taking her on as your new cause. Your career can't handle much more scandal." She clutched his arm suddenly. "You didn't— Please tell me you haven't had sex with an addict. Or tell me you used a condom.''

"That's none of your business." Zane shook her off, even as his own gut clenched. Then he remembered Roan's terror when he'd forgotten protection.

He saw Annie's hurt. Jesse's snapping dark eyes wanting the same answer. "Give me a minute with Jesse, please, Annie?"

Her shoulders were stiff, but she did as he asked.

He lifted his gaze to his brother's. "I'm not talking about it with you, either, except to say that I wasn't stupid." *But I sure wanted to be.*

Jesse's censure drained away. He placed one hand on Zane's shoulder. "And I won't ask. But tell me you're not still thinking you can save her." His fingers squeezed to comfort. "You know addicts can only save themselves, little brother."

Zane wasn't sure what he knew anymore. With her valor, Roan O'Hara had touched a place inside him that no one else had. "She's trying to do it all by herself, Jesse, working her heart out to make it. I understand now…she needs to prove she deserves to survive." He glanced up. "I—she's different. She's not Kelly. If you met her, you'd see that." New urgency struck him. She was out there alone, more so than ever now that she knew who he was and thought—

Zane groaned. "I was afraid to tell her because she was clinging to her pride, not asking for help from anyone, and she could see I had money because of that stupid car and it bothered her a lot. She didn't want anyone's pity.'' He turned tortured eyes on his brother. ''I can't just walk away, Jess. Help me find her.''

Jesse's expression was grave. ''And then what? You sweep her off to L.A. so she can be surrounded by all the temptation that did Kelly in?''

Oh, God. Zane faltered. How could Roan possibly fit into his world? What might it do to her?

He rubbed at his forehead, drained. ''Find her, Jesse, please. Once I know she's safe, and—'' Resignation settled into his heart like lead. Jesse was right. He couldn't be responsible, not again.

''For her sake,'' he whispered. ''I'll stay away.''

Jesse patted his shoulder and left.

ROAN STARED at the drink in front of her, its dark honey color casting her back in time. She lowered her head and inhaled the too-sweet aroma that would always make Roan think of her mother.

One hundred proof alcohol, the perfume that scented so many lost nights and desperate days of her youth.

She hated this stuff, but once again the symmetry was nearly amusing. She'd spent years trying to escape becoming her mother, only to wind up no different.

Might as well complete the circle with her mother's drink. She wasn't up to hunting an unfamiliar town for what she really craved to smooth out the edges. To help her forget.

"You just gonna stare at it all night?" the old guy down the bar asked. "Oughta go sit in the back with Charlie." He hitched a shoulder. "Preacher man in here nearly every night, wantin' to save us all."

Roan glanced in the direction he'd pointed. A slight man, middle-aged, stood beside a booth in earnest conversation, his hands filled with pamphlets. "Why would a preacher come here?"

"Says he used to be a drunk and saving others is his mission." The old guy snickered into his glass. "Got to give him credit for tryin', but he don't drum up much business. Better drink up. He'll smell fresh meat and be bendin' your ear all night."

Roan turned away. "I'm in no hurry." Trembling fingers curved to surround the glass, not touching yet, only...guarding.

She didn't have enough to pay for more. This one would have to last her until she figured out where she would go from here.

"When's closing?" she asked.

"Two," the bartender answered.

Roan nodded. "Good." She had time.

Someone walked up right beside her. "Want to dance, honey?"

She shook her head, smelling sweat and beer. "No, thanks."

"I'm a hell of a good dancer, and you're here alone." He pushed closer.

"I just want to sit, thanks." She shifted to put space between them, still not looking.

"Hey, it's not like you're pretty or nuthin'." Anger-laced fumes assaulted her.

She hunched over and gripped the glass.

"Leave it, Bobby," the bartender said. "The lady said no."

"Bitch, don't you ignore me!" One ham-handed fist clamped on her shoulder.

"Bobby, I told you—"

But Roan had had enough. She shoved to her feet and faced him. "I'm not ignoring you now, all right?" She forced herself to stand straight. "But I'm not dancing with you or anyone else in this whole godforsaken place, got that? I—" To her horror, her eyes began to burn. "I've had a really bad day, that's all. It's not a day to dance."

The man's gaze scanned her face, lingering on the bruise Frank had bestowed. Past the haze of all he'd had to drink, she saw something like understanding. "Yeah, okay." He shrugged. "Maybe later."

"Yeah," she whispered as he lumbered away. Astonished at her own temerity, Roan didn't move for a couple of minutes.

Then she resumed her spot on the barstool and stared once more at the glass.

She had all the time in the world. No use getting in a rush.

CHAPTER THIRTEEN

ZANE TOOK THE CELL PHONE from his brother. By the grin on Jesse's face, he could already guess where the call had initiated.

"Son," his father boomed. "I want to hear you tell me yourself how you're feeling. For your mother's sake, of course. You know how she worries about her chicks."

Zane's smile was sincere for the first time since he'd awakened in the hospital. "Hi, Dad. I'm doing fine." How good it felt to connect with home. "So are you a grandfather yet?"

"You better believe it. The best-looking young fella since one future movie star was born."

Zane laughed. "I was the ugliest baby in the nursery. Even Mom admits that."

His dad chuckled. "Well, you cleaned up pretty good."

"So Diego and Caroline have a son. What are they calling him?"

"They did an old man proud—" His dad's voice caught. "They named him Roberto MacAllister Montalvo. Eight pounds fourteen ounces, twenty-two inches long."

Way to go, Diego, Zane thought. Class act. Hal wasn't his sire, but Diego had managed to honor both his own father and the man who'd raised him after his own dad died. "A great name, Dad, and richly deserved." His own throat felt a little tight. "Just under nine pounds, huh? Sounds small."

"Small?" Hal boomed. "Easy to tell you're a bachelor. That's a strapping big boy. He'll fit right in with the rest of us."

"How are the proud parents?"

"That oldest boy of mine is something, son. Delivered his own child and did a fine job of it. Who would have ever thought Miracle Malone would give birth at home?"

Zane chuckled. *Miracle Malone* had been Caroline's nickname as a renowned cardiac surgeon. When she and Diego had met, they'd locked horns on many subjects, but medical practices had led the list. "She's mellowed a lot since she met Diego."

"She's a pistol, that one. Couldn't be prouder of my girl."

"Her sisters and everyone there?"

"The whole kit and caboodle. Speaking of which, your mama finally let Diego have his baby back and is tapping her toes wanting to talk to you."

"Congratulations, Dad. Give little Roberto a kiss for me and tell Diego and Caroline I'm happy for them."

"Come home and do it yourself." His father

paused. "Son, Jesse says you're worried about that woman."

Zane didn't like the impersonal term. "Her name is Roan, Dad. She's…" He stared at the wall and wondered how to explain. "I want to be home, but I just can't go until I'm sure she's safe. The doctors say I have to stay at least two days, but Roan is so vulnerable up there. I don't even know how she's getting back, since she left my car here. I don't like thinking of her out on the road alone."

"Zane, don't you rush things. Let Jesse help—he said he's willing."

Zane shot his elder brother a glance. "Dad, you remember how Jesse is in his G-man mode. He'll scare the hell out of her."

Jesse stood across the room, dark eyes shuttered, arms crossed over his chest in full protective big-brother pose.

"Son, this is Jesse's arena, not yours. This woman sounds like trouble—haven't you had enough?"

"I don't think she's like Kelly."

"What about her effect on your career if she's got those problems?"

"Hang my career, Dad—this woman saved my life. Twice. She was barely hanging on by her fingernails, and now she's in more danger than ever. I can't just walk away."

"Easy, son. You have to decide what's right, and I trust you. I just don't want you to take any more chances. When I think about what could have happened if that knife had gone in a few inches higher—'' Hal cleared his throat noisily. "Listen, I can be in North Carolina tomorrow, if you need me.''

Zane had no doubt he meant it. Anyone who knew Hal MacAllister understood that family was everything to him. "I lied to her. I wasn't intending to hurt her, but I did and now I have to see her and explain. There was something between us, but…'' He dropped his head back. "If she really does have a drug problem, my world is the last place she should be.'' He sighed. "I wish I could bring her home with me and let her get acquainted with Mama Lalita. Roan's grandmother was what they call a wise-woman around here, something like Mama Lalita. I suspect her grandmother was the only person who ever made Roan feel truly loved.''

"Sounds like someone else has some pretty strong feelings for her, too.''

Zane stared at the ceiling. "It can't go anywhere. And she'll likely spit in my eye the next time she lays eyes on me, anyway.''

"A spirited woman is a treasure, son. I'll testify to that—so will your brother Diego.''

Zane found a smile. "Roan's spirit got broken somehow. I intended to help, but I'm afraid I just made things worse for her. I have to try to fix that before I can leave.''

"I understand. You make me proud, Zane.''

"I love you, Dad.''

"You get home soon or I'll be coming after you. Now, here's your mother."

Zane met his brother's eyes. Jesse's warmed with sympathy.

"Sweetheart, I could be there in the morning if I leave for El Paso now and catch the last flight."

"It's okay, Mom. Jesse's already appointed himself my mother. He scares me almost as much as you."

Grace MacAllister laughed. "I'm sure he considers that a compliment. But I'm serious. I can pack in twenty minutes and be on my way."

"I swear I'm in good hands. The nurses barely give me a chance to ask for anything before it appears, and Annie's here to be my fire-breathing dragon. And then, of course, there's my pain in the behind bodyguard who ought to be in La Paloma with the rest of you."

"Be nice to your brother, Zane Harold. The willow tree is flourishing."

"No, not the willow switch threat." Zane rolled his eyes in mock horror.

Jesse grinned.

"Tell me about the baby, Mom."

"Oh, he's just so precious…" His mother was off and running, and Zane settled back, simply enjoying the sound of her voice, the respite from his worry for Roan.

Jesse gave him a thumbs-up for the effective distraction. Zane blew on his fingernails and polished them on his chest.

"But you'll see little Roberto soon enough," she said. "How long before they release you?"

"Maybe a day or so."

"A day or so? That doesn't sound nearly long enough. I'll have Caroline call them. You could have died."

"Mom, Mom—whoa. Caroline's a little busy now, and I didn't come close to dying. I bled and my hard head got knocked around a little, but I'm fine, I swear." He was making light of it, but his mother should be enjoying this special time. What she didn't know wouldn't hurt her.

"I'm going after Roan, Mom."

To her credit, his mother didn't argue. Grace MacAllister was a woman to admire—opinionated, yes, and fierce about her offspring, but eminently practical. Both strong and compassionate. They were incredibly lucky to have been raised by her.

Roan hadn't been so fortunate.

"Bring her home, Zane. We'll take care of her."

He smiled. "Annie and Sal think I should ditch her the first second possible. Jesse thinks I'm bad for her."

Jesse frowned.

"The way you speak of her and hearing about her courage in protecting you, at the very least this family owes her our heartfelt thanks. Bring her here, sweetheart. Let's see what's broken."

"She's strong in her own way, Mom, just... damaged." He leaned back, exhausted. "Jesse's probably right. My lifestyle would destroy her."

"Then change it. I think you're getting a little tired of playing around, anyway, honey.. Don't you?"

Zane hesitated. Was he? He had a life millions envied. Was he ready to give it up?

Especially for a junkie? questioned an inner voice. *Remember Kelly. Are you so sure Roan is different? She tried to kill herself, too.*

"I don't know, Mom." He stared into the distance. "I just don't know."

ROAN LIFTED the glass to her lips. Did her best to avoid inhaling the sickly-sweet bouquet. Imagined the burn of it down her throat, then, in a few moments, the welcome warmth in her stomach spreading through her chest.

Into her frozen heart.

She was so tired of being afraid, drained by the constant edge. For too-brief instants, she'd been brave—turned aside a drunk, forced Frank away, gotten Zane to safety...

Opened herself to love.

You should be proud of yourself. Green eyes alight.

When had she last felt any scrap of pride? She'd done so much wrong. Harmed others. Hurt herself.

But where did one begin to create a new life? How

did a person make it out of a deep, dark hole? Was she entitled to happiness in some distant future existence? When would she have paid enough?

What was it that those AA pamphlets said? She frowned. *Just for today*—that was it. *Just for today, I will…*what?

Roan stared at the drink in her hand.

Then set it down.

I won't take this drink. I won't escape.

Maybe tomorrow she'd feel weak and terrified again. Perhaps even later tonight.

But she'd been strong today, stronger than she'd realized she could be. It was a start.

There was a café not far away frequented by truckers. If she was careful and patient, maybe she could find a safe ride.

And go home. She'd be alone again, but life had taught her that, in the end, everyone was alone.

She slipped from the barstool and left temptation behind.

A WHILE LATER, Roan huddled in the corner of the booth at the café, struggling to stay awake now that she was warm. Across the way, she saw the preacher from the bar enter, head up to the counter and order. He glanced around, spotted her and smiled.

Roan didn't respond, though it might be wise to capitalize on his interest. Maybe he knew someone, could help her find a ride.

She was so sick of needing assistance from others.

She'd thought, before she ever left her old life, that if she just got to Gran's cabin and hunkered down, she could manage alone.

"You want more coffee, hon?" The big blond waitress paused beside her.

Roan quickly straightened. "Please." She couldn't reveal that she was only killing time, though that was exactly what she was doing, trying to screw up her courage to hitchhike. After the price of that untasted drink, coffee was all she could afford.

Her stomach growled loudly.

"You ready to eat yet?"

"No, not quite." Roan couldn't meet the woman's gaze.

"You in trouble, hon?" Concern laced the woman's voice. "I don't want to pry, but I couldn't help noticing the bruise on your face. If you need help, I can get the police for you."

Cops again. Roan caught her breath. "Thank you, but nothing's wrong."

"Have it your way, but if you change your mind—"

"Jolene, baby, your man's back in town." Roan was spared the need to continue when a big, burly trucker walked up and laid a big kiss on Jolene.

Jolene slapped one scarlet-tipped hand against his chest. "You seem to forget I'm married, Hank."

"Naw." His gap-toothed grin revealed tobacco-stained teeth. "I figure you're just waitin' on me to make enough money to cart you away to Bermuda."

His eyebrows waggled good-naturedly. "White sand, tiny bikini…"

Jolene's robust laugh shook her ample frame. "If I wasn't already too old for a tiny bikini, I'd sure be that way by the time you made that much money." She turned back to Roan. "You can stay a bit, but the manager won't like having people waiting too long for a table. I'll be back and we'll figure something out, all right?" Without lingering for Roan's answer, she nodded toward a booth nearby. "Come on, cowboy. Let me pour you some coffee."

Roan stared at the cup with regret, aware that she had to go now before Jolene returned. The burning told her that she couldn't consume more strong coffee on an empty stomach, anyway.

She gathered her purse and emerged from the booth, pondering again her decision not to take Zane's rental car. With it, she wouldn't be reduced to hitchhiking back to the cabin. Wouldn't feel so alone and exposed.

But she already owed him too much. She'd figure out where to send his money, once she got back to Gran's cabin. He'd appreciate being shed of her, no matter how he'd been raised to behave.

He didn't really need her measly funds, she understood now. Zane MacAllister might have hit a bump in his upward path, but he was basically rich, handsome, well adjusted and on top of the world. Chivalry had forced him to stop and help her, but if he understood what a mess she'd made of her life, he'd be only too happy to have nothing else to do with her.

He'd deceived her, but that didn't cancel her debt. Regardless of his motives, she would repay him if it took the rest of her days.

She put money on the table, including a tip for Jolene she couldn't really afford, then headed toward the front door and the parking lot.

Just then, a state trooper walked inside, surveying the room. He stopped at the cashier's stand and engaged in conversation.

The cashier nodded toward the booth where Roan had been sitting.

Roan ducked into the hallway leading to the rest rooms, starting to shake. Surely he wasn't looking for her, but—

The police will want to talk to you. Eldred.

A very important man had been stabbed, and she was the only witness.

And she had a record.

Roan spotted an exit door that didn't seem to have an alarm. She slipped down the hallway and through it. Once outside, she scanned the lot for eighteen-wheelers, wondering how she'd ever decide who to trust. She wished she had more time, but that cop might be looking for her.

She hadn't a minute to waste.

She took a deep breath and crossed the endless expanse of asphalt, puddles of water gleaming like oil-slicks in the darkness.

A brisk wind sliced through her thin shirt, and Roan wrapped her arms around herself. She couldn't have brought those bloodstained quilts with her; it would be like waving a flag, courting every predator in sight. But she mourned the loss of something that had come from Gran's beloved hands. Perhaps Zane would be thoughtful enough to send them back to her one day.

Thoughtful. The word settled into her chest, choking off her air. She didn't know what to make of him, for he had indeed been considerate in many ways.

All the while aware that he was deceiving her on the most basic level.

A game, perhaps. A part he'd played. That made sense, now that she considered it. Simple research for a role.

It didn't hurt any less, though.

Behind her, Roan heard a car approach. She glanced back over her shoulder to figure out which way to dodge it.

The car, old and battered, rumbled to a stop beside her. She searched the vicinity for a place to hide. A man emerged, and Roan poised to run.

"Are you okay, miss?"

She swiveled her head. The preacher from the bar.

Roan began to retreat, seeking refuge. "I'm fine."

He stopped as if he could sense her fear. "Listen, I don't want you to worry. I'm not...I won't hurt you. I saw you in the bar. I know you didn't take that drink. I wondered if I might help you.''

Roan backed up a step.

"If it makes any difference, I'm married.''

She couldn't help a quick, derisive laugh.

His smile was patient. "Listen, I'm a preacher. I mean you no harm. I think you're troubled, and a lady like you shouldn't be out here by yourself. Do you want a ride, or is there someone I could call?''

She'd never felt so alone in her life, not even in that dingy motel room. "I'm fine. I don't need any help.''

Zane's green eyes rose in her memory. *Don't say you don't need me, Roan. I'm not buying it.*

"Begging your pardon, miss, but I've been in your shoes. I'm an alcoholic, too. I can't go driving off until I'm certain you're safe.''

Safe? That was a laugh. She'd finally let herself feel secure in a man's arms, only to discover that she'd been duped.

She glanced across the intersection. "I'm not an alcoholic. And you're mistaken. My car is parked over there.'' She pointed to another café across the street.

"No offense, but I don't believe you. You would have gotten coffee over there if that was the case.'' He exhaled. "Look, I'm not out to make your life harder or mine, either. I saw the expression on your face when the trooper came in. Are you in some kind of trouble? Someone after you?''

She peered at him. "Why do you care?"

"Miss, the good Lord tells us 'Do unto others as you would have others do unto you.' It's my Christian duty to help out where I can."

He was barely her height and not much heavier, his expression solemn and kind.

"So I'm a good deed?"

In the headlights, she saw color rise in his cheeks. "If my wife were in your shoes, I'd sure want someone to step in and render aid."

Your wife would never be in my shoes, Roan thought.

What choice did she have, though? Either throw herself at the mercy of law enforcement and risk all the questions that would be asked if she were connected with the stabbing of Zane MacAllister— something she suspected neither of them wanted—or find another ride. Or walk back sixty-odd miles to Gran's on an empty stomach. She had no friends here.

He seemed like a nice man. Earnest.

Serial killers often appeared "nice" and "normal" to their neighbors and co-workers. It had been a long time since Roan dared trust her instincts, but everything within her said that this man meant her no harm.

Of course, Zane MacAllister, too, had insisted he only wanted to help her.

But within Roan, a fragile sense of strength was growing. She'd bested the guy in the bar, had faced down Frank—much bigger than this man and fueled by a venom this man lacked. Yes, Zane had intervened, but when he'd been wounded, she'd forced Frank to back down. She had no shotgun here, but if life had handed Roan one lesson in the past few years, it was that there was no perfect safety. She would be alone in Gran's cabin, and she had no choice but to survive without help because no one on the mountain would care if she lived or died.

This chance might not be ideal, but it was all she had right now.

You're crazy for trying to kick this on your own, her counselor had said. *You need to be attending meetings and have support.*

"What's in those papers you were handing out at the bar?"

"The Twelve Steps of Alcoholics Anonymous."

She only knew the first: *Admit you have a problem.*

"I'm not a criminal, I promise. I'm not an alcoholic, either, but my mother is." She met his gaze. "I chose to set a new family trend. Started with Valium and worked my way down."

He smiled. "I know where there's an early-morning meeting, starts in a couple of hours." He gestured toward the truck-stop café. "Since you're not too keen on going back inside, how about I take you home and let my Martha cook you some breakfast while we wait? You want to call her on my cell phone to make sure she's real? Or I could get Jolene to come out and vouch for me.''

Roan felt something inside her warm, just a bit. ''Won't your Martha be asleep?''

He shook his head. ''She's always ready for me to bring a lost lamb home. I'll call her, anyway, so she can put the coffeepot on.'' He opened the scraped and dented passenger door with a knightly flourish. ''My name is Charlie Sellers, miss.''

''I'm Roan O'Hara.''

''Come on, Roan O'Hara. My Martha makes pancakes lighter than an angel's wings.''

Friendship and food, too. Her head was light, her strength waning. She was running out of choices as well as strength.

Roan settled onto the worn, patched seat. She could eat and still keep her guard up. Be ready to run.

''You won't be sorry,'' Charlie said.

Could he know how much she wanted to believe the warm reassurance in his voice? Roan's fingers clenched, but she unbent enough to give him a small, hopeful nod.

CHAPTER FOURTEEN

JESSE PULLED the SUV to a halt in sight of Roan's cabin. "Good God."

"I didn't ask you to come," Zane reminded him. "I could have made the trip by myself."

Jesse snorted and shot a glance at Zane's heavily bandaged side. "Oh, yeah. One, I'd never be allowed home again, even for your funeral, and two, you'd have been lucky to make it out of the parking lot." He shook his head. "This is stupid, Zane. You should be in bed, not—" He exhaled. "Whatever the devil it is you think you're going to do up here."

"I told you. I have to make sure Roan's all right. Now, get me closer before she spots the car and takes off through the trees. I'm not up to chasing her this time."

Jesse's eyebrows rose. "*This* time?"

"Long story. Just drive." Zane's side would hurt less, yes, if he'd take the pain pills the doctor had prescribed, but he hadn't wanted a fuzzy head when he encountered Roan again.

Nothing, he was sure, would make his stomach stop jumping. Not until he saw how she reacted to him.

But no one came outside. Zane slid down from the seat and landed with a jarring impact. He grunted softly.

Jesse rounded the hood. "You could wait a damn minute for me to help. You had a knife slide into your gut only three days ago."

"Just nicked my side," Zane grumbled.

"They had to give you two pints of blood, pea-brain."

Zane knew Jesse was only carping because he was worried. He leaned gratefully against his brother. "Maybe you and Diego and I can compare scars sometime."

"You'd lose."

"Yeah." Diego's body was a mass of scars from the firefight that almost killed him; Jesse had been shot twice and stabbed once. "I was just kidding."

"You're missing the point. Diego and I got hurt, but it was part of the job. You didn't have to put yourself in harm's way, but you did. I'm proud of you, little brother."

Jesse's praise warmed Zane, but Roan deserved it, too. "Give Roan the credit. She fought him both times, out-manned as she was. She's got strength, Jesse. I swear she's not Kelly."

Jesse didn't answer, too busy assisting Zane up the steps. All Zane could figure was to let Jesse get to know Roan and make up his own mind.

At the door, Zane lifted a hand to knock, but

paused. Did he truly have the right to intervene in her life again?

"Go on," Jesse urged. "You'll always wonder if you don't." In his brother's voice, Zane heard regrets.

So he knocked. And waited. Knocked once more.

The brothers traded glances. "We could come back," Jesse said.

"There's no lock. I meant to get one put on, but…" Zane opened the door and froze. "Oh, no." He walked inside. "She hasn't been back. Everything's just the way it was the day we left."

Blood-soaked rags on the floor, dried stains on the bedsheets, furniture knocked askew…

He twisted to face Jesse. "I thought the reason the cops hadn't turned her up was that she was already home." Fear dug spurs into his gut. "Where is she, Jesse? What's happened to her?"

Jesse's look was grim. Zane was aware that his brother had seen a wealth of horrors in his job.

"Sit down," Jesse urged. "I'll make some calls."

Zane sank to the bed where his lifeblood had poured out, the bed where he'd taught Roan about passion and discovered a new depth of it in himself…. *Please.* He buried his head in his hands. *Let her be okay.*

She'd run because of his deceptions.

If anything happened to her, he would never forgive himself.

THE NEXT MORNING, Zane rose with the sun, wincing as he climbed from the bed Jesse had insisted he use. He slipped quietly past the brother sleeping on a pallet in front of the fire and moved outside.

For a couple of bachelors, they'd managed pretty well last night. Jesse had done most of the work of putting the cabin to rights, threatening Zane within an inch of his life if he didn't rest. Between what Jesse recalled of Mama Lalita's woodstove cooking and Zane's own memories of Roan, they'd put a creditable meal together.

Zane clasped a hand over the bandage Jesse had changed before bedtime. Arguing that Roan wasn't likely to appear after dark, he'd bullied Zane into taking a pain pill along with the antibiotics.

Mom would be proud. Nurse Ratchet had nothing on Jesse Montalvo when it came to barking orders.

Where was Roan? Zane looked out over the mountains, squinted in the faint light at repairs he'd done. Perused weeds he'd cut by hand, wood he'd chopped. Felt a pride of accomplishment he hadn't experienced in a long time. A sense of homecoming he'd only known in Texas.

He could live here, he realized.

Zane dropped his head in a silent laugh.

As if she'd let him. He should probably be grateful Gran's shotgun and .22 were still in the cabin instead of in Roan's hands, pointed at him.

He glanced around and cataloged the changes he'd bring about if it were up to him. Not as many as he would have expected when he'd first arrived and examined the setup with horror.

Oddly enough, the place grew on you.

But the point was moot. He had to go, just as soon as he knew she was safe.

Where the hell was she?

The cabin door creaked. "You never used to be an early bird." Jesse's jaw cracked with a huge yawn. "Need a pain pill?"

Zane rubbed absently over his bandage and shook his head. "Nope. Got some things I want to do today while I wait."

"Zane…"

He pinned Jesse with a glare. "You can leave anytime. I'm staying put."

Jesse rubbed his eyes, then held up both palms. "I got it, I got it. I won't ask again." He turned. "I'm going to make coffee."

Zane watched his brother with regret. Jesse had been there for him every step of the way. He didn't know how much sleep his brother had missed while dealing with the furor in Asheville, and no telling how hard he'd been working before he arrived. Jesse's job was one of unrelenting tension; a hostage situation could go on for hours, even days, and once he established a bond with the hostage taker, Jesse lived on adrenaline.

His eyes held shadows deeper than usual. Jesse might need to go home more than he himself did.

Zane headed for the door to apologize. Maybe, for

his brother's sake, he should depart, since Jesse wouldn't go without him.

But how could he, not knowing where Roan was? He'd gladly let her blast him up one side and down the other if he could just see her safe and whole.

He turned the knob and pushed at the door…

And heard a sound that made his heart falter.

THE MOUNTAINS weren't as soothing as Roan had hoped. She sat beside Charlie, hands clasped tightly in her lap. She dreaded seeing the cabin, still turned upside down from Frank's attack and the frantic race to get Zane to the hospital.

But you didn't win a fight if you gave up the field. Roan was determined to fight.

The cabin was hers, by God, the only thing she had left of Gran. She'd broken Gran's heart by leaving; maybe Gran would know somehow that she was back. Perhaps Gran could see the progress made already, even if much of it had been Zane's doing.

Their list was unfinished, but Roan would complete it herself.

"I know you're nervous," Charlie said. "But I'll stay until it's set to rights, and you heard Martha say she'd welcome you back if you changed your mind."

"I won't." She turned and smiled. "I can't, Charlie. Not and live with myself. I've run enough."

"You'll use that cell phone I got you?"

Roan flushed. "It's not right for you to pay the bill. You've got others who need you."

"You'll be covering it soon enough. I have faith."

"I wish I had your confidence." She faced him again. "But I'm going to make it. I'll never be able to thank you enough." He'd taken her to meetings, sat with her and talked for hours. Fed her and let her sleep.

The older man shrugged. "You're the one who put down that drink, Roan. Don't forget it." He leaned forward. "I think you got company, girl."

Roan's head swiveled. She saw Zane's car and let out a small moan of distress.

Then she spotted Zane himself.

"Who is it? I won't let him hurt you, I promise."

He already has, she thought, but couldn't keep herself from greedily devouring him with her eyes.

The mustache was gone, she realized. His face was drawn in lines of strain, and he wasn't standing quite straight, one hand pressed to his side.

The side where Frank had stabbed him as he battled to save Roan.

Zane walked to the edge of the porch, his eyes intent on her, his expression solemn.

Then another man came out of the cabin, tall and dark. Handsome in a different way. He asked Zane a question, which Zane answered with a sharp nod.

Over the dark man's face slid a glare directed at her.

"I'll go talk to them," Charlie said. "Send them on their way."

"No." Roan cast him a tight smile. "I have to handle this."

She stepped from the car.

Something had changed about her was Zane's first thought, but he couldn't pin down what it was. She walked past the front of the car, then paused.

Zane descended the steps toward her.

"Zane…" Jesse called, low and cautious. "Wait."

But Zane couldn't wait anymore. He narrowed the distance between them, wishing he knew the right words to say, his gaze locked on hers.

He'd seen those blue eyes in many different moods, but never quite like this: worried and nervous, but somehow…strong.

"I wouldn't blame you if you hated my guts."

Her head rose swiftly, her eyes rueful. "I tried. Mostly I was—" She stopped. Glanced at the ground.

"Hurt?" he ventured. "Roan, I never meant that to happen. I just… After Kelly and all the reporters hounding me and then when you didn't recognize me, I only wanted to be taken for myself."

Her head snapped up, eyes heating. "You're not Hal."

"Actually," he said. "I am. My middle name is Harold, after my dad." He took a step closer. "It wasn't all a lie, Roan. Only the name."

He could see in her eyes that she was remembering everything, as he was. For a second, he felt again what it was like to hold her in his arms, to press her against him.

"It doesn't matter," she said. "It's over now."

Zane grasped her arm. "No."

"Hey there!" An older man emerged from the car. Moved toward them. "I don't know who you are, fella, but this little lady's had a rough time. I may not be as big as you, but I won't hesitate to defend her. You take your hand away."

Zane dropped his hand, seeing himself through another's eyes. Stung to be considered a threat as if he were like Frank. "Who the hell are you?"

"I'm her friend. I'll ask you the same. What are you doing in Roan's cabin?"

Who was he to her? Lover, friend…deceiver? "We've been looking for her." He met Roan's stare. "I had to be sure she was safe."

Roan shifted her gaze behind him.

Zane turned. "Roan, this is my brother Jesse Montalvo. Jess, this is Roan O'Hara and…?"

"Charlie Sellers," the man offered. "And your name?"

Zane steeled himself.

Roan saved him the effort. "This is Zane MacAllister, Charlie. The movie star."

"Damn it, Roan, forget that." He lifted his eyes to the older man. "It's not important. I'm Roan's friend, too." He tilted his chin. "She never told me about you."

Amusement skipped over the man's features. "She

never mentioned you, either. That mean neither of us is real?''

''Where have you been, Ms. O'Hara?'' Jesse asked then. ''I've had this state crawling with cops, looking for you.''

Roan shrank from his tone. ''Why?''

''Because there seem to be some things you didn't tell Zane, either.''

''Stop it, Jesse,'' Zane warned.

Inside, Roan jittered. *Cop* was written all over him, and his contempt was clear. She started to retreat.

No. No more running.

She faced him head-on. ''Such as the fact that I was arrested once? Or that I've had a problem with drugs?''

His expression was stony. ''Yeah. Zane doesn't deserve any more trouble in his life.''

''I don't need you to speak for me. If you can't be civil to Roan, then get the hell back in the cabin or better yet, leave.''

Jesse didn't back down. ''I'm going nowhere without you.''

Zane turned on his brother. ''She hasn't earned the third degree from you.''

Roan saw it then, in Jesse's expression, the determination to protect his own. No matter how he felt about her, she could forgive him that.

She grasped Zane's arm. ''No, Zane. He's right. It's part of why I left the hospital.''

Zane turned back to her. "I never meant for you to find out who I was that way."

"How did you mean for it to happen? You had plenty of chances to tell me yourself."

But then she remembered him bleeding, struggling to talk. *Roan, something…have to tell…*

"You tried, didn't you?"

He glanced away. "Not hard enough."

She let go. "It doesn't matter." She faced Charlie. "Would you like to come inside and rest before all of you leave?"

Charlie started to answer, but Zane clasped her shoulder first and turned her to face him. "I'm not going anywhere yet, not until we talk."

"There's nothing to talk about." She shook off his hand and slipped past. She looked at his brother. "He should rest. Will you escort him inside while I make all of us breakfast? You'll want a good meal before you hit the road."

Jesse nodded solemnly, but she thought she saw approval flit through his gaze.

"Roan…" Zane called.

The least she could do was what was best for him, so she pretended she hadn't heard him and stepped inside.

ALL HIS LIFE, Zane had been known for his sunny disposition, but he could find none of it now. With simmering impatience, he endured a largely silent meal, punctuated only by Charlie's attempts at small talk and, astonishingly, Jesse's reciprocation.

Jesse, the Sphinx of the MacAllister-Montalvo clan, the man who never used two words when one would do, except in his work.

At another time, Zane would have kicked back and enjoyed the sight. Savor every detail for sharing with the folks at home. But not today. It was all he could do to remain civil. When Jesse had dragged out Zane's antibiotic and tried to slip in a pain pill, Zane had nearly bitten his head off.

Roan fared little better, returned to the silent wraith he'd first met, her frame tense, face tight with strain.

He wanted to tell her to lie down and rest—she looked like hell. Wanted to snatch her into his arms and cuddle her until she relaxed.

But her manner made it very clear that she preferred him to keep his distance.

And to go.

Finally, Zane could stand no more. He slapped down his fork and rose. "I need to talk to you, Roan." He glared at his brother and Charlie. "Alone."

Her jaw spelled mutiny. "There's nothing to say."

"Fine. You can listen. I'll talk."

He straightened and headed for the door, prepared to drag her out if required.

Except that when he reached the door, he had to stop for breath. Damn it.

"You shouldn't be up," she said, hurrying to his side.

Hell, if he'd known all he had to do was fall prey to weakness to bring her close, he'd have collapsed when she'd first arrived. Zane gazed down into her worried eyes. "I'm fine. Come outside with me. I promise I'll sit."

"You sure about this, Roan?" Charlie asked.

"She's safe with my brother," Jesse snapped.

Roan nodded at Charlie. "He's right."

She shouldn't feel too safe, Zane thought. His thoughts were running on the primitive side at the moment. He might just grab her up and take off.

Then he turned too quickly and gasped as his wound made a liar of him.

"Come here," Roan ordered, leading him to the rocking chair.

He dug in his heels. "No. I don't want anyone listening. I can make it to the barn."

Her eyes narrowed. "Zane, there's not that much to talk about. You've said you're sorry, and I am, too. End of story."

"If you believe that, you're lying to yourself." He grabbed her arm and marched down the steps, ignoring his body's protests and leading her across the yard and into the barn.

She slipped from his grasp and put distance between them. "Sit down, will you? I won't be responsible for putting you in the hospital again."

"You weren't responsible the first time, Roan.

Frank was.'' He realized she wouldn't know. "You don't have to worry about him anymore. He's been arrested and charged with aggravated assault and attempted rape.''

Her eyes opened wide. "How did that happen?''

"Jesse's an FBI agent. He worked with the local sheriff to get Frank brought in. He made sure Frank's bail was set too high for him to be released before his trial.''

"Trial.'' She stiffened visibly. "I-I'll have to testify.'' Panic crossed her features. "With my background, they'll never believe me.''

He rose to his feet with less skill than he'd like. "They'd better. Your past isn't the issue.''

She uttered a small laugh. "Oh, sure. Tell that to Noah. Or anyone else around here.''

"Roan, you're not alone anymore.''

Blue eyes met his. "Yes, I am.'' She touched his arm. "But it's all right. I can handle it now, Zane. I've done a lot of thinking since—'' She shrugged.

"Since you saved my life?''

She shook her head.

"You did, Roan. Give yourself credit. Frank would have killed me if you hadn't been there. And you drove me to the hospital in time.''

"I'm no hero, Zane.'' She smiled sadly. "That's your role.''

"I'm not,'' he said. "But you make me want to be one.'' He stepped closer. "Roan, I want you to go to Texas with me. Meet my family.''

"Why? What would be the point?"

"It would be good for you."

"There's nothing positive that would result from any further involvement. Your reputation will surmount Kelly's death, but it won't survive involvement with me, not with my background."

"I don't care." To his surprise, he actually meant that.

She faced him squarely. "I can't live in that world, even if you wanted me. I'm an addict, Zane. I'll always have to fight it. You said it yourself, people in your world take narcotics for a hangnail."

"I don't."

Her smile was sad and soft. "But I'm not as strong as you. I have to be more cautious. Charlie says—"

"What does Charlie have to do with it?" he growled.

"After I left the hospital, I went to a bar. I wanted something stronger, but I had no connections in Asheville. No way to score." She stared at him. "Hear that? Score, Zane. That's the reality of the past few years for me. I was married to a man who didn't love me, and I didn't mind because he was my ticket out of these mountains and out of my mother's insane, alcoholic life."

She gazed away. "I lost a baby," she said softly. "My precious Elise." She was silent for a long span. "I became an embarrassment to my husband, living on pills to ease the pain. I found a man who could provide something stronger, and I kept sliding down and down into the warm blanket of a life where I didn't have to feel anymore, where everything had a nice, soft edge.''

Her eyes flashed then. ''I took the easy way out, Zane, and I became no better than my mother, with her constant parade of men and booze. Then came the day that my dealer showed me how to feel really good.'' Her voice twisted with bitterness.

''Roan, you don't have to tell me this.''

''Yes,'' she insisted. ''You have to understand that you're better off without me. I'm no different from your Kelly—in fact, I'm worse.'' Her frame trembled. ''I let him introduce me to heroin, Zane—got that? Only once, but I loved it. It was the best feeling I'd ever had in my life until…''

Her eyes met his, and memory sparked. Both were silent for a long moment.

Roan broke the connection. ''Then he showed me the price. I had no money, see, but he liked my looks. That night when I crashed from the high, I found myself in his bed and when I realized what I'd become…'' Her voice dropped to a whisper. ''I rented a room in a fleabag motel, and I crawled into the tub with a razor blade.''

Zane grabbed her then and pulled her into his arms. ''But you didn't, Roan,'' he murmured into her hair. ''You didn't die. You knew you wanted to live. That's what you've been fighting to do ever since.''

She trembled against him, and her hands clenched in his shirt.

Zane couldn't help clasping her tighter.

Roan leaped back. Retreated to the other side of the barn.

Zane started after her.

"No." She held out a hand, her eyes pleading. "Please, Zane. Don't."

He ignored the plea, desperate to surmount the distance between them somehow. "I don't care what you did. I know who you really are, and I want to help you."

Her laugh was bitter. "That gentleman your mother raised you to be, right? I don't need your pity, Zane. I don't want to be your charity project. I'm going to make it—I promise you that—but I have to do it by myself. You can't imagine how badly I want to lean on you, but I have to prove that I can stand on my own two feet and beat this."

"But—"

"You couldn't save her, Zane. You can't save me, either."

He recoiled as if she'd slapped him.

"That's not meant to hurt you. It's simple fact. Don't blame yourself for her and don't chain yourself to my fate. Maybe one day…" She stopped.

He seized on that *maybe*. "One day what? How long do I have to wait for you, Roan?"

"Don't wait." Her eyes were merciless. "I can only think about one day at a time right now. If you want to help me, Zane, don't expect anything of me and get on with your life. An addict's battle is never over, and the outcome is always in doubt.''

Zane could only stand and stare at her, searching for the right combination of words, the facile argument at which he'd always excelled to get his own way.

But charm was useless, and debate moot. To think of leaving her tore his guts out, but her determination was clear, even if he didn't like it. Experience told him that she was right. He couldn't do this for her, no matter how badly he wished that wasn't the case.

But to sever ties for good—

"How can you expect me to just walk away?" he asked her, voice hoarse. "And leave you in this place alone?"

Roan's eyes glistened. Her hand stroked his face. "Because I know you'll come in a heartbeat if I call."

"Will you?" he asked, leaning into her hand. "Damn it, I hate this." He glared at her, fury and sorrow battering hope. "I won't ever stop worrying about you, Roan O'Hara."

"I know." She rose to tiptoe and touched her lips to his.

"I'm going to wait for you." Zane gathered her close again, tempted to sway her with passion and make her relent. She was tearing out his heart. "Call me, Roan. Soon."

It was then that Zane knew he truly loved her, because instead of sealing his mouth to hers and drawing her into the sensual spell he knew he could weave—

He pressed one last, broken kiss to her lips—

And walked away.

While he still could.

CHAPTER FIFTEEN

By Christmas, Zane was losing hope.

Here in his parents' home, beloved and familiar, fragrant with the scent of hot spiced cider and creamy eggnog, pungent evergreen garlands and sweet vanilla candles, alive with the colors of the Christmas tree and the chatter of a big family, he should have felt warmed and cherished as always.

But inside him was an emptiness he couldn't seem to fill.

When he'd come back from North Carolina to recuperate, his family had hovered over him until he'd left for the film, then called him daily to show support.

He'd wrapped principal shooting on his latest film; his director, at first perplexed, had decided that Zane's unaccustomed reserve brought a new and promising depth to the role that had begun as standard action, adventure and sex.

Sal had been less enthusiastic when Zane had announced that once his next commitment wrapped, he was taking a year off. Annie had groused and grumbled because Zane didn't have the heart to hit the hot spots and keep his profile high.

But the only person Zane really wanted to hear from kept totally silent.

He'd intervened with Noah, who, it turned out, had a grandson with a serious case of idol worship. With proper encouragement, Noah had been willing to thaw relations with Roan and lend a helping hand.

Charlie was in contact with Roan on a regular basis and, though maddeningly circumspect, would deign to take Zane's constant calls and issue sketchy reports. She was attending meetings. She had enough to eat. Was staying warm.

Jesse kept Frank's case under surveillance and eased Zane's mind that Frank would be no threat.

But the man who had everything couldn't obtain the one thing he desired most.

A call from Roan.

He'd arrived home today, Christmas Eve, but Zane, usually the most enthusiastic of the clan, couldn't dredge up any sincere interest in the holiday fuss. Even the traditional tamale dinner he'd always loved failed to stir his appetite. Tired and edgy, he dropped down on the overstuffed sofa beside Mama Lalita.

"*Cielito,* your heart is so troubled." She patted his hand with hers. "You must come visit me. We will talk."

Zane clasped her small hand in his and tried to relax into her soothing touch. "I don't think there's anything to say, Mama Lalita."

She pressed back. "Then we will be silent and let

love speak for us." She met his gaze with her own boundless reserves of calm and acceptance.

"Thank you." He closed his eyes and leaned his head against hers for a minute.

Footsteps sounded across the wood floor. Zane saw Caroline approaching with her and Diego's nearly four-month-old Robbie. He straightened and pasted on a holiday smile.

"Here, Uncle Zane. Your nephew's been asking for you."

Zane rolled his eyes at her. "He can't talk yet."

"I'm his mother. We have a bond that doesn't need words." Her eyes warmed with sympathy.

He took the little guy. "Oof—what a chunk. You've grown, fella." Robbie gave him a wide, gummy, irresistible grin.

Zane couldn't help grinning back. "Good for you, bruiser. Your mom provides good grub, huh?" He marveled at how Caroline had changed from the high-strung burnout case he'd first met. Her blond hair was longer, her face softer. "Motherhood suits you. You look great, sis."

"Stop flirting with your brother's wife, Zane." His sister, Jenna, long and leggy and seldom still, plopped down on the arm of his chair. "Just because you can't get your own girl is no excuse."

Zane saw Caroline shoot his redheaded sister a frown. Leave it to Jenna to drag out in the open what everyone else tiptoed around. "Smooth move, big mouth. Hit a man when he's down," he jeered affectionately. "Why don't you go steal some kid's Christmas toys while you're at it."

Jenna looked only slightly remorseful. "You've been moping around over her for almost four months. I don't know why you don't just go to North Carolina and bring her home."

He'd wondered the same thing. Often. "It's not that simple, brat. She asked me to give her time, and I'm trying to be fair."

"Fair, schmair." Jenna flapped one wrist. "What if she's embarrassed? Or maybe she thinks you've gone on with your life and don't need her."

Need her. Thunderstruck, Zane could only stare. He'd never once told Roan that he needed her, only the ways in which she needed him.

Caroline's younger sister Chloe, a psychologist, spoke up. "I don't mean to intrude, Zane, but the look on your face makes me wonder if you've thought of that angle."

Robbie grabbed Zane's ear, but Zane barely felt the tug. "I—" He shook his head. "Nope."

"Roan not only has her chemical dependency to deal with, but she's also the child of an alcoholic, and they have other battles." Chloe hesitated.

"Please, go on." Zane cuddled the baby, his attention riveted on Chloe.

"Control is a huge issue for children of alcoholics. They realize very early that being vulnerable is dangerous and always has negative results. They learn how not to want so that they won't be disappointed, because the alcoholic parent has let them down over and over. They have to be their own parents and possess a powerful hunger for nurturing.''

She tucked a strand of her long blond hair behind one ear. ''These children often suffer from depression, and they are terrified of trust. They feel safer being isolated and often have great difficulty believing they are worthy of love.'' She sat down on the ottoman in front of Zane with her characteristic grace. ''Jenna may seem insensitive—''

''She is insensitive,'' Cade teased from the doorway.

Impatiently, Zane waved him off. ''Please. Finish.''

''She might be on the right track, though,'' Chloe responded. ''We've all been trying to give Roan room to heal, but from what you report, she's surviving on her own just fine.''

''So what now? I told her I'd come the second she called. She begged me to stay away until she did.''

Chloe's older sister Ivy, honey curls bouncing, smiled, ever the little mother. ''You're Zane MacAllister, you goose. A woman far more secure than Roan would have trouble summoning the nerve to contact you. And I'd guess that the more time that elapses, the easier it is to imagine that you've moved on without her.''

Zane rested his head on Robbie's fine dark hair. ''I don't think I'll ever put her behind me.'' He straightened. "But the fact remains that my life in L.A. would be poison to her."

"Linc moved his business to Palo Verde from Denver to be with me." Ivy cuddled her toddler, Amelia, and cast a smile at her husband. "And Caroline and Diego found a compromise living in both places they were needed."

Chloe's detective husband, Vince, walked up behind her and twisted one finger in her hair. "It would be understandable if Roan was intimidated. I was sure a mutt like me could never fit into a society girl's world." Chloe lifted her shining gaze to his, and he answered with a grin both rueful and intimate. "And I'm arrogant as hell. Maybe Jenna's right." He touched Chloe's cheek. "And Doc here is seldom wrong."

For the first time in months, hope stirred inside Zane, right alongside unaccustomed fear. He remembered the plea in Roan's eyes, understood how hard her road had been. What if he'd waited too long? What if she'd come to prefer life alone?

"Man." He rubbed the heel of his hand over his breastbone. "I think a woman's got me scared."

"About time, Mr. Irresistible." Jenna kissed his cheek. "Go get her, big brother."

Zane smiled at Jenna, then peered down at solemn gray baby eyes. "What do you think, buddy? Want to ride shotgun to North Carolina?"

"He should be weaned first." Diego lifted his son into his arms. "Dad just called you."

"Son…" Hal MacAllister's voice rang out from the front door. "Can you come here a minute?"

Zane rose, already planning what he'd pack. "I have to book a flight." Driving would take too long. "Airlines fly on Christmas Day, right?"

"In a hurry, Zane?" Laughter followed him to the front door, where his father and mother stood greeting a guest.

"Dad, Mom, I'm leaving in the morning for North Carolina. You'll forgive me, right? I have to—"

His parents stepped aside.

Zane went mute.

"I hope you haven't bought your ticket yet, sweetheart," his mother said, patting his arm as she and his father left the room.

"Hi," Roan said, her stance tentative. "Merry Christmas."

Zane couldn't seem to find his voice.

"I, uh, I know this is a family time, but…" She fell silent, her gaze filled with nerves.

"You look different," he finally managed. "But good, Roan. Really good." Stronger somehow, not so desperate. Not starved or haunted. Her hair was past her ears, softly curling, and her face had filled out.

His heart sank. She didn't need him after all.

"You look like a movie star."

Zane swore beneath his breath. "I can't help that, Roan. But it's not who I am." He paused to summon his arguments.

"I only meant that…you're more like your pictures in magazines or on the screen now. I'm not used to seeing you with blond hair." Her hands clenched into fists, and she tucked them into her coat pockets.

"It was always blond, except—" *When you met me.* Sorrow swept over him at the subterfuge that had hurt her. "I'm sorry."

"It's okay. I understand why you did it."

Silence fell between them once more. Zane hadn't felt this awkward since junior high.

He decided to go for broke. "I was coming to get you."

Her head rose. "What?"

"I couldn't wait any longer. I mean, I haven't forgotten that I promised you, and God knows I can't afford to be making any more mistakes where you're concerned, but—" His gaze locked on hers. The room narrowed to her face and what her expression would reveal. His heartbeat drummed in his ears. "I thought that maybe you should hear that you might not need me, but…" He took a deep breath. "I need you, Roan."

Her eyes widened. "You…" She blinked and stared at him for endless seconds.

Finally, she gave a faint, shaky laugh. "I was certain you'd forget me once you got back to your glamorous life. You'd be better off if you had."

"You're wrong on both counts."

She frowned. "Charlie told me last week about all

your calls. I'd wondered why Noah was helping me, so I asked him. He admitted that at first it was because of you, but..." She shook her head. "He said that he thought Gran would be proud of me after all." Tears gathered on her thick, dark lashes.

"Gran had no use for cowards, though. I've wanted to call you a thousand times, but—" Her voice grew hoarse. "I wasn't sure you'd want to hear from me. It took a while to work up my nerve, but I had to say this in person."

Zane tensed as she squared her shoulders. "I've proven to myself that I can live without you, Zane, but...I miss you." At his sudden stir, she held up a warning hand. "Not the movie star, but the guy with the blisters. The man who washed my hair." She swallowed. "Who taught me about passion. Who made me remember how to laugh." One tear fell.

"You miss me," he repeated.

She nodded.

"Thank God." Zane closed his eyes for a second in pure thanksgiving. "All I've wanted since the day I left was to hear from you."

He stepped forward and gathered her into his arms.

When their bodies touched, they both sighed. Settled.

Zane could finally breathe. "Let me be with you, Roan. I only have one more film I'm obligated to do, and then I'll quit. You can go with me on location or I'll come to you every day off," he whispered fiercely into her hair. "I'll live wherever you want, sweetheart, just don't make me live without you any-more.''

"I don't want to," she murmured, tightening her arms around his waist. Her head rose suddenly. "You're all right?" She touched his waist. "The wound doesn't hurt?"

"The place that hurts is higher." He lifted her hand and placed it over his heart. "And I think you've got the only remedy."

She worried at her lower lip. "I'll always be an addict, Zane. There's no cure for me. The gossip columns will have a heyday if my name gets linked to yours."

"If I'm not acting, I'm old news. They won't care." He stroked her cheek. "And your name is definitely getting linked with mine, if I have my way."

"You shouldn't quit acting. You're too talented."

"I already told my agent I'm taking a year off after the next film. I have enough money, and there are other things I can do. We'll have time to think about the next step."

She looked troubled. "Caring about me has already cost you too much."

He tried for a jest. "Maybe I want to try something new. Get fat and bald."

A tiny smile curved her lips, but her eyes remained uneasy.

"Are you happy in the mountains? Do you have plans that can't include me?"

"I...it's lonely there, but it's peaceful." She chewed at her lip. "But I have to do something right with my life, Zane, more than just staying clean. I was thinking..." She faltered.

"What?" He tilted up her chin.

"There are other women like me, some of them in jail. They don't have hope. They don't believe they can win. I want to figure out a way to help them get a new start, but I'm not sure if I'm the right person."

Zane smiled at her. "You absolutely are." He could see the doubts shimmering and redoubled his efforts. "I understand that you'll always have to deal with battles I won't, but I believe in you. You'll make it, and I want to be with you all the way. Not because you can't do it alone, but because...I love you, Roan O'Hara."

Her eyes went wide. "How can you be sure?" she whispered. "We were only together for a matter of days. It's too soon to make such a big commitment."

Zane's heart sank, but he tried to keep in mind what Chloe had said. "Is it that you don't have feelings for me? Or are you afraid you can't trust me?"

"No," she said. "It's not you. I—" She glanced away. Pressed her fingers to her mouth.

Then she looked up at him, wet blue eyes searching. "I knew I loved you before you ever left, but..."

"But what? I love you. You love me. What else matters?"

Her voice was so soft he almost couldn't hear her. "This…you…it's too much like a dream. I'm afraid of dreams, Zane. They vanish just when you need them most."

"Not this one. We won't let it. It's too important, and we're both too stubborn to let it slip away." He held her securely within the circle of his arms. "Stay with me, Roan. Build a life with me, I don't care where. I've got plenty of money and a knack for making more. Let me share it. Maybe we can do something for those women with it. And I'd like to pamper you, but I'll live with kerosene lamps if that's what you want…the *with you* part is all that's important. I was happier chopping your wood than I've been since you sent me away."

"Being apart was miserable for me, too, but—"

"No more *buts*." He silenced her with gentle fingers. "Have Christmas with us. Spend time with my family and see if you like it here. If you don't want to come with me on the next film, this would be a safe place to stay. My family and friends won't let the media bother you."

"I couldn't impose."

"Roan, I can't lose you again. I want to marry you." He focused on the blue eyes that would determine his future. "Please…give us a chance. Fight for us the way you've struggled to save yourself. You're my hero, Roan O'Hara."

"I'm not." She lifted herself to tiptoe, clasping his collar. "You'll never know what you did for me.

How you brought me hope. You're the real hero.'' She pressed her lips to his.

"I don't care about top billing," he said, holding on for dear life. "As long as I get the girl." He slanted his mouth over hers in a kiss as achingly sweet as it was powerful. "Say yes, Roan."

"I..." She hesitated.

He held his breath.

Then she smiled, bright and free of shadows. "Yes."

Zane let out a shout and kissed her hard, then picked her up and twirled her around, their shining eyes locked on each other.

Behind them, the house erupted into cheers and fond laughter.

*   *   *   *   *

Look for Jesse's story,
Most Wanted,
from Harlequin Superromance
in August 2004.

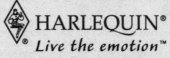

What if you discovered that all you ever wanted were the things you left behind?

John Riley's Girl
by Inglath Cooper
(Superromance #1198)
On-sale April 2004

Olivia Ashford thought she had put her hometown and John Riley behind her. But an invitation to her fifteen-year high school reunion made her realize that she needs to go back to Summerville and lay some old ghosts to rest. After leaving John without a word so many years ago, would Olivia have the courage to face him again, if only to say goodbye?

Return to Little Hills by Janice Macdonald
(Superromance #1201) On-sale May 2004

Edie Robinson's relationship with her mother is a precarious one. Maude is feisty and independent, and not inclined to make life easy for her daughter even though Edie's come home to help out. Edie can't wait to leave the town she'd fled years ago. But slowly a new understanding between mother and daughter begins to develop. Then Edie meets widower Peter Darling who's specifically moved to Little Hills to give his four young daughters the security of a small-town childhood. Suddenly, Edie's seeing her home through new eyes.

Available wherever Harlequin Books are sold.

Visit us at www.eHarlequin.com

HSRGBCM

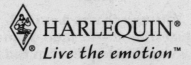

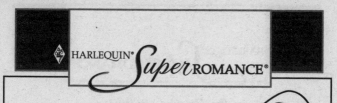

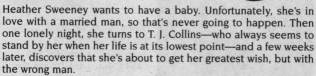

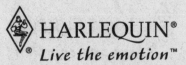